JOSH AND THE CARGAN

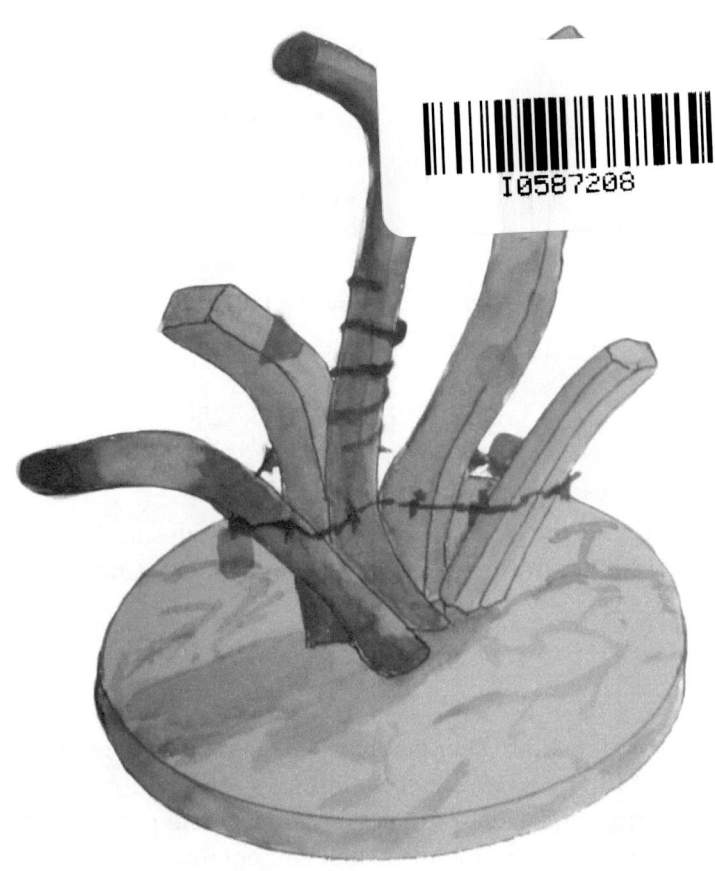

M. L. Hollinger

TotalRecall Publications, Inc.

TotalRecall Publications, Inc.
1103 Middlecreek
Friendswood, Texas 77546
281-992-3131   281-482-5390 Fax
www.totalrecallpress.com

ISBN: 978-1-59095-125-5
UPC: 6-43977-41255-3

Printed in the United States of America with simultaneous printings in Australia, Canada, and United Kingdom.

FIRST EDITION
1   2   3   4   5   6   7   8   9   10

To Joseph and James who used to
believe my tall tales.

Author M. L. Hollinger

received an Aeronautical Engineering degree from Purdue University in 1957 and went into the Air Force right after college. He worked on several space program projects including; Titan III Space Booster, Space Shuttle, Star Wars and several other special studies for the Air Force. He attended the Air Command and Staff College and the Air War College. He served in Viet Nam from 1971-1972. His decorations include The Bronze Star Medal, Meritorious Service Medal, Air Force Commendation Medal, The Vietnamese Honor Medal First Class, The Vietnamese Gallantry Cross and five unit excellence awards. He retired from the Air Force in 1980 with the rank of Lieutenant Colonel and came back to Indiana where he joined the Indiana Corporation for Science and Technology. He is now fully retired.

Acknowledgement

The author gratefully acknowledges the editorial advice of several friends and relatives as well as other readers including; Mr. Fayez Phillipe Hanna, Mrs. Paul Concha, Mr. Joseph Concha, Mr. James Concha, Ms. Julie Murphy and my lovely wife.

I also wish to thank my critique group for their contributions. They are; Nicole Amsler, Stephanie Ferguson, Laura Baugh, Jim Meeks-Jonson, Marcia Kelly and Garrett Hutson.

Preface

This story is my favorite. During the awkward days of puberty, every man experienced Josh's problem with girls . For some of us the problem continued on into high school.

When I finally overcame my shyness and learned how to speak coherently to the opposite sex I was baffled by their attitude toward boys. Considering the hormones raging inside my body, I wondered why females didn't experience the same drive.

A key factor in my puzzlement was the fact that I grew up in the 1950s. Morals were much tighter then, and any girl who was known to have 'played around' was branded as 'loose'or worse. Girls knew boys couldn't keep a secret when it came to that sort of thing, so they refused to believe my honest proclamations of confidentiality.

I often thought it would be good if there were another planet where sex was safe, confidential and free of guilt. On such a planet girls would feel no compunctions about sex. It would be a Nirvana. Little did I know that Earth would become such a planet in the 21st Century.

CHAPTER 1

It was Charles Bastin's first creation, and now it constituted his last hope. Sheer willpower forced his reluctant arms to move the wheelchair toward the cold, metal table beside the institutional bed. With his last ounce of resolve, he compelled his rigid fingers to grasp the one thing offering any means of escape. He pulled the ugly, silver-gray tangle of metal into his lap, and bony, gnarled hands discolored with brown splotches grasped familiar locations. The pain now caused his breath to come in sharp gasps. His vision began to blur, and his throat constricted, but he could still hum the first note of Dixie.

A kaleidoscope of colors flooded his vision. He fell through a deep hole surrounded by streaks of red and blue light, always falling toward the bright glare at the bottom, laughing with wild abandon.

CHAPTER 2

Heavy metal guitar chords flew through the air like shrapnel, rattling the windows and threatening the existence of every brittle object in the room. To the welcome relief of the wallboard, they died in a crash of drums and cymbals. It was Tuesday, practice night for the rock band and its lead guitarist, Josh Smith.

The band practiced at Rodney Barnes place because Rodney's parents owned a rather large estate with an old carriage house separated from the main residence by enough distance to dampen out the band's insult to the atmosphere. It was also far enough from neighbors to avoid irate phone calls.

"That was great guys. The middle part still needs some more work, though."

"God, Josh, we've done this thing a dozen times tonight; and each time you say it's great, but you want to change something. Make up your mind, for Christ's sake."

"You're doing good on the bass part, Rod. I think we need more work on the keyboards, though."

"It'd be nice if we had some music to go by." Willie Jenkins said.

I don't know why I let some high-brow pianist join the band. He's a real pain in the ass.

"You want to write it out?" Bill Thompson, the drummer, said. "We do okay just winging it. I trust Josh's ear. He knows when it sounds right."

Josh looked at his watch and decided he'd prodded his guys enough for one night. "I think it's time to wrap it up anyway. Same time on Friday. Okay? Remember we've got our first gig in two weeks."

A flurry of half-hearted affirmative responses signified everyone would be back for more practice. Josh turned off the recorder and lifted the disc from the holder.

I'll play this back tonight and figure out what we need. Oh shit, I need a ride home.

"Give me a ride home, Will." It was more of a command than a question.

"Sure, you leavin' your stuff here?"

"Just the amp. I'll take the axe home."

Will nudged Josh in a friendly manner. "How'd you make out with Mary Sadler last night?"

"Not much there. Ralph Mitter said she does it, but she wouldn't let me do more than feel her boobs."

"Too bad. I was hopin' you'd put in a good word for me when you were through with her."

"Don't worry about it. Mitter was giving me a line of crap about her. I don't think he did her at all. I guess I'll never get to screw a girl."

"Hey! Don't get down on yourself. You got personality, looks, and your old man's rich. Maybe you just ain't found the right girl yet. I think Judy Rosser has the hots for you. Try her."

"She would. She's nothin' but skin and bones, and she's got more hang-ups than my Mom's closet."

"Like the man said, 'It's all good, just some better 'n others.'"

"She'd have to be the best piece in the world for me to do it with her."

"Maybe she is."

"I don't think so, and she's not my type anyway. You know, you'd think in this day and age girls wouldn't have so many hang-ups about sex."

"Yeah, you'd think it was 1950 instead of 2015."

* * * * *

The boys who couldn't yet drive piled into Jenkins' van for the short ride to their houses.

Once home, Josh opened the door to find his father listening to a CD of Beattles music. Roger Smith rose and turned off the stereo. "You guys practiced late tonight," he said checking his watch in an automatic gesture.

"Yeah, the guys just couldn't make it come out right for some reason. Why you up so late?"

"Aunt Kathy called today. Great Grandpa Charley died last night."

"That's too bad. I used to love his tall tales, but he was pretty old, wasn't he?"

"Yes, he was ninety six. We'll be going up to South Dakota on Thursday for the funeral, and you'll have to come along."

"Dad! I told the band we'd practice again Friday night. We've got our first real job in two weeks. I mean, I loved Great Granpa and all that, but I can't go to South Dakota right now. Why can't I stay here by myself? I'm old enough."

"No negotiating on this one, Josh. I'm not asking you; I'm telling you."

"You'd think I was a baby or something."

"Just make whatever arrangements you have to make

tomorrow. Good night, Son."

Josh stomped up the stairs to his bedroom suppressing the urge to argue further.

This sucks. Now I have to call all the guys and listen to their bitching. This really sucks.

He flopped into a chair to remove his shoes, and a new thought crossed his mind. *Hey! Everybody always said that old mansion's haunted. It'd be really cool to run into a ghost there.*

He paused as he dropped one heavy sneaker to the floor. *Scared? Nah, I wouldn't be scared. At least, I don't think I'd be scared.*

He untied the other shoe and dropped it on the floor in reasonable proximity to its mate.

I might be scared for a second or two, but that's all. What do you say to a ghost? How's haunting? I'll bet any ghost'd have a really creepy story to tell. Yeah, and I could use it for inspiration for a hit song.

He lay back in the chair and mused a moment. *Maybe this trip won't be so bad after all.*

CHAPTER 3

The flight from San Francisco through Denver to Rapid City was typical of modern air travel; a long line to check bags, a degrading process at the security check point, and a screwed up seat selection. Josh read three chapters on his notepad book before the plane left the gate, and another three chapters waiting in line to take off. At Rapid City, they had to wait what seemed to be an eternity to his bladder for their gate to clear.

Inside the terminal Josh emerged from the restroom to find his Aunt Kathy and Uncle Walt greeting his parents. Josh joined the group and waited his turn to be pressed by the aunt and uncle he rarely saw, but who were, at least, "cool" enough to appreciate his music.

Kathy offered her hand to Josh. "Hi Josh, sorry we had to get together under these circumstances. How have you been?"

Great, she remembered I don't like hugs from old people. "I've been fine, Aunt Kathy. My band's about ready for its first gig."

"How exciting! Where's it going to be?"

"There's a teen club in Oakland that wants us for a one night stand. There's no pay, but at least we'll have a real audience."

He felt a large hand slap his back. "Hey, soon we'll be able to say we knew the famous rock star when he was just a kid." He turned to see his Uncle Walt.

It's always some kind of macho bullshit with him. "I hope so, someday, Uncle Walt."

"What hotel are we in?" his mother, Evelyn, asked as they walked toward the baggage claim area.

"We thought we'd save everybody money and put them up at Grandpa's mansion," Kathy replied.

"Cool! Maybe we'll see some ghosts," Josh said.

"Josh, you know there's no such thing as ghosts," his mother admonished.

"You've seen 'em, haven't you Dad?"

"I've seen some strange things there, but I really don't think it's haunted, Josh. Old houses like that make funny noises, that's all, and if you want to see something strange, you'll see it."

"Kathy, wouldn't it be less trouble for the household staff if everyone just stayed in a hotel?" Evelyn said.

"There are so many people coming in for the funeral the one hotel in Spearfish can't hold them all, and Rapid City's too far away. It seemed a waste not to use the old mansion especially since Charley ordered it kept fully staffed and in first class shape," Kathy said.

After collecting baggage, the family headed for the small town of Spearfish and Charley's lavish country estate. The dull gray sky and the stinging cold warned of the bitter, white blizzards lurking just over the horizon, ready to pounce on the countryside at any moment.

During the drive, Josh texted his band members while Kathy filled his parents in on the details of Grandpa Charley's death.

"Charley didn't come to the dining room for dinner that night; so, Lyle went to check on him and found him dead."

"Who's Lyle?" Roger asked. "I thought that nurse, what's

her name...?"

"Rosie, dear," Evelyn prompted with a sigh of disgust.

"Yeah, I thought Rosie was taking care of him."

"She usually did, but she was out that night for some reason," Kathy explained. "Anyway, Lyle, the maintenance man, found him slumped over in his wheel chair holding on to one of those horrible statuettes of his."

"That doesn't surprise me. He loved those monstrosities, but I didn't think he had any heart problems," Evelyn said.

"We didn't either. He was having these miniature strokes, but we all thought his heart was pretty good. Goes to show that you can never be sure of anything when it comes to a man his age."

Josh was able to ignore the small talk until the van turned into the drive and up to the big iron gates guarding the grounds. His eyes were drawn immediately to the huge stylized initials C. E. B. set into an ellipse on each one. They stood open, and above the drive an arched, wrought iron sign read, *Wanagiyata*. The huge crow perched just above the "G" gave the whole scene a Gothic touch straight out of Edgar Allen Poe. Josh expected the bird to croak "Nevermore", as they passed.

A uniformed security guard stepped out of the gatehouse and motioned for them to stop.

"Oh, good morning, Mr. Bowden," he said as he touched his cap in greeting. "Go on down to the house. I'll tell them you're on your way."

"Thanks, Bill," Walt acknowledged and drove on.

"Why did he ever give the place that screwy name?" Josh asked as they drove under the ironwork entry. A recent paint job covered up any trace of corrosion, but the dull, black color made it look centuries old. The arbor seemed to blot out the sky far too long, and Josh felt relieved when the car passed into the open again.

"I don't know. He never told anyone why," his father said.

"It means 'place of the spirits' in Lakota Souix," Kathy said. "I guess he wanted everyone to think it really was haunted."

"The old man was half crazy when he built this place 30 years back," Roger added. "I think the sudden wealth did it to him. He never had two nickels to rub together until that old gold mine of his turned out to be full of uranium. If you ask me, it was just too much for him."

The van stopped in a large, pea-gravel courtyard before a huge mansion. The three-story structure stretched for two hundred feet on either side of an ornate entryway held up by carved limestone columns. Leaded glass windows showed no signs of life. They gaped at the world like blind eyes craving sight. Numerous blackened chimney pots marked the many rooms with fireplaces, and the slate roof exacerbated the impact of the overcast sky. The big house faced north so the formal gardens on the south side would get the benefit of the sun all day. Jensen, the butler, and two maids stood ready to assist as they pulled up.

"Jensen," Roger called as he stepped from the van. "I thought you would have retired by now."

Josh smiled as he watched his father embrace the frail little man. *That guy's older than dirt.*

"Roger, for God's sake be careful! Jensen isn't a young man anymore," Evelyn sighed.

"I'm all right, Mrs. Smith," Jensen assured her. "I won't

break. It's good to see all of the family again. It's been a very long time."

"Too bad it had to be on such a sad occasion," Kathy said.

"It's good to have people in the house again," Jensen said. "You don't know how it is around here when the place is empty." Jensen shuddered.

"Why Jensen, you don't believe in ghosts do you?" Walt chided.

"I've served here over 25 years, Mr. Bowden. I won't say I've ever seen any ghosts, but there are some rooms in this place that make you shiver just going into them. It doesn't matter anymore, though, sir. I suppose they'll be selling this place now that the Master's dead."

Really cool! The old fart's convinced the place is haunted, and he lives here. Ghosts, here I come.

"That's for the will to decide, Jensen," Walt said. "It's getting cold out here. Let's get in."

Kathy led a procession up to the West wing where two floors of bedrooms waited to house the guests.

"Josh, this is your room." As she opened the door, the sun broke through the clouds, bathing the room in light. Dust specks danced in the golden shafts as if to protest the disturbance to the stale-smelling air. It was furnished in Victorian style with a canopied, four poster bed and ornately carved dressers, chests, and tables. Pictures of stern looking men and women hung in heavy gold frames on each wall.

"Hooo! Smells like it's been closed up for a while," Evelyn said, waving a hand in front of her nose.

"I'll open the windows a crack, madam," the maid commented as she set down the bags and cranked out the leaded glass panes.

"Are these relatives?" Josh asked scanning the portraits.

"Heavens no!" his father said. "We didn't have any relatives wealthy enough to afford a portrait before your great grandfather made his fortune. These are just some things he bought for decoration. God only knows who they are."

The fresh air seemed to brighten the atmosphere to match the sunlight. Kathy handed Josh a key. "Here, you won't really need this; but in case you want some privacy, Jensen assures me all of the locks are in working order. Take your time settling in. Dinner won't be until eight."

"Hey, maybe I'll find a ghost before the others get here," Josh said.

"Everyone thinks the conservatory, where all his old sculptures are, is the haunted place," his father said.

"I know, I know, but I really need to check my blog and answer my emails. You guys go on. I'll catch up with you later."

The group left Josh and his laptop in cyberspace peace and moved on.

Catching up with events in the real world required less than a half hour, but it served Josh's purpose admirably. *Now, I can go to the conservatory and check it out without Mom and Dad hovering over me. If that's where the ghosts are, that's where I want to be.*

Josh sped off to the central staircase and bounded down two steps at a time. He opened the door to a large, windowless room dominated by dozens of sculptures. Massive oil paintings hung on every wall but one, and that one held a huge map of the world.

Josh moved about the room inspecting the sculptures. They stood on circular marble bases, and though fairly uniform in diameter, they varied in height from less than a foot to over four feet. They consisted of round, square, and triangular silver-gray metal bars twisted together in strange formations. Some were dotted with randomly shaped bits of silver, brass and copper. Some were wrapped with aluminum wire or steel screening material. They looked as if they were hastily thrown together and brazed in place wherever the pieces happened to fall. Nothing about them gave the impression of fine art. They looked more like old cars crushed into blocks in preparation for the melting pot at the steel mill. His father's voice startled him.

"Charley made all of those himself. It was his one hobby," his father said. "He didn't play golf or tennis, and he considered most other things people do to relax a waste of time. He told me he only bought these paintings because he needed something fancy to hang on the walls. I never understood why he liked to sculpt, but a lot of things Charley did defied explanation."

"Hey, Dad, Mom, you surprised me. I guess you knew I'd be in here?"

"You said you were interested in finding a ghost, and I knew you'd go right to the sculptures," his father said.

"Do you suppose they're worth anything?" his mother asked.

"I doubt it," Roger said. "He never showed them anywhere. Only the guests at Wanagiyata ever got to see them. He'd spend hours and hours alone with these things–sometimes he even slept in here. He'd come in and lock all the doors and wouldn't open up for anything. Later, he'd come out smiling and refreshed, ready to take on the world again. Nobody ever figured out what it was about these things that enthralled him so much, and he wouldn't talk about it. He'd only say that 'communing with his creations', as he called it, was necessary from time to time."

"If we're lucky, they'll stay with the house?" Evelyn said as she fingered a particularly grotesque sample of Charley's art.

"Depends on how the will reads," Roger said. "He was pretty proud of these things. I imagine they'll go to someone in the family. He'd probably think he was doing that person a favor by bestowing his life's work upon them."

Roger laughed, but Evelyn only eyed the pieces with disgust. "None of this trash will enter *my* house."

"I doubt we rate high enough in Charley's favor to get any of *this trash*, in *your* house," Roger said. "They'll probably go to Uncle John." Roger changed the subject. "We're going to get a snack. Want to go with us?" he asked his son.

"Not right now, Dad. I'll get something later. I think I'll stick around here for a while and look for ghosts."

Evelyn and Roger suppressed their laughter. "Okay, but we'll be in the big sitting room if you want something."

They left, but Josh stayed behind fingering the sculptures. *I remember great grandpa's weird stories when I was little. They were really a kick, but all of 'em involved some strange power he possessed. He never told us exactly what it was, though he did hint to me one time it had something to do with these things. Funny, they all have worn spots where it looks like somebody's been holding on to them. Why would you want to hold these things? Hmmm, maybe that's where the maids held 'em while they cleaned.*

One of the paintings caught his eye. It depicted several

naked women trying to pull a satyr into a pond. A sculpture much smaller than the others sat on a shelf under the painting.

As he studied the strange piece of art, he thought he noticed a movement in his peripheral vision. He turned to see who was there, but the room was empty. He resumed his inspection. The metal bars on this piece were worn down in two areas, like the other sculptures, but this one was more polished. He suddenly felt a cold chill, and heard a distant voice whispering, "Go there."

Startled, he turned to find the room unchanged and empty. He rubbed the back of his neck and looked around for a possible source of the chill. Nothing he saw could account for it.

Was that a ghost? If it was, it wasn't like any kind of ghost I've ever read about. That was really creepy.

He strained his vision scanning the room, but nothing else stirred, and he heard no more voices. He was beginning to feel very uncomfortable and decided it might be a good idea to rejoin his parents. The painting and the sculpture begged him to stay, but he left the room glancing back over his shoulder several times.

* * * * *

That evening the funeral guests assembled in the huge dining room for a sumptuous dinner. Kathy hadn't bothered to designate seating, and Josh found a chair next to Caroline, his younger cousin. The age difference was only one year, but Josh hadn't seen her in over six years. She'd grown more mature in that time, much to his delight.

"Hi, Caroline."

The girl looked up at him and smiled. "Josh, it's been a long time."

"Can I sit next to you?"

"Sure, have a seat." She patted the plush velvet of the chair seat next to her. "What are you doing lately?"

Josh felt the warmth of her body and the scent of her perfume nearly made him faint. He fought off the sensation. He figured he needed to get comfortable around girls if he wanted to find one who would have sex with him. Caroline was not a candidate, but she was good practice for approaching other girls. "Oh, school and my band."

"Do you play an instrument?"

"Electric guitar. I have my own rock group, the 'Spacing Guild'."

"Oh, like in *Dune*."

"Yeah, we've got our first gig next week."

"That's cool. My best girlfriend sings with a band. I don't have any talent like that."

"Did Mitch come with you? I was looking forward to seeing him again."

"No, he's got exams this week. You won't believe what a nerd he's become. He only thinks of school and his GPA these days. I talked to him on the phone yesterday, and he said to tell you hello," Caroline said.

"He always was more interested in school than anything else, but I'm sorry he can't make it. By the way, have you toured the mansion yet?" Josh asked, hoping it would lead to more time with Caroline.

"No, I don't need to. My Mom and Dad used to come here all the time to check on the place after Great Grandpa Charley went into the nursing home."

"Oh, what do you think of the conservatory?"

"Duh! It's haunted."

"I was in there today and had the strangest feeling someone was talking to me, but nobody was there."

"I know, every time I go in there I feel cold chills even with the heat up full blast."

"They say ghosts are cold and you can tell when they're around by the cold feelings."

"If that's true, the conservatory is definitely haunted."

"Why don't we go there after dinner, and I can show you where it happened?"

Caroline looked at him as if he were some kind of mad man and shifted in her chair to give him more space. "Not on your life. There's no way I'm going in there after dark."

"I think it'd be a blast to actually see a ghost. I mean really see one, not like on those TV shows."

"Those TV shows are 100% phony. They never really see anything."

"Yeah, but now that I've felt one, I really want to see one. Don't you? If we stick close to each other, we should be safe."

"Well, it might be an adventure. I'll go with you."

* * * * *

When the adults adjourned to the salon for after-dinner drinks, Josh and Caroline wandered back to the conservatory. Josh found a light switch by the door, but only the small lights over the paintings came on.

"What a spooky place," Caroline said as she hugged herself tightly.

"This is the one I felt the ghost at this afternoon." Josh led her to the satyr painting and the small sculpture.

"I can see why you'd be drawn to this one." Caroline gave

him a disgusted look.

Josh blushed a bit but composed himself quickly. "Well, you have to admit it could have a certain appeal for guys. Which one do you like?"

Caroline wandered about the room perusing the paintings. She stopped next to one showing a dark castle set on a high crag overlooking a stormy sea. "This one's intriguing. Remember all those stories Great Grandpa used to tell us?"

"I sure do. They were really cool, but they couldn't be true."

Caroline looked at him with a surprised expression. "Why not?"

"He always had some kind of special advantage in all of them. One day I asked him what it was, and he wouldn't give me a direct answer. He only said that he'd make sure I found out someday. I think he was just nuts."

"Well anyway, this painting reminds me of one of his stories." She passed her fingers over the canvas as if trying to coax the words out of the picture.

Josh pointed out the worn spots on the sculpture below it. "See where this one's worn smooth? Put your hands on those places."

Caroline gave him a wary look. "What's going to happen if I do?"

"When I did that to the one over there, I felt the ghost. Try it."

Caroline tentatively placed one hand on a spot and held the other hand over the remaining location. "I don't know about this, Josh."

"Go ahead! It's harmless. I grabbed the one I showed you, and I'm still here, aren't?"

She placed her free hand on the sculpture and closed her eyes. In only a moment her eyes snapped open and her hands flew from the artwork. "Oh my God! I felt a ghost." She stumbled backward into Josh's arms.

Wow! What a rush. Stay calm, Josh. God, that perfume!

"Tell me what you felt," Josh asked.

"It was a cold sensation, like I just stepped into a freezer. Brrrr!" She suddenly realized where she was and delicately separated herself from Josh. "Sorry, I didn't mean to embarrass you."

"Don't worry about it. I kind of liked it."

She pushed Josh playfully. "You would. I should have guessed that after seeing what picture you liked."

They fell into playful laughter to relieve the stress. Caroline recovered first. "That was awesome, but that's enough ghosts for one night. I think we should leave now."

"Sure, I think Dad said they were in the 'main salon', or something like that."

CHAPTER 4

The viewing was just as boring as Josh expected. He retreated to one corner of the large room and passed the time texting his band members until his mother summoned him for a command appearance with a relative he hadn't seen in years.

"Come over here, Josh. Your great-aunt and uncle want to see you," she said.

Josh joined the group and went through the expected routine. He smiled when his great-aunt remarked how much he'd grown, and replied as expected to all the questions about his ambitions. He did a better job of hiding after that.

The funeral was not much better. The family sat uncomfortably close to the minister for Josh's taste. He tried to use his cell phone to text as surreptitiously as he knew how, but his mother caught him.

"Put that away. Show some respect, Josh," she said.

* * * * *

Sunday and the reading of the will was his next ordeal. The assembled group filled every chair in the big sitting room at Wanagiyata, and the servants brought in several folding chairs to accommodate the overflow crowd.

This time his father stopped the texting. "Listen up, you may be in for some money."

Fat chance. He never even sent me money for Christmas. He stowed the phone in his coat pocket.

Mr. Lansky, Charley's lawyer, entered and took a seat on the sofa, laying his briefcase on the coffee table. As he opened it, the click of the latches brought an immediate silence to the assembled family.

"Ladies and Gentlemen, I believe you know who I am; but I will introduce myself anyway. I am Isaac Lansky, Mr. Bastin's lawyer. I have here his last will and testament, which is dated three months before he entered the nursing home. All of us can attest that he was in complete control of all his faculties at that time. He never made any move to alter the will from the day he signed it until the day he died. It contains some unusual provisions, but I trust you will recognize them as typical of the man."

Lansky cleared his throat and waited for any protests. There being none, he produced the usual blue, legal-sized folder from his briefcase and folded back the cover.

"I'll skip the boilerplate and go right to the meat," he said. "'I leave to each of the current servants and employees at Wanagiyata the sum of fifty thousand dollars in recognition of their faithful service over the years'. He goes on to name six people who are all still with the estate. 'To my great grandchildren, Caroline Elizabeth Bastin and Mitchell Dean Bastin, I leave the sum of two hundred and fifty thousand dollars to be held in trust by their parents until they graduate from college. Should they fail to graduate, the money will revert to their parents. It is my hope that each of them will use the money to start their own business. Working for someone else is slavery by another name, and I hope this bequest will free them from that curse. To my Son, John MacArthur Bastin, I leave my interest in the Bastin Mining Corporation, the estate at Wanagiyata and all of its contents except for my collection of sculptures.'"

Josh felt his mother grow tense at that announcement.

"'To my grandson, Roger Morrison Smith, I leave my sculpture collection and all of my remaining assets on condition he insures compliance with the instructions in this will."

"Oh shit!" Evelyn blurted out.

Is that Mom? She never cusses. He looked around and noticed the other guest's startled expressions. *She'll really be pissed now.*

Lansky stopped to acknowledge the interruption and looked at Evelyn as if waiting for a more complete response.

"Sorry," Evelyn apologized to the assembled family. "Go on Mr. Lansky."

At the back of the room another voice expressed disappointment, but no one could see the individual or hear his voice. Only the chill felt by a distant Bastin cousin gave any clue that a spectral presence witnessed the proceedings.

Lansky resumed reading after clearing his throat. "The only exception to this provision is the unit located under my copy of the painting 'Nymphs and Satyr' by W. A. Bouguereau. That sculpture I leave to my great-grandson, Joshua Marcus Smith. I feel he will appreciate it more than any other member of my family. I sincerely hope it will help him to become a man once he finds its true value…

Josh wasn't listening any more. *Crap! Mitch and Caroline get $250,000, and all I get is one of those stinking sculptures. I guess Great Grandpa did like them best after all. At least it's the one with the ghost. I know Mom isn't pleased with the idea of having any of them around the house. I could put that little one in my room, but where would they put the rest? Oh well, no use worrying. Dad'll* *have to take care of that part.* Lasky's voice broke through his wall of indifference.

"... stipulate that my sculpture collection must be established as a permanent exhibit in an appropriate location befitting its dignity and high intrinsic value. These sculptures are the culmination of my life's work, and must remain a unified whole. They contain my very soul, and as the Pharaohs cursed those who would spoil their tombs, I will have my vengeance on any who defy my wishes in this matter. Should my grandson, or his heirs, fail to abide by this provision, they will forfeit all claim to any remaining portion of the assets delivered to them as a result of this will.'" He read on through several minor bequests and announced he was done. Placing several copies of the will on the coffee table, he returned the original to his brief case, and snapped it closed.

The room cleared quickly, and Josh asked his mother, "Can I go get my sculpture now?"

She didn't answer him. She sat in her chair stunned.

"Mom! Can I get my sculpture now?"

"No, Josh, I won't have those monstrosities in our home. You'll have to leave it here."

"What's the harm, if he keeps it in his room?" Roger asked. "It is *his* sculpture, you know," Roger said.

Evelyn glared at her husband before turning to her son. "Oh all right. You can go get it, but make sure the staff knows you have it."

"Sure, Mom."

Josh ran off to the conservatory and found his sculpture quickly. He placed his hands on the worn places and spoke. "Well, Mr. Ghost, you belong to me now. I'm going to take you home and put you in a special place so you can inspire me to write a hit tune. I know you'll like California. It's a lot warmer than here."

Once again, he felt a chill and heard a voice inside his head. "G# Josh, remember G#."

The cold feeling left him, and he scanned the room for what he now knew was a ghost of some kind. *It must be a musical ghost. It wants me to remember G#. Maybe that's the key for a song this thing'll inspire me to write? We'll check it out at home.*

He picked it up and was surprised by its weight. *This thing must be made of lead, or something.*

He found Jensen and informed him of the will's provision.

"Very good, Master Smith. I'll make a note of it. Congratulations on your inheritance."

"Thanks, Jensen, but no money came with this thing."

"Mister Bastin always valued his sculptures rather highly. You should feel honored that he willed one to you, personally."

"I guess so. I'm taking it up to my room now, okay?"

"Certainly, it's yours now."

Josh carried the sculpture up to his room and placed it on the night table near his bed. "Take it easy. I'll come back and pack you up later." He figured he'd better reassure the ghost he was not forgotten.

He went back downstairs to find his parents talking with the lawyer. He interrupted. "Mom, Dad, I got the ghost sculpture, and I told Jensen about it."

"You interrupted our conversation with Mr. Lansky, Josh. That's rude," his father scolded.

"I'm sorry."

Roger turned to Lansky.

"This is our son, Josh, Mr. Lansky." Roger introduced him.

Lansky offered his hand to Josh. "Congratulations on your inheritance. Your Great Grandfather was quite proud of those things. Giving you one was very generous of him."

"Thanks, Mr. Lansky, but I'd rather have had the money."

The adults laughed at Josh's response.

Roger resumed the conversation. "Mr. Lansky, besides the sculpture collection, the will mentioned all 'remaining assets'. How much money are we talking about?"

"I'd say on the order of four to four and a half million after the estate taxes are paid and probate's settled. Of course, the assets will have to be liquidated to realize that, but you should clear at least four million at today's prices."

"Oh my God, I never realized it would be that much," Evelyn said.

"Mr. Bastin invested very wisely and bought during bear markets when everyone else was selling. With the recent bull markets, his portfolio has grown to a considerable sum. He used the income from the business to finance this house and to cover his other expenses. He never touched his stocks and bonds. I knew the family's opinion of the collection, and I advised him to settle a considerable sum of money with them in order to insure his wishes would be respected."

"You'll have to excuse our surprise, Mr. Lansky. We didn't think anything near that much money would be involved. Do you have any idea how soon we'll we have to take possession of the collection?" Roger asked.

"It'll take six to eight months to get the estate through probate, but you can take the sculpture collection any time you want. Charley had it insured, and that policy will establish the value to the estate.

"Well, I know my wife is in no hurry to take possession of the sculptures. I guess we'll leave them here until John decides what to do with the mansion. Thanks, Mr. Lansky. I assume we'll be in touch again as soon as the estate is settled?" Roger asked.

"I'll call you as soon as that happens, Mr. Smith. Have a safe trip back home." Lansky shook Roger's hand and nodded to Evelyn and Josh before he resumed his path to the door.

"God, Roger! That changes everything," Evelyn said as the lawyer moved out of earshot.

"Dad, does that mean we'll have all the sculptures at our house?" Josh asked.

"Let me talk to your great uncle John and find out if he has any idea what he's going to do with the mansion. Maybe we could just leave them here, or donate them to a local art museum, or something. I'll be right back."

"Can I go now, Mom? I noticed they were fixing lunch in the kitchen, and I'm hungry."

"Yes, you may, but we'll be leaving in the morning. Make sure you get packed tonight. Will your sculpture fit in a suitcase?"

"I'll check it out. What if it won't?"

"Then have Jensen pack it for you."

"I will. See you later." Josh vanished into the closest hallway.

* * * * *

Josh was busy with the lunch buffet when his parents found him. They filled their plates then joined him.

"What'd you find out about the rest of the sculptures, Dad?"

"Your great uncle John hasn't given much thought to what he'd do with the house? He has an idea about letting the state have Wanagiyata as a museum. He also thinks there might be someone interested in it as a fancy hotel or something, though there isn't much to see around these parts besides Mount Rushmore. In any case, he said we could leave the things here until the estate's settled."

"I'm glad I can take mine now," Josh said.

"Why do you want to bring one of those *things* home?" Evelyn asked her son.

"I think this one has a ghost with it," Josh beamed. "I was in the conservatory looking at it the other day and got a funny feeling in the back of my neck. I think I'd like to write a song about it for my band."

"As long as you keep it in your room," Evelyn added. "I won't have one of those things where guests might see it."

"Okay, Mom," Josh agreed.

* * * * *

Josh held his sculpture a moment before packing it. *If you have a ghost, I sure hope it follows us home.* He looked around the room. *If you're here, ghost, please know you can tell me your story any time.* He wrapped the thing in some dirty clothes and placed it in the suitcase. *I'll bet that's why great grandpa left it to me. He knew the ghost would help me with my music.*

That evening, Walt drove them to the airport in Rapid City but could not stay to say good-bye. Other relatives were waiting back at Wanagiyata.

Josh's packing job had to be torn apart when TSA became convinced it was some new form of bomb. Fortunately, they'd allowed plenty of time thanks to Roger's suspicion it would trigger every sensor in the airport. Roger was pleased to learn his son's name was not on the FBI's latest list of dangerous characters.

As the jet liner lifted off, Josh was engrossed in his earphones tapping out the rhythm on his armrest. He decided the sculpture made the trip worthwhile after all.

*****

Evelyn gazed out at the bleak landscape slipping by below and said a silent prayer requesting Charley's collection remain at Wanagiyata. There was certainly no room in their house for such junk, though most people would consider her home a mansion with ample room for anything. The storage space over the garages might work, but she would have to move out some of their things to make room. It might be a good excuse for a garage sale.

Evelyn snickered at the thought of a garage sale in their neighborhood. Their house sat on twenty acres of California shoreline just north of Santa Cruz. "Exclusive" was probably the word the average person would use to describe the area. It was a beautiful house featuring modern architecture and furnishings, with a spectacular view of the ocean.

Roger was truly a good provider. He'd worked his way up at Theta Industries from a lowly computer engineer to Executive Vice President. The generous salary and bonuses from that position coupled with the substantial inheritance from his father and some fortuitous turns in the stock market made them millionaires several times over. In spite of that they couldn't just throw away four million.

Four million dollars just to see the collection was kept intact. No matter how much she disliked them, some way would have to be found to comply with the stipulations of Charley's will. They had enough land to accommodate a small building for the things away from the main residence. It wouldn't need to have any windows, and she could tell people it was a storage shed. For four million she would find some suitable answer.

Roger finished reading the same paragraph in his book for the fourth time and let his mind return to what was really bothering him. *Why would Charley leave a sculpture to Josh? I know the great grandkids used to love his tall tales, but what does that have to do with his sculptures? Oh well, I'll ask Josh if he knows anything when we get home.* Roger closed his book and turned to his wife. "A penny for your thoughts."

"How about four million?" she said and smiled back at him.

"Thinking about the sculptures, eh?"

"Yes, we could always put up some sort of building for them, couldn't we?"

"Sure, but I imagine John'll find someone to take over Wanagiyata who'll allow us to keep them there as a tribute to Charley. If he gives the place to the state, he can make that a condition of the deal."

"Let's hope he can do just that." Evelyn said.

* * * * *

Josh missed all of this conversation. He was oblivious to anything but the opiate being piped into his head through the black, plastic tubes.

CHAPTER 5

Once back home, Josh gave the odd looking sculpture a place of honor on his computer credenza under his poster of Lady Gaga in a skimpy outfit. He thought of the sexy painting and the eerie voice more felt than heard. He still remembered the sudden chill at the back of his neck and shuddered as he re-lived the moment. He sat staring at it, trying various combinations of notes on the keyboard, and evaluating their impact on his vision of the sculpture. Everything was normal until he hit one particular note.

He hit the key several times, but only a fraction of the normal sound came from the speaker. "Shit! What a time for this damn thing to act up," Josh said to the empty room.

"Josh, will you stop making so much racket," his mother's head poked through the doorway. "It's after eleven, and I have a headache. Go to bed."

"Mom, I have to practice. The band's got a gig a week from Friday."

"Well use your headphones, then. I can't get any rest with that God-awful noise blaring from your room."

"Okay, Mom." Josh put on his offended expression for her benefit.

He switched the keyboard to the headphones and tried the same note. This time he heard it clearly. *Must be a bad connection*, Josh thought.

Josh checked all of the cables and found no problem.

"Okay, let's try this again," he mumbled to himself. He switched the keyboard back to speakers and hit the note. Once more only a muted sound reached his ears. He tried the headphones again and heard the tone at full volume.

Now wait a minute. You can't have just one note bad in the speakers. It must be something wrong with my keyboard, he thought. He picked up his electric guitar and connected it to the same speakers.

That was a G sharp. Let's try it with the guitar. Wait a minute! That's the note the ghost told me about. What was it trying to tell me? I'll try it again.

He fingered the proper fret and struck the string. Again, the note was muted. He switched to headphones and heard the full tone once more.

Weird. The ghost must be around here somewhere making sure G# doesn't play. He glanced around the room, looking for any sign of a specter, then he noticed the sculpture. One of the twisted metal bars showed a light coating of frost. The rest of it looked normal.

"Wow, that's awesome," he whispered to himself. He touched the metal to verify his perception and immediately pulled back his hand.

Could this thing be absorbing the sound? Josh decided to test his theory. He lifted the sculpture and carried it into the hall bathroom. After returning to his room, he tried the note again. G# sounded loud and clear through his speakers, using both his keyboard and his guitar. At that point his father's head appeared in his doorway.

"Josh, I thought your mother told you to knock it off and go to bed fifteen minutes ago."

"I'm sorry, Dad. I'm shutting down right now."

"One more sound from this room and you're grounded for a week, understand?"

"Yes, sir."

Josh waited as he pictured his father walking back to his bedroom and closing the door. After a suitable interval he retrieved the sculpture from the hall bathroom.

Well, now I know it's this thing absorbing the sound, but why? He studied the sculpture more carefully. The felt covering the bottom of the base was loose in one place. He peeled it back and noticed the bottom of the base was removable.

Hmmm, wonder what's under there? He peeled off the felt then fished a screwdriver from his toolbox and removed the panel. *Jeez, look at all the electronic stuff. This is more than just a crummy-looking sculpture. This thing must be some kind of radio or computer or something.* Josh inspected the thing for someplace to plug in a power cord, but there was none. There was also no place to put a battery. *It has to get power from somewhere, but where, and what does this stuff do?* He traced the wires from the circuit board to connections on different parts of the sculpture's metal rods. *Beats me. Maybe it's just there for show. Dad could figure it out, I'll get him to have a look at it tomorrow.*

He replaced the panel and turned the item over in his hands. *Look at those two worn spots. Obviously, somebody's been holding on to this thing, and that somebody was probably great grandpa. Maybe holding on to this thing and humming G♯ is the big secret?*

Josh remembered the painting hanging above it in the conservatory. The full figured, naked women playing with the satyr, and the voice telling him to go there. He placed his hands on the sculpture covering the worn spots. His fingers wrapped naturally around the rectangular bars with no discomfort from the edges. He hummed G# and felt the metal grow cold as he thought of the painting.

The cold worked its way through his hands and wrists and began to climb his arms. Strangely, it was not like being cold in the winter. The chill did not seem to be penetrating below his skin. He could keep his hold on the piece without fear of freezing to it. He was about to give up and go to bed when he felt a sudden lightness as if he were filled with helium. His vision went gray, and he felt himself floating above the chair.

Maybe this was the way Great Grandpa got high? What a kick! He had a wonderful sense of well-being as if he were in the palm of some mighty hand. He let himself be carried away down a tunnel of red and blue lights.

A bright flash of light restored his vision, and he found himself standing in a forest next to a large sycamore tree. The scene was eerily similar to the one in the painting at Wanagiyata, but there were no naked women and no satyrs. The sounds of the forest assailed his ears, the birds, the rustle of the trees in the wind, the sighing of the pines, the music of a small stream nearby.

Then he noticed his arms were imbedded in the tree trunk. He pulled them back quickly and sucked in his breath—they were transparent. He touched one hand with the other and could feel the flesh as if it were still visible. The rest of his body had the same ghostly appearance. *Hey, I've never been a ghost before in my dreams. This is cool.*

Josh inhaled deeply to take in the scents of the forest, but there was no sensation of smell—no scent of decaying leaves, no spicy aroma from the underbrush. It dawned on him then—he must be dreaming. That was it; he fell asleep holding on to the sculpture, and he was dreaming about the painting. He tried to remember if he smelled things in his dreams before, but he couldn't be certain. All he had to do was wake up, and the dream would end; but no matter how hard he tried to regain consciousness, the dream persisted.

This is really weird. I've always been able to wake myself up from a dream before. I don't understand what's going on, but I'm sure if I keep on trying, I'll eventually wake up. I'll just walk around for a while, and maybe, that'll do it.

The path ahead wound deeper into the forest, and he remembered a book he once read where the hero stepped into a painting and explored the world behind the canvas. Now he had the same opportunity. He felt almost weightless as he moved with incredible ease along the rough pathway, but this was a dream, wasn't it? He was familiar with dreams of gliding, even flying, from place to place.

A satyr, like the one in the painting, interrupted Josh's thoughts as it jumped onto the path in front of him. The sudden appearance of the half man, half goat startled him; and his first thought was for his own safety. The creature was almost a head shorter, but his muscular upper torso and wiry goat legs indicated it would be a formidable opponent. He braced himself to receive its charge, but the satyr passed right through him as if he weren't even there. Josh nervously inspected his body for damage but he seemed to be fine. He felt a bit faint from the realization a satyr just passed right through him, and sat down next to a large tree to compose himself.

The satyr plunged back into the brush again, calling out

softly in a strange language. A sound caused him to look up at a very curious squirrel who seemed to be studying him. The squirrel scampered down the tree trunk not two feet from his face and stopped at eye level. Josh spoke to it, "Hey Mr. Squirrel. How's the acorn business these days?"

The animal cocked its head to one side and stared at him. To test his ghostly powers Josh raised his hand to pet the creature, figuring it would bolt the moment it detected movement. He was shocked to see it did not flinch. He touched the animal's head, but his hand passed through the creature, just as the satyr passed through him. The only sensation was a warm feeling in the back of his head. The squirrel's only reaction was bristling its fur and tail as if it suddenly felt a winter chill.

Figures, ghosts are supposed to be cold.

The squirrel scampered back up the tree and resumed its study from a safer distance.

Funny, it acts like it can see me; but that satyr didn't seem to know I was there. Maybe he was just distracted. He was looking for something, or someone, that's for sure.

A crash of broken twigs caused Josh to turn just in time to see an amply built, stark naked lady enter the clearing to his right. She stopped and studied the open area carefully, but her gaze bypassed Josh, who was glad to be a ghost at this point.

The lady emerged cautiously and paused to listen. She, too, was a copy of the woman from the painting. By modern standards she was heavy, but she had a pleasant figure in spite of her bulk. Soft, innocent dark brown eyes darted from side to side, giving her the look of a startled doe. She was by no means what he would call pretty, but Josh felt aroused at the sight of her.

She, too, moved past him without noticing; but her body

brushed against him as she did so. In that moment he thought he could smell her. It was a combination of perspiration and some kind of flower. Like an aphrodisiac it roused his manhood, and he was embarrassed.

Josh jumped as the satyr pounced on the woman. She shrieked in terror, and the smile on the beast's face left no doubt about what he had in mind. He threw the woman to the ground face down and pinned her there with his body while he twined her long hair around his free hand. As the satyr maneuvered into position, Josh composed himself and decided he must act to save the poor female from being raped.

He ran to the satyr and tried to grab it, but his hand only passed through the creature's body. He tried to grip a fallen tree branch to use as a club with no more success. Then he noticed the woman was purring contentedly in the same language the satyr used earlier.

Maybe these people just like some kinky things? Josh stood back to watch the drama unfold. The woman and the satyr assumed some positions Josh never imagined, but since he had no first-hand experience with women himself, he put it down to his own naiveté. It was quite a show, and he hated to leave it, but someone was calling him from the other side of the clearing. The voice was faint and seemed to be very far away, but it sounded like his mother. He ran in the direction of the sound, and it grew louder and louder as he approached the tree where his dream began. Instinctively he reached back into the trunk and felt something metallic. It had a familiar shape, and he grasped what he knew were the same worn spots on the sculpture in his room. He hummed G#.

* * * * *

"Josh, wake up!" Evelyn shook her son violently since calls and prodding produced no response.

"What? Huh?"

"Josh, are you okay?"

"It's okay, Mom. I just dozed off, I guess." Josh removed his hands from the sculpture and rubbed them together to restore warmth.

"Why didn't you go to bed when I told you to? You know you shouldn't be up this late on a school night," his mother scolded.

"I was working on a new song for the band, and I guess I just fell asleep."

"What were you doing with that sculpture?"

"I was just using it for inspiration. I must have been holding on to it when I fell asleep." Josh watched the frost melt from the artwork as the room's temperature rose. Everything seemed so real, yet it had to have been a dream.

"I turned up the thermostat for you. You really shouldn't let it get so cold in here," his mother admonished as she moved to close the open window next to his bed.

"Sorry Mom. I guess I was just wrapped up in the music."

"Well, get in bed and don't let me hear a sound from this room until morning." She pecked him on the cheek knowing he hated mushy kisses.

Josh climbed into bed as his mother turned out the light and closed the door. He lay there for a moment staring at the sculpture. *What a rush. No wonder Great Grandpa had such a high opinion of 'em.* He looked at his alarm clock and read 11:37. It seemed like he'd been asleep a long time, but only a few minutes had passed on the clock. *Oh well, that's how dreams are,* he thought.

CHAPTER 6

In Miami, Florida another person knew of Charley's death, but Mark Wycham was more concerned about the fate of the sculpture collection than the death of his old client. At 73, Wycham was well beyond the age when most men retire, but, as with many men, the thought of doing nothing was more fearful than dying from job related stress. A rigorous fitness program kept him in good physical condition, but the ravages of time and gravity were beginning to prove too much for his personal trainer and professional dietician to overcome.

If money could buy health, Mark Wycham would be the healthiest man on the planet. He spent whatever he felt necessary on doctors, fitness programs and fad diets, but those expenses did not even dent his income from the many businesses he owned. As one of the richest men in the world, he was prepared to go to any lengths to achieve his goals, and fitness was his primary objective. Right now, however, Charley's sculptures were running a close second.

"Charley Earth is dead, Wycham. What is your plan for obtaining his Cargans?" The voice belonged to Manjahba, a ghostly specter standing in front of Wycham's large, mahogany desk. Wycham didn't seem to mind that the person addressing him would be invisible to anyone else entering the room. The specter spoke with a heavy accent resembling Russian, but including a hint of something else Wycham couldn't put his finger on.

Manjahba stood nearly six foot six inches tall and was built to match his height. He wore the usual full-length robe characteristic of his people featuring long sleeves hiding his hands, and a stiff collar fitting closely against his neck. A heavy, gold chain with curiously shaped links draped across his shoulders, and a gaudy gold ring dangled from his right ear.

Wycham feared this apparition. Not because he was afraid of ghosts, but because the thing standing before him wielded great power on a planet far away and could easily make or break Wycham's fortunes here on Earth.

"I was there when they read the will. His grandson, Roger Smith, inherits them, but I'm sure he has no idea of their real value. Everyone in the family thinks the things are ugly junk. I thought it'd be no trouble at all buying them from whoever got them, but Smith gets $4 million if he retains control. It won't be easy convincing him to sell."

"Bah, $4 million? Offer him twice that, you can afford it," Manjahba said.

"If I offer that much, he'll get suspicious and do some investigating. I think my approach will be as a friend of his grandfather who wants to do something to honor the old man's memory. I'll think of something. Just leave it all to me, Manjahba."

"I will check with you in seven Earth days, Wycham." With that pronouncement, the ghostly image disappeared through one of the wood paneled walls of Wycham's office.

Wycham leaned back in his plush swivel chair and breathed a sigh of relief. He was always uncomfortable around Ulans, and Manjahba was even more imposing than most of them, but if he could put up with his sense of dread long enough, he could increase his fortune tenfold.

CHAPTER 7

Roger was glad to be back to work Monday morning. "Good morning 'Nita." Roger always left off the "An" part of his executive assistant's name.

"Good morning, Mr. Smith. Sorry to hear about your grandfather. How was the funeral?"

"Thank you. It was a lovely service 'Nita–just what he would have wanted. Anything break while I was gone?"

"No, but Mr. Bryson has called a meeting on the Mystic project for one this afternoon. I put the folder in your basket. Better check your calendar over carefully. I made several appointments for you while you were gone. Let me know if I need to change any."

"Okay, 'Nita." Roger opened the door to his office and smelled the familiar blend of wood polish and window cleaner. The wall behind his desk consisted of a solid row of large picture windows, giving him a good view of the green campus composing Theta Industries.

As he sat down to start on his emails and computer memos, the intercom came to life. "There's a Mr. Wycham on line one for you, Sir. He says he was an old friend of your grandfather's. Will you take the call?"

"Yes, put him on, 'Nita." Roger picked up the phone and waited for the click telling him he was connected.

"This is Roger Smith."

"Mr. Smith, thank you for taking my call. My name is Mark Wycham, and I knew your grandfather, Charles Bastin, very well. We were business associates for many years, and he was one of my mentors for several years before that. Please accept my deepest sympathy for your loss."

"Thank you, Mr. Wycham. What can I do for you?"

"I understand you inherited Charley's... I'm sorry; I don't mean to be disrespectful. I always called him Charley, and the habit's hard to break."

"No offense taken, Mr. Wycham. Everyone called him Charley, that's the way he wanted it. Go ahead."

"As I said, I understand you inherited Charley's sculptures. Your grandfather was one of my mentors when I was starting out in the mining equipment business. I was a green kid just out of college, and Charley took me under his wing, so to speak. I owe him a lot, but what I'm calling you about is his sculpture collection. I'd like to buy it. You see, I'm an art collector, and I have a good-sized gallery in my home. Don't get me wrong, it's not that the gallery is full of old masters, or anything like that. I collect the art my friends create, for the most part, and I'd love to have Charley's sculptures as part of my collection. I hoped you would be willing to sell them."

"Normally, I'd be happy to give them to you. My wife abhors the things, and we don't have any place in our home to display them even if we wanted to. The problem is my grandfather's will stipulates that we keep them together in one place under our control. A substantial sum of money is contingent on the fact that we do just that. I'm afraid they aren't for sale."

"That's too bad. I so had my hopes up they might be

available. Do you have any plans for the collection?"

"No, they'll stay at Wanagiyata until we're forced to move them. I haven't given it much thought beyond that. There's always the possibility they can stay with the house."

"I see. I wonder if you might be open to a suggestion?"

"Let's hear it," Roger said.

"I'm sorry you aren't in a position to sell, but what about displaying them in a museum or art gallery?"

"I know my wife doesn't want them in our house, but what art gallery would take that bunch of junk?"

"With your permission I'll check around. I'm a major contributor to several artistic organizations around the country. Perhaps one of them might be willing to cooperate given a large donation to support the exhibit?"

"You certainly have my permission to try."

"Good, I'll let you know if I find anything. It's been a pleasure speaking with you Mr. Smith."

"You can drop the formalities. Just call me Roger."

"Thank you, and please call me Mark."

"I'll look forward to your next call."

"Thank you, let me give you my contact information."

Roger copied down the information and hung up the phone. Perhaps this Wycham fellow could solve all of his problems with the collection. He filed the contact data in his computer.

* * * * *

As Roger was speaking with Wycham, Josh was reliving his dream several times during school, much to the consternation of his math and English teachers. At home he continued the internal debate in his room.

That was so real. Should I tell Mom and Dad about it? This decision didn't require much thought. *No, they'd just tell me it was a dream, but it was more than a dream—I know it. I also better hold off on letting Dad look at that circuit board.*

He picked up the sculpture and studied it carefully. *I sure wish Great Grandpa Charley were alive so I could ask him what they really are. Whatever they are, that was a cool dream. I'm going to try it again tonight.*

"Josh, supper's ready." His mother's voice on the house intercom halted any further contemplation.

Over supper Roger told of his conversation with Mark Wycham. Evelyn brightened visibly at the thought the collection might find a home other than hers.

"Well, I'm glad somebody wants those things. I hope he calls you with a plan before we have to get them out of that old mansion," she said.

"John'll call me when they've made a decision on the mansion. We should have plenty of warning if we have to move them. Phil thinks there's a good chance the state will take the place over and use it as a park. If they do, we can throw in the condition they keep the sculptures on display as a memorial to Charley. If Wycham comes up with something before then, so much the better," Roger said.

"Hey Mom, I think it'd be neat if Dad could put up a pole barn out back, and the band could use it as a practice studio."

"You have a very nice facility for the band at the Barnes'," Evelyn said. "You don't need another one, particularly around here."

Oh no, I'd really like to see what dreams come with the other ones. I sure hope we have to take them all.

CHAPTER 8

Manjahba appeared in Wycham's office promptly at 9:00 AM exactly one week after their last discussion. Ulans were nothing if not prompt, and they never forgot an obligation.

"What did you find out, Wycham?" the ghostly figure demanded.

"My sources tell me the old mansion house and grounds will be picked up by the state as a park. The agreement will stipulate that the sculptures be maintained there as a permanent exhibit."

Manjahba stroked his chin. "That would mean they'd be under the control of some bureaucrat who might do anything with them. I don't feel very comfortable with that arrangement."

"Their hands would be tied by the sale agreement. They'd have to leave them alone."

"I've seen your government forget about agreements whenever it was convenient for them to do so. You have to come up with a plan for taking control as soon as possible. I don't think I need to remind you that your future success is riding on control of those Cargans. We must have them under our complete control if we want to place our own people in key positions on those planets. The future of Ula depends upon it. Without the Cargans my people will remain slaves to the powers on Mica. Earth is the only place we can operate with impunity."

"I know what's riding on them. I'm just as interested in the gold as you are in replacing those Mica politicians with Ulans. I also know you couldn't pull off an entity transfer scheme anywhere else but Earth. The Grand Council would shut you down almost instantly anywhere else but here. Don't worry, I'll have a plan in a few days, and I'll come to see you when it's ready. Meantime, I'd appreciate it if you'd leave. I'm expecting some clients in a few minutes, and it's very disconcerting to have you in the room when other people are here."

"I'll go for now, but I'll be back in three days to hear your plan if you do not come to me by then." Manjahba vanished through the far wall much to Wycham's relief.

CHAPTER 9

Josh lay in bed staring at his computer credenza. The moonlight filtering through the curtains gave the scene a ghostly quality, and the shiny places on the metal bars flashed and dimmed as the trees outside his window swayed in the wind. They shifted the shadow patterns such that the thing seemed to be beckoning to him. Josh remembered the satyr and the woman and he smiled at the thought of witnessing more of their sexual activity. He'd heard stories of XXX rated movies, but had not yet seen one. He couldn't imagine a movie being any better than his last dream. Why not?

Josh rose from his bed and moved to his desk. The polished places were clearly visible. He gripped them and hummed G#. The cold crept up his arms as it had before. He concentrated on the painting.

Once more he found himself in the forest with his arms inside the sycamore tree. This time he knew what to do. He started down the same path he'd used before, but instead of seeing a satyr, he noticed the ghostly figure of a young girl. She looked human, but her clothes were not like any he'd seen before. The leather-like, red sleeveless top had a high collar, and the front was open to her waist, revealing only the hint of breasts. Her black skirt was very short, but high black boots came nearly halfway up her thigh. Deep green eyes shone beneath ridiculously long lashes, and her hair was siff black spikes. The paleness of her skin accented the garishness of her appearance.

He stopped not knowing just how to proceed. The girl smiled at him and spoke in a language he did not understand.

Oh my god, she can see me, and I can see her and hear her. The satyr couldn't see me, but she can. I guess I'd better see if we can talk to each other some way so she can tell me what's going on. "I'm sorry, I don't understand you," Josh said with a shrug of his shoulders and hands upraised as if in defense.

The girl spoke again in a different language just as unintelligible. He shook his head. The girl thought for a moment then beckoned for him to follow her. *Why not? She's not bad looking. Maybe we can have a ghost date?*

The girl led him through the trees to a clearing and put one arm inside an oak tree. A satyr and a naked woman appeared out of the bush and stood quiet before her. She beckoned to Josh again and indicated the satyr. Josh shook his head to indicate his confusion. The girl put her hands together and made a motion as if she were diving into the satyr then stood back and waved to Josh to come forward. Josh shrugged again. She seemed exasperated, but indicated he should watch her. Josh nodded his understanding.

The girl melted into the naked woman, and the slightly plump nymph seemed to come alive. The woman waved her hands in front of her body as if she were smoothing the wrinkles in a dress and pointed to Josh then to the satyr.

"You want me to melt into him?" Josh said as he pointed to the half man, half goat.

The woman nodded vigorously, and Josh moved into the strange body.

What a rush! He tried moving his hands and feet and found they obeyed his wishes just like his own limbs. *It's like I'm looking out a window from inside his head. I can even feel his thoughts. He sure is horny.* A girl's voice interrupted his thoughts.

"There, can you understand me now?"

"Yes, I can. What's happened to us? How come I can understand you now? Why could I see and hear you when nothing else around here can see or hear me?"

The woman giggled. "Silly, you've possessed the satyr. The satyr and nymph speak the same language. When you're an entity, you can see and hear other entities—it's that simple. Now we can have sex."

"What?"

"Isn't that what you came here for?"

"What do you mean? I'm just dreaming. I'm asleep in my room at home."

"I understand that's where your body is. Let me ask another way. What planet do you live on?"

"Earth, but I haven't left it."

The woman laughed again. "You're so silly. Look, I'm from Brem, and my name is Oriana, what's yours?"

"Josh."

"Don't you speak any Giran?"

"I don't even know what Giran is."

"Most entity travelers speak a little Giran. It's the universal language."

"Entity travelers? What are they?"

The woman cocked her head to one side and gave him an incredulous look. "Wait a minute, are you telling me you didn't deliberately come to Mythos for sex?"

"Not really, I guess. I was holding one of my great grandpa's sculptures and humming its note just like before. I only wanted to see the creatures here making out. I had no idea you could do it for real."

The woman smiled knowingly. "Well, now you have a chance to do more than just watch. Come on." She lay down on the soft grass and reached out to Josh.

"Wait a minute, I hardly know you."

"That's what it's all about, stupid. You have sex, but you don't really have sex. I mean, it's not you, it's the satyr, and it's not me, it's the nymph. We get all the pleasure with none of the complications. I don't get pregnant, and there are no entangling relationships. You're not supposed to be in love with me."

"But, these people we've…we've…"

"Possessed, stupid. We possessed them," she said.

"Don't they care?"

"They're androids, dummy. They aren't people. Come on, get with it." She reached out to him.

Josh stared at the woman for a moment. *God! I've wanted to make out with a girl since I was twelve, and here I can do it with no problem. She even wants me to do her.* He looked down at the satyr's manhood. It stood erect. *Why not?*

* * * * *

They lay on the grass together afterward with the woman in the crook of his arm. She spoke first.

"That was pretty good. Was it your first time?"

Josh thought a moment before answering. "No, no, er, I've had lots of girls before."

"How many?"

"I don't know, two or three."

The woman rose on one elbow and gave him an evil smile. "You don't know if it was two or three?"

"It, it, it was three. There were three of them."

The woman relaxed again. "What were they like? Was I better than them?"

How do you answer that? I guess there's only one way. "Oh, you were much better than they were."

The woman laughed again. "You're lying. You were a virgin, weren't you?"

"Yeah, I was. How many men have you had?"

"No actual men. I really am a virgin back home. I just come here for pleasure. I've had three satyrs, one centaur, and two unicorns. Most of those were as a female, but I did two as a male, one unicorn and one centaur."

"You mean you can do both?"

"Sure, want to switch and do it again?"

He thought for a moment. *This is fabulous! I can have sex as often as I like. Wait until I tell the guys in the band about this. Wait a minute, I can't tell them, they'll want to come here too. I'd better keep this to myself. Come to think of it, it might be cool to try it as a woman.* "Sure, I'm game."

They switched, and Oriana went to work on him with the confidence of prior experience. It didn't take him long to get into the swing of playing the woman's part. In fact, he thought his female orgasm was much better than the male one. Again, they lay on the grass together.

"That was great!" Josh said.

"Which do you like best?"

"I think I liked the female orgasm, but I'd rather just do the male part. I feel funny being a female."

"Yeah, I don't think you guys have nearly as much fun. Let's switch back."

They switched, and Josh sensed a subtle change in the atmosphere inside the satyr. He caught a faint odor of perfume mixed with perspiration he'd found normal in the nymph, but seemed out of place in the satyr. It passed quickly.

"This is unbelievable," Josh said.

"Did you really not know what this planet is all about?"

"I had no idea, really."

"Let me explain it to you. The thing you used to get here is called a Cargan. They let you travel around the universe as an entity."

"Entity?"

"Yeah, entity. You can't travel faster than light, but your entity can. I don't know any of the science behind it, but I know you can travel all the way across the galaxy in a few minutes. My school class took a field trip to Gora 4 last year, and that's a long way off."

"My great grandpa had thirty or more of those 'Cargans'. Do they all go different places?"

"Duh, there's a different Cargan for each planet. The one you used took you from your planet to here. Hey, would you like to come back to my planet with me and see what it looks like?"

"I don't know I'd better be getting back home before Mom checks on me. Besides, I have to go to school tomorrow, and I won't get much sleep now."

The woman laughed again. "I guess you don't know about the time thing either. When you entity travel, time slows down back home. You can be here for hours, and only a few minutes will pass back home. There's no hurry."

"Not now, maybe the next time," Josh said. He wasn't sure his mother wouldn't decide to check on him and find him glued to the Cargan again. He wasn't ready to answer her questions yet.

The woman stood up, and Josh did the same. "Tell you what, the next time I come to Mythos I'll come get you. Show me the tree with your Cargan."

A light went on inside Josh's head. "Ah, the one I was stuck in when I got here."

"That's the one."

"It's back along that pathway." He indicated the way by pointing.

"That's the long way. I know a shortcut," Oriana said, and led Josh into the forest.

On the way they passed some trees bearing strange-looking fruit.

"What are those things?" Josh asked.

"They're energy trees for the creatures here on Mythos. Don't try to eat any of them," Oriana said.

"You mean the nymphs and satyrs eat those things?" Josh said.

"Sure, they're androids. They don't need food or water, but they have to get energy from somewhere. Those glob things are what they eat. They're really gooey and sticky. I like to throw 'em at things. They make a real mess."

Oriana moved to one of the trees and carefully plucked a grapefruit-sized globe. She hurled it at a nearby tree, and Josh watched it splatter and run down the bark in a green, molasses-style pattern.

"Yuck, what a mess," Josh said.

"That's what makes it fun," Oriana said. "Come on, your tree's probably in that next clearing."

She led him out of the trees, and Josh recognized his tree.

"This is it," he said.

The woman looked around to get her bearings. "Okay, I know where it is now. Give me the note for activating it."

Josh hummed G sharp for her, and she hummed it back to him several times. "Okay, I've got it. Where is the Cargan in your house?"

"It's in my room."

"Good, I won't disturb your parents. Is it night on Earth now?"

"Yeah, how about on Brem?"

"Late afternoon. I'm supposed to be studying, but my folks both work, and they don't know what I do until they get home. I sneak downstairs and use my father's Cargan for Mythos. He thinks it's well hidden, but I had no trouble finding it. I'll see you next time, Josh." She emerged from the woman, and her ghostly image drifted off down the path. She waved to him as she moved out of sight.

Josh left the satyr and moved to the tree. He put his hands inside the trunk and felt a familiar shape. He grasped the thing he now knew was a Cargan and hummed G sharp.

He woke up in his room shivering cold. He put an extra blanket on his bed and lay awake for a while thinking about entity travel. *What a cool experience, and me and great grandpa are the only ones who know about it. This was what he was talking about all the time. His special edge was invisibility. I see it now, and he left me this Cargan because he thought I needed the experience of Mythos to make me a man.*

A wicked smile crossed Josh's face as he pictured his great grandfather romping through the forest in pursuit of a nymph. *That old fart must have had a great time on Mythos. I suppose your entity doesn't get old like your body. Even if it does, once you're inside the satyr, you're only as old as he is. Thanks great grandpa. I promise to keep your secret for you.*

He drifted off to sleep content in the knowledge that, technically, he was no longer a virgin.

CHAPTER 10

Mark Wycham was also thinking about entity travel, but his destination was a desolate planet called Ula, the home of his fellow conspirator, Manjahba. He pressed a button on his intercom.

"Miss Burdsong, I'm going to be resting for a while. Please see that I'm not disturbed."

"Yes, Mr. Wycham." Nancy Burdsong was accustomed to her boss taking long periods of rest in his special, hidden room. No one knew where it was or how he got there, and any questions on the subject were met with stony silence and a wicked glare which clearly conveyed the message, "It's none of your business."

He moved to a bookcase on one wall of his office and pulled out the first volume of H. G. Wells' *Outline of History*. Reaching into the empty slot, he pushed back on the wood paneling. In response to his action, one section of the bookcase swung back to reveal a small room. A comfortable-looking chaise filled one wall, and the nightstand next to it held his personal Cargan.

Wycham remembered how he forced Charles Bastin to turn over one of his prized possessions. Once while attending a party at Wanagiyata, he'd caught Charlie after his host had consumed a few too many martinis and asked him about the ugly sculptures. Charlie offered to show him a ghost and led him to the conservatory expecting his guest to see nothing at all.

To his surprise Wycham saw several "ghosts" moving about the room and decided to speak to one. He quickly discovered the "ghosts" were from other planets and confronted Charlie about it. The fact Wycham could see entities while not an entity himself, puzzled Charlie, but he put it down to some genetic aberration. Realizing he'd let the cat out of the bag, Charlie offered him a Cargan to keep quiet about the secret.

The bookcase door closed behind him while Wycham moved to the chaise. He pulled a knitted comforter over his legs and grasped the Cargan. The first note of the National Anthem chilled the room and put the old man into a catatonic state.

* * * * *

Wycham always felt uncomfortable in the Ulan terminal. There were no flowers or brightly painted artwork to contrast with the dull gray Cargans and no windows to mix sunlight with the cold fluorescent hues of the fixtures above them. Less than a dozen Cargans sat on the main floor, and only a few Ulan entities moved between them. They were a sinister looking lot with heavy builds, bald heads and fat hands. None of them smiled or offered a greeting to him.

All of them wore the same loose fitting robe hanging to their ankles. The long sleeves were bell shaped, and some of the entities used them to cover clasped hands like an old Chinese Mandarin. Each one wore a heavy chain around his neck. The chains were of various designs with curious-looking medallions hanging from them. There seemed to be no two alike.

Wycham made his way to the compass rose and set off for his destination. He could have used Manjahba's personal Cargan, but he decided a flight through the early morning air might be invigorating.

The countryside below him was as bleak as the terminal. It was mostly mountains and desert with only sporadic oases containing villages of somber, gray stone buildings. It was night on this side of the planet, but few lights showed from the windows. He crossed the terminator into daylight and entered an only slightly more hospitable landscape. The few meandering rivers supported some farming along their banks before ending in huge areas of swampland. He passed over some small towns, but the only major city in view was a metropolis located in the delta where one of the larger rivers met a small sea. Wycham descended to the city and a white, 10-story office building. He passed through a wall into Manjahba's outer office.

"Good morning, Malliba," Wycham greeted the bald woman seated behind a plastic console. She also wore the bulky robe, but her chain and medallion were more delicate and contained precious stones.

"Good morning, Mr. Wycham. Manjahba is expecting you. Go on in." She seemed to consider the sudden appearance of a ghostly image as part of her normal routine. Unlike humans on Earth, the people of Ula could see and hear entities quite easily. They could also manipulate physical objects while they were in entity form and possessed the ability to control other entities. Wycham feared these people. They were one of the few races capable of serving as policemen in the business of entity travel, but they were also quite valued as agents for all sorts of marginal activities involving their special gifts. Wycham passed through Manjahba's door into a spacious, but spartan, office.

Everything in the room was plastic. Wood suitable for building houses or good furniture was a rare commodity on the planet. Everything was functional. No frivolous figurines, plaques or paintings adorned the room. The walls were textured with geometric designs suitable to the peculiar religious beliefs of the Ulans and painted in soft shades of gray and beige. Fortunately for his allergies, Wycham's entity could not detect the scent of night-blooming jasmine pervading the room. It seems the Ulans valued this aroma over all others, and the whole planet reeked of it. Manjahba looked up as he entered.

"I sensed you outside, Wycham. Do you have a plan for gaining control of the Earth Cargans?"

"Yes, but it will require your help."

"As you Earth people say, 'I'm all ears'." Manjahba was always amused by Earth sayings. The people of that planet had not progressed beyond reference to their own physiological make-up to illustrate many emotions and attitudes. He was particularly fond of their use of a slang term for the anus as a personal insult.

A smile spread across Manjahba's face as he listened to his co-conspirator. These Earth people were almost as devious as Ulans. Wycham was the perfect Earth partner for his venture.

"A key element is securing Smith's cooperation, but he doesn't suspect anything at this point. According to my sources, the family's negotiating with the state to leave the Cargans at Charlie's old mansion. If we can stop that, the only other alternative is for Smith to take them to his home. His wife hates the Cargans and doesn't want them in her house. I think Smith would be open to any plan that keeps his wife happy. Now, I'm ready for you to do your part.

We'll have to be sure the politicians balk at taking the

Cargans. One state senator is the key to that. All we have to do is take control of him, and the Cargans will be out of Wanagiyata. After that I'll approach Smith with my museum idea again. He'll jump at it, and if he doesn't, his wife will force him into it. If all works as we planned, the Cargans should be under our control in a matter of weeks."

Manjahba relaxed a bit, and his face lost the contorted sneer Wycham saw earlier. "Good! I'm ready. Do you have a picture of this politician I am to possess?"

"Yes, but we'll have to go back to my room for you to see it. As you know entities can't carry physical objects with them when they travel."

"Very well, we can use my personal Cargan." Manjahba led Wycham into his Cargan room. Wycham grasped the Cargan and vanished. Manjahba sat down and hummed the proper note. Soon, both were standing beside a row of filing cabinets in Wycham's secret room. Wycham opened a drawer and pulled out a folder. He opened it and handed a photo of a smiling, gray haired, distinguished-looking man to Manjahba.

"This is State Senator Mitchell. He heads the committee investigating the purchase of Wanagiyata by the state of South Dakota. He's known to be a bit on the eccentric side, so it won't be a surprise to anyone when he baulks at accepting the Cargans as part of the deal. Just be sure you don't tip our hand by acting too rashly."

Manjahba snorted in disgust.   "I was manipulating politicians for 30 years before you were born, Wycham. This Earth twit should be easy. Are you sure you can convince Smith to release the Cargans to you?"

"I have an appointment with him the day after tomorrow to

discuss future plans for what he thinks will be an art museum. The committee on the purchase of Wanagiyata meets that day also. It might take you a few days to pull off your part of the scheme, but Smith will want some time to think about the deal, I'm sure. The news of the state's refusal to accept the Cargans will cause him to look for an alternative, and he'll jump at my offer of temporary storage until the museum is completed."

"I'll report back to you as soon as I'm successful in Pierre. Be sure to let me know immediately if there is any slip up with Smith," Manjahba said.

"I'll be in contact with you at Mitchell's office either way. Now, I have some important preparation to do, if you don't mind."

Manjahba took the hint. He grasped the Cargan, hummed the note and vanished.

* * * * *

Back on Ula he smiled as he rocked back in his office chair. Soon, he would be able to end the economic monopoly of Mica, and bring prosperity to Ula.

He often wondered why he was cursed to be born on the desolate half of a two-planet system, circling their sun in orbits only 50,000,000 kilometers apart at their closest approach. Earth reminded him of Mica with its green fields, forests, lakes and lush plains in contrast to the deserts and swamps of Ula. Mica's mountains contain rich deposits of minerals and precious stones while the low ranges of Ula yielded only hard rock and a few semi-precious crystals.

He thought of his childhood on Ula with his parents eking out a living farming the dry soil. He'd migrated to Mica at an early age, but he found himself treated as a second class citizens and working low paying jobs.

His only other alternative was signing on for duty as an entity travel Marshall, but the Marshall academy only accepts the top five percent of all applicants. When he was forced to return to a hardscrabble existence on Ula, he vowed that one day he would bring down the arrogant powerbrokers on Mica and give Ula control of both planets. He'd done whatever it took to amass his fortune, legal or illegal, and now he was ready to begin his conquest. The Earth Cargans and Wycham would play a key role in that plan.

CHAPTER 11

The night for the band's first gig came, at long last. Rodney Barnes borrowed his father's van to transport the instruments while the rest of the group rode to the teen club in Willie Jenkins' old VW microbus. Bill Thompson and Josh were not yet old enough to drive, and Willie was the only one who had his own car.

The club was a converted retail store in a once-fashionable strip mall. The stage was small, but they managed to set up in a reasonable fashion. The teen club's manager was a young man in his mid-twenties named Bob Karrasnik. He barely acknowledged their arrival.

"After you guys get set up you can use the space behind the curtain to change. Remember, you're not on all night. The DJ goes first, and then I introduce you. Stay out of sight until then. You got one hour to play then the DJ takes over again. Got it?"

"Yeah, we got it," Josh agreed.

"Okay. You can pack up and clear out as soon as you want after that, or you can stick around and dance; but no free drinks or food. You pay for everything."

"We understand," Rodney echoed Josh.

Karrasnik left the boys to attend to other matters he obviously considered more important.

"What an asshole," Jenkins said.

"He's just making sure we don't screw up." Josh tried to put a good face on it. "Let's practice a little before the crowd gets here. I want to check out the acoustics."

The band sounded great, but Josh knew the presence of a few hundred screaming teenagers would produce a severe case of butterflies in all of them. Only Willie Jenkins had played before a live audience before, and that was a group of adults at a piano recital. Josh was not even sure how he would react to an audience of his peers.

Josh closed the curtains around the stage, and the boys changed into the outfits they carefully selected for their debut. As avant-garde musicians of the early twenty first century, they were obliged to look as radical as they hoped their music sounded.

They donned various wigs sporting multi-colored spiked hair, long black tresses or mullets. Those whose parents would not allow piercing glued studs and other decorations to their ears, nose and lips. Studded leather vests covered scrawny bare chests, and ragged jeans ended at the top of black leather boots. The bass drum bore their logo, a bug-eyed green alien holding up a vulgar one finger salute. They were confident their clothes would "wow" the crowd even if their music didn't.

Behind the curtain the boys sipped soft drinks, Josh's treat, and listened to the crowd building up while the DJ's music reminded them what amateurs they really were. Karrasnik's head appeared around the back curtain.

"You guys ready?" he asked.

"We're ready when you are," Josh said as the boys took up their positions.

"Okay, you're on in five minutes." He held up one hand with the fingers spread to make sure they understood and then vanished.

Josh heard the song end and the DJ announce, "And now, a brand new band for your listening and dancing pleasure, the 'Spacing Guild'."

An uncertain response from the assembled teenagers greeted the opening of the curtain, and Josh stared out at a sea of zit-marked faces challenging him to entertain them. He planned to introduce the band first, but the cold stares told him he needed to do something quickly before they became hostile. He turned to the group to see three deer-caught-in-headlights expressions.

"Okay guys, hit it!" he commanded as he slammed a starting chord at maximum volume. The sound of the guitar seemed to invoke a reflex response in the other band members. They joined their leader in wailing out the unusual sounds of Josh's music, but he could see it wasn't going over well at all. The final explosion of drums and guitar wails produced what could only be called luke-warm enthusiasm.

"Thank you, thank you. That was one of my own little compositions called, *Dead Rat Pie*. I hope you liked hearing it as much as we liked playing it." Again, a brief smattering of applause was his only answer. Josh felt his throat going dry and his knees getting weak. Cupping his hand over the floor mike he turned to the band. "We'd better play some dance music or these guys are going to walk. Let's go with number 12."

As insurance against the failure of their main menu, the boys had prepared several standard numbers they could revert to in a pinch. Unlike Josh's compositions, these numbers did have sheet music. During the lull accompanying the band's frantic shuffling of papers, the crowd grew restless.

"Hey, play somethin' we can dance to," one boy shouted.

"Yeah, that stuff sucked," another barked.

"God, aren't they nerdy!" a girl giggled.

Josh hit the downbeat and the band launched into more familiar territory for the audience. The ribbing soon ended as the couples concentrated on gyrating sensually to impress whoever happened to be watching. Josh knew they only had five sets of sheet music; so, he stretched the first song as long as possible. The climax of the number produced a much warmer reaction with an occasional shout of, "Okay, that's more like it."

The band managed to fill the rest of their allotted time with the remaining numbers at their disposal, plus an introduction of the band between the third and fourth songs. Josh was never so glad to see anything in his life as the curtain closing around the stage in spite of the more than generous applause and calls for more.

"God, I'm glad that's over," Bill Thompson sighed.

"Did we bomb, or what?" Jenkins said as he threw his hat to the floor in disgust.

"I didn't think we did so badly," Rodney Barnes insisted.

"They seemed to like our standard stuff," Josh tried to assure them.

"They sure didn't like our best stuff at all," Jenkins said as he began to pack up his keyboards.

Karrasnik appeared through the curtain. "Good job, guys. Any time you want to come back let me know. I'll pay you $100.00 for the hour next time. If you can keep the crowd happy, I'll make it more after that; but lay off that heavy metal stuff."

"Sure," Josh was overwhelmed. "I'll call you, Mr. Karrasnik," was all he could manage.

"Whooo hoooo!" Barnes shouted. "He liked us. What do ya think about that?"

The boys packed up, changed, and decided to celebrate their opening triumph with a beer at the Jenkins house. Willie's parents were out for the night and could not object. Willie said his father never missed beer from the huge refrigerator in the basement area off the family room as long as it was replaced from the vast store of cases stacked beside it.

CHAPTER 12

Roger Smith sat at his desk staring out the picture window wall of his plush office. Mark Wycham would arrive any minute now, and Roger would hear the details of his plan for the sculptures. The negotiations with South Dakota's politicians were not progressing well, and whatever Wycham proposed, Evelyn would be glad the things were not bound for her house.

The intercom interrupted his thoughts.

"Mr. Wycham is here for your meeting, sir." The voice of Annita, his secretary, was always pleasant but official.

"Oh yes, 'Nita. Please send him in."

In a moment the door opened, and Annita showed Wycham in.

"Good to see you Mr. Smith." Wycham offered his free right hand to Roger while cradling a large presentation folder under his left arm.

Roger took the offered hand and almost recoiled at the touch. It was like grasping the hand of a cadaver, but the old man's grip was like iron. "Good to meet you in person, Mr. Wycham. Please call me Roger. Would you like some coffee or something to drink?"

"Oh, no, thank you. I never drink coffee, and please call me Mark," Wycham said.

Roger nodded at Annita, and the woman left the room

closing the door behind her.

"Sit down, Mark. I understand you have some plans for an art museum."

"Yes, I'm sure you'll agree that leaving the sculptures at Wanagiyata indefinitely is not a good idea, particularly since the mansion is to come under the supervision of the state government," Wycham said.

"I hope to hear from my cousin in the next few days about that. The state committee responsible for such acquisitions is due to have their final meeting soon. With any luck we can leave the sculptures at Wanagiyata, but I'm open to other ideas," Roger said.

"Which is why I'm here. I have some architectural drawings of a permanent home for them and a large part of my private collection." Wycham opened his portfolio and spread a large drawing on Roger's desk. "This is a concept drawing for the Charles E. Bastin Museum of Modern Art. How do you like it?"

Roger perused the drawing. It was a very modern building with a large sculpture in front of the main entrance and fountains on either side.

"Very impressive, Mark. I think Charlie would have been proud of this," Roger said.

"Yes, I think he would."

"Where would this be located?" Roger asked.

"I was thinking of the San Francisco area somewhere. That would put it closer to you so it could be properly supervised and still conform to the provisions of Charley's will. My people have located some property that might be suitable." Wycham rummaged through his portfolio again and produced a map showing the proposed location.

"Whew!" Roger said. "That's some pretty high priced real estate. What would all of this cost?"

"The current owner of the property is in some degree of legal trouble with the IRS. He must sell his assets to avoid a prison sentence for tax evasion. The price would be quite reasonable, I assure you. As for the building, my architect estimates a cost of some $25 million. If we get the land for what I think we can, the total cost should be under $30 million."

Roger sat back in his chair and tapped his fingers together pensively. He was silent a few moments before responding. "That's a lot of money. Where would it come from?"

"Naturally, I would provide some of the funds, but I was anticipating a major contribution from the Bastin family. I understand you inherited some of Charlie's money."

"He left a small sum to me, but I want to put most of it into a trust fund for my son. I wouldn't feel right putting it into our venture."

"I understand. My lawyers have set up a 501(c)(3) foundation for the museum, so all contributions would be tax deductible. We had to do that to get any federal money anyway. I myself am willing to contribute $10 million. Charlie was responsible for a good portion of my personal fortune, after all. I was hoping you would help a little and use your influence to persuade Bastin Mining to contribute something. We should be able to raise several million from the federal government. With those sources, and what we can raise from the philanthropic community of San Francisco, we should be able to cover the construction expenses."

"What about the operating costs after the museum's completed?" Roger asked.

"The annual operating fund could come from private donations and foundations." Wycham sat back in his chair with a satisfied smile on his face and waited for Roger's reaction.

"Please understand I'm in no position to help you with the grant proposals and the other paperwork associated with this effort. Who will do that work?" Roger asked.

"I have some staff people willing to do the job on a volunteer basis. Two of them are retired college professors who have extensive experience in grant writing. I'll take care of all that," Wycham said.

"I'm still curious as to why you're willing to sink this kind of money into a building housing what the rest of the world would call scrap metal," Roger said.

Wycham leaned closer to Roger and spoke softly. "I'll be honest with you, Roger. I'll make a lot of money next year on some investments that are panning out rather well. I'll need to offset those gains with a sizeable deduction of some kind to avoid a ridiculous tax bill. My accountants tell me this museum fits the bill nicely, but I can't swing the whole cost without liquidating other assets. I hope you understand."

"That makes sense," Roger said. "I think it's an excellent plan, but I want to pass this by my lawyer for his review and sound out Bastin Mining."

"Of course. I've included some draft contracts and agreements in this package." Once more Wycham produced a sheaf of papers from the portfolio.

Roger shuffled through the stack in a cursory manner, and laid it on the drawings. "I'll give it my full consideration and let you know as soon as I can. In the meantime, we can leave the sculptures at Wanagiyata." Roger said.

"I have a suggestion in that regard also," Wycham said leaning forward in his chair again.

"What's that?" Roger asked.

"I have a property in the Miami area that would make an excellent temporary location. It's an old warehouse of mine that's only about half full these days. I'd be willing to wall off a segment of the building for the collection. One of my companies provides security for the building already, and, of course, there would be no rental charge for its use."

"That's very generous of you, Mark, but I think I'll wait to see what happens with the state of South Dakota and Wanagiyata before I agree to that."

"Understandable, Roger, very understandable. My offer is open indefinitely, however." Wycham looked at his watch and said, "I hate to rush off, but if we have no more business to conduct here, I'm due in Atlanta this evening."

"I think we've covered everything." Roger rose and extended his hand to Wycham. "Is there anything my secretary can do for you? Confirm a flight or a rental car?"

"That's all taken care of. Thank you, Roger." Wycham took Roger's hand and closed up his portfolio leaving the papers it held with Roger. The two men walked to the office door where Roger bid his potential partner a safe trip.

Roger walked back to his desk and sat down facing the windows. *I think I'll check this guy out more thoroughly. I know he said he needs the tax write-off, but anyone willing to invest $10 million in Charlie's art has to be in big tax trouble. It all seems too good to be true. John's having trouble with the state legislature, and Wycham appears out of the blue to provide an easy answer. There's more to this than he's telling me, and I have no idea what it is.*

CHAPTER 13

A week later, Josh was still on cloud nine over his experience on Mythos. Even Willie Jenkins' nagging couldn't faze him.

"When are we going to play that club again, Josh? I could sure use the money," the keyboard man pleaded during lunch recess.

"I have to call that guy and set it up," Josh said in an effort to put him off.

"We have to practice more, too. We need to put together some arrangements of more popular stuff. Your tunes didn't go over very well."

"I know, I know. Let it drop for now, Will. I've got more important things on my mind."

"Like, what's more important than our band and making some money?" Jenkins asked.

"I can't tell you about it right now. It's personal." Josh gave the first excuse that came into his mind. He couldn't tell Willie, or anyone else, about the Cargan at this point.

"Josh, are you okay?" Willie's voice held a note of serious concern.

"No, nothing like that. It's just I'm going to be very busy for the next few days on a, a, a... project for my dad." Josh felt himself sliding into a deep hole. He hated to lie, but he knew he had no choice.

"Anything I can help you with?" Willie asked.

"No, I have to do this one on my own," Josh said.

Normally, Josh would be grateful for any assistance on a parentally assigned project; and Willie knew it. Turning down help was only more likely to arouse suspicions. Josh was not surprised when Willie continued to pursue the issue.

"Something real secret, huh?"

"No, I just can't tell you about it right now. Maybe in a few weeks," Josh offered.

Willie Jenkins went away with a knowing smile on his face, and Josh knew he would soon have to share his knowledge with the rest of the band. What would he do when they all began to press him about the subject? All of them would love to take part in the sex stuff, but he knew none of them would be able to keep their mouths shut for long. The parents would find out, and that would be the end of it. No, he had to come up with some kind of cover story for their benefit, and it had to be credible—but what?

* * * * *

That night he felt a cold sensation as he sat at his desk doing homework. "Oriana, is that you?"

A warm glow bathed his brain as he felt her enter his body. "Hey, you really do like me, don't you?"

"What are you doing? Get out of my head." Josh tried to make his mind a blank, but she kept digging deeper into his subconscious.

"I'm possessing you. Entities can do that, but it's really illegal to possess someone without their permission," she said.

"Well, I didn't give you permission to possess me."

"Hey, we've made love to each other. I think that constitutes permission." Her laughter rang inside his head. "Besides, it's the only way I can talk to you to let you know it's me."

"Okay, okay, just cut it out!" He felt her presence leave his mind and moved to the Cargan. "See you on Mythos."

Oriana was waiting for him at the sycamore tree. This time her outfit was just as provocative as before. The top's soft fabric revealed the shape of her breasts, and the long pants were more like tights. Her boots had been replaced with platform shoes of some kind of shiny plastic. Her hair was now a garish purple color instead of the previous raven black. She spoke, but he still couldn't understand her. She laughed merrily and led him off to another tree. This time two unicorns appeared instead of a satyr and nymph. Josh entered the male unicorn.

"Okay, now we can talk," Oriana said.

"I suppose you want to have sex as unicorns."

Oriana laughed. "If you want to. I only chose these so we could talk. What I really want you to do is come back to Brem with me so you can learn Giran."

His unicorn pawed the ground, but Oriana's didn't seem to be interested. "Learning a language takes years. I can't stay away that long."

"On your planet maybe, but on Brem you can learn it in a few hours."

"And how do I do that?"

"Come along and see. My Cargan's this way."

Oriana galloped off, and Josh followed. The horse sensation filled his brain with images of wild stallions dashing across the plains. It was very pleasant, but he still felt his unicorn's urge to mount Oriana's.

They stopped at a large beech tree, and Oriana left her

unicorn. Josh followed suit. She hummed a note he figured was the activator for her Cargan. Josh hummed it back several times until she smiled and stuck her arms into the tree. She vanished immediately. Josh felt inside the tree and found the Cargan. He was not quite sure where to grasp it and tried several locations before he found himself in what was obviously a girl's room. The décor was what would be considered very modern on Earth, but the soft colors and smooth fabrics left no doubt about the sex of the occupant. Oriana stood there in person. Josh thought she was just as beautiful in the flesh as she was while she was an entity. She motioned for him to follow and led him to a garage where what looked like a convertible with no wheels rested on blocks. Oriana slid into the driver's seat.

Josh tried to sit down on the passenger side, but he fell through to the garage floor each time he did. Oriana only laughed and made flapping motions with her arms. Josh nodded his understanding and thought of himself as a bird. He moved his arms and soon found he was floating above the car. Oriana nodded her approval and pointed out the garage door.

She pushed a button on the dash, and the vehicle seemed to come to life with a low bass humming sound. The car lifted off the blocks, and she drove out of the garage into a residential street with Josh hovering just above her. The houses were very functional-looking with no superfluous trim. They looked like children's blocks scattered over a playroom floor. They appeared to be composed of some sort of concrete, and each one was dyed a soft pastel color. The grounds surrounding them were planted with strange-looking shrubs and gnarly trees with very little grass. The cars passing by were totally silent, gliding along a few inches above the pavement. Oriana drove to a large building in a downtown area.

She led him through glass doors and stopped at a reception desk. She spoke to the receptionist who smiled and pointed to the elevators. Once more Oriana beckoned Josh to follow. They took the elevator to the sixth floor and found an office marked by writing he could not decipher. Oriana walked in and spoke with another receptionist who rose and led them to a small room with one desk, what looked like a desktop computer and a chair with a large hood. Josh thought it looked like the hair dryers in beauty shops back home. The receptionist motioned for him to sit in the chair.

His recent experience told Josh it might be impossible for him to sit, and he was surprised when his bottom didn't fall through the leather seat. The receptionist positioned the hood over his head and the lessons began.

Thoughts began to flood into his brain until Josh thought his head might explode. He tried to move his hands to signal the woman to stop, but the chair seemed to hold him in a vise-like grip. Images and conversations raced across his inner sight, and pain like a severe headache accompanied the visions. After a few moments the pain eased, and he found he could understand some of the phrases being spoken by a distant voice deep inside his skull. Soon he was actually conversing with the voice mentally though he said nothing. His mind went blank, and he fell asleep.

When he woke he found Oriana leaning over him, and the receptionist smiling down on him from the other side.

"How do you feel?" the receptionist asked.

Josh felt strange words forming in his mind and spoke them.

"I think I'm okay. Am I speaking Giran?"

The women laughed merrily as he sat up. Oriana spoke. "Yes, but you have a funny accent."

"We could eliminate that with another lesson," the receptionist said.

"I like it," Oriana said. "Besides, I can't afford another lesson."

"You paid for this?" Josh asked.

"Yes, silly. It wasn't free," Oriana said.

"I can repay you. How much was it?"

"It cost me 200 Platinas."

"How much is that in Earth money?" Josh asked.

The women only laughed, and Oriana replied, "First of all, I have no idea what Earth money is worth on our planet since we don't ever see it. Second, you couldn't bring it with you anyway. Entities can't carry things with them."

"But, I'm wearing my clothes," Josh protested.

"I know. Nobody ever told me why entities can't carry things but can bring the clothes they wear. I'm just glad we can."

"My head feels like someone hit me with a sledge hammer."

"I think he'll be all right," the receptionist said.

"Come along, Josh. Now that you can understand me, it's time for our date." Oriana dragged him back to the car and they drove to her house.

"Where are we going for our date?" Josh asked as they drove.

"We're going to Regulus to see the museum. I have a friend who says it's a really cool place."

Josh looked at his watch, but it stopped when he grasped the

Cargan. "How long have I been here?"

"Only three of our hours. I don't know how many Earth hours that is, but don't worry. Remember the reverse time compression factor. You'll be back on Earth in no time as far as they're concerned."

At the house Oriana led Josh to her room again and brought out a different Cargan. "I have to take Dad's Mythos Cargan back then we can go to the terminal." She flitted out the door with the Mythos Cargan and returned in a few moments with a different Cargan.

"Now take hold of this Cargan here and here." She indicated the grips. "And, hum this note." She gave Josh the activation note and he soon found himself in what looked like an airline terminal. Oriana appeared beside him in entity form almost at once.

"Where are we?" Josh asked.

"You're in the Brem Terminal. All of these Cargans go to different planets. The one for Regulus is over here." She led Josh through a swarm of entities appearing and disappearing at various Cargans. Most of the entities looked human, but a few were a bit on the bizarre side. They even passed several who were stark naked.

"I suppose they're going to Mythos," Josh said.

Oriana laughed. "Josh, you're so funny. Those are Andrans, and they never wear any clothes. This way."

She stopped at a Cargan almost four feet tall and read the notice on its base. Josh followed her gaze and found he could also read it.

"I don't know this note," Oriana said.

Josh scratched his head after reading the placard. "You guys use a different notation system than Earth. I have no idea what tone 'õ' represents."

"I do know it's the next note after 'õ', will that help?"

Josh checked several other Cargans until he found one requiring the õ tone. He waited until an entity approached and listened to that note before returning to Oriana. "I think it's this one." He hummed what he thought was the correct note, and Oriana copied him. She put her hands on the indicated spots and hummed. Josh was surprised when she vanished, but he did the same and soon found himself standing next to her in another terminal.

"Josh, you're a genius. How did you know it would be that note?"

"I really didn't. I just assumed your scale had the same intervals as ours. The note I heard was a middle B, so I figured our note would be middle C."

"Are you a musician, or something?"

"Yeah, I play electric guitar and have my own rock band."

"What's a 'rock band'?"

It was Josh's turn to laugh. "Don't you guys have rock music on Brem?"

"Never heard of it."

"You'll have to come to Earth again so you can hear it. You'll love it."

"I'll do that, but we'd better get to the museum

CHAPTER 14

"I don't know where the museum is, but we can ask the Helper," Oriana said. She glided off toward a green door on the far wall and Josh followed. She pushed a button, and the door slid open to reveal a short, plump, balding man with a bilious green complexion.

"Yes, madam, how may I help you?"

Josh found his accent familiar. He heard it from the Pakistani man behind the counter every time he went into the local convenience store back home.

"How do I get to the museum, please?"

The little green man gave her instructions and closed the door abruptly.

"He's a funny duck," Josh said.

"He's a Sellan, most of the helpers are Sellans. They're good with languages."

"Any of them speak English?"

"I doubt it. You're the only person I've ever heard of from your planet. The museum's this way."

She led Josh out through a wall and into a city street. Traffic was more like Earth here, and the cars had wheels though they were still silent. They found an impressive building made of a stone much like marble on Earth but with bizarre patterns embedded in the rock. They glided up to the door and passed through it.

Josh stopped as he noticed a ticket counter. "How are we going to pay for this?"

"Entities don't pay. We just go through the scanner, over there, so they know we're here. Come on."

Oriana passed through a portal much like the airport security units back on Earth, and Josh followed. A green light above the opening illuminated, and a uniformed guard nodded their way.

"Can he see us?" Josh asked.

"No, he's just acknowledging the light."

In a moment they were standing in the lobby. The swirling mosaic pattern of the marble floor almost made Josh dizzy. The walls were black stone of a type Josh had never seen before, with veins of a golden metal zig zagging through it like lightning bolts. The hall contained several statues made with a marble-like material depicting what Josh assumed were historical figures from the Regulun past.

"This is awesome," Oriana's mouth gaped open as she surveyed the scene.

"And this is just the entrance," Josh replied from his dazed state.

As they approached one of the statues a light illuminated it and a voice began a commentary in what they supposed was the language of the Reguluns.

"It's all automated," Josh said.

"I wish we could understand Regulun," Oriana sighed.

As they spoke, another entity moved up beside them. He was rather short and had only a small patch of hair at the back of his head, the remainder being quite bald and shiny. Two large blue eyes radiated kindness, and his mouth curved into a perpetual smile. He spoke in a language quite different from Regulun, and when he saw it was useless, resorted to signs.

He pointed to his eyes and then to himself then looked inquiringly at Josh and Oriana.

"I think he wants us to watch him," Oriana said.

"Go ahead," Josh said as he made a familiar gesture with his arm.

The man nodded and moved closer to the sculpture. Again, he pointed to his eye.

Josh nodded again, and the man vanished into the statue.

"Oh, I see. We're supposed to possess the statue!" Oriana said.

"I guess so." Josh's eyes were also wide with wonder at the sight of the man actually blending into the statue.

In a moment, the man's head appeared poking out of the statue's chest. His smile was bigger than ever. The rest of him appeared from inside the stony form and he stood next to the couple again. He cocked his head and made a sweeping gesture toward the statue.

Oriana turned to Josh. "Better let me try it first in case there's any kind of problem. I've got more experience with possessions." Oriana moved to the statue and felt into it with her hand. A cold, tomblike sensation met her inquiry. The little man seemed to sense her hesitation and made a pushing motion to indicate she should continue.

Slowly Oriana melted into the statue. She was not inside long before she emerged with a look of sheer terror on her face.

"What happened?" Josh asked.

"I think this is more for the guys than the gals, you try it."

Josh shrugged and melted into the statue. He found himself

surrounded by a vicious battle. All around him men were wielding battle axes and strange-looking curved swords. He found he was holding a sword, and was about to drop it when a warrior charged him. Surprisingly, he was able to wield the weapon very expertly and dispatched the opponent easily. He fell into the mood of the scene, enjoying his role as a hero, but decided it was time to return to Oriana. He emerged with an awestruck expression.

The little man laughed at the look on Josh's face and promptly vanished into the next statue.

"That was a real trip!" Josh's eyes were wide with surprise. "It's like you can see the reason the artist made the statue. I can understand why you didn't like this one. God! I must have killed six or seven people while I was in there. It was pretty awesome!"

"Okay, I'll try that one over there," Oriana pointed at a white marble statue of a Regulun female. Josh was not impressed by the fact it had no clothes. The short, stocky build of the Reguluns did not make their women the most physically desirable creatures.

Oriana melted into the statue, but again she pulled out quickly.

"What was wrong with that one?" Josh asked.

"It was really creepy. I was in this strange garden with a beautiful fountain playing into a pool beside me. I was the woman of the statue admiring my image in the water. It was so peaceful and beautiful. I was about to leave when a large beast jumped from the hedges behind me and sunk its teeth into my shoulder. It pushed me to the ground and began to eat me. It was terrible." Oriana shuddered.

"Let's go through that door over there," Josh said. "It looks like there're paintings in that room."

They moved into a large gallery with huge impressionistic paintings. None of them made any sense to them, and they were about to move on when the little man reappeared. His smile was large as ever, and he motioned for them to join him at one of the pictures.

Oriana and Josh did as he indicated and watched as he passed his hands over the surface of the work. He felt into every corner of the piece then indicated they should do the same.

"I'll try this one first," Oriana volunteered.

She moved both hands over the painting and felt an electrifying sensation in the back of her skull. Her mood changed to one of deep depression, and she wanted to die rather than go on; but something told her to move her hands again.

This time she felt a crushing sadness for a loss too great to bear. In spite of herself, tears streamed down her cheeks. Once more she moved her hands.

Now she was light as a feather and happiness flooded her body. She looked at Josh and saw him as a knight in armor. She giggled to think that she had put him into her favorite fantasy, but quickly pulled her hands away to stop it.

The little man applauded silently and went on his way.

"That must have been a strange one," Josh said.

"Try it and see what you get," Oriana said.

Josh moved his hands over the painting and pulled them back instantly. The horrible scene made him recoil in terror.

"Wow! That was really scary." Josh shook his hands as if

he'd just pulled them from a bath of cold water and was trying to drive out the numbness.

"I think I'll just look at the rest of these," Oriana said as she moved to another canvas splashed with vibrant colors.

"Good idea," Josh agreed.

The rest of the museum was devoted to ancient artifacts of the Reguluns, and the two teens perused them superficially before returning to the terminal. They found the Brem Cargan and used the same note they'd used before. Back on Brem, Oriana led him to a   Cargan where a line of entities queued up.

"Why the line?" Josh asked.

"This is the universal Cargan for Brem. You see, they can't have a Cargan here for every family on the planet, so they have one that allows you to return to your own personal Cargan."

"Personal Cargan?"

"Yes, the one we used at my house was our family's personal Cargan. We use it so we can go to the terminal in entity form. All I have to do is punch in my Personal Cargan Number, hum the note, and we're home."

"I wish we had this back on Earth. It'd sure save a lot on parking. But, why can't I just use the Mythos Cargan here in the terminal?"

"Because there is no Mythos Cargan here. Our government doesn't approve of Mythos, so they won't have one. That's why my Dad keeps his secret."

"Kinda like pornography back home, I guess."

Oriana laughed and entered the line. Soon they were at the Cargan where Oriana placed her hand inside a thing like a transparent shoebox and pushed some buttons.

"The code is in Giran so most people can use it. My PCN is

5859, and you heard the note before. Okay?"

"Yeah, I got it 5859."

Oriana vanished and Josh found it strange his fingers could push buttons inside the box when they were useless everywhere else. He appeared beside a flesh and blood Oriana.

"That was a lot of fun, Josh. Maybe you could take me someplace on Earth if I came to visit?"

"I'd love to, but how could we manage that?"

"I'll figure something out. I'll come see you the next time I can get a full day to myself."

Oriana seemed to be expecting something, but Josh wasn't quite sure how an entity would kiss a real person. *Oh well, I'd better try.* He pursed his lips and moved toward her. She broke into laughter.

"Josh, you're so funny. An entity can't kiss a person, stupid. You just brush cheeks to say hello and goodbye." She presented her cheek to him, and Josh brushed his against it. He felt a very warm glow and lingered a bit before she pulled away.

"That's enough, unless you want me to go back to Mythos with you."

Josh looked at his stopped watch out of sheer habit. "I'd better get back home. Can you get me the Mythos Cargan?"

"I put it back in case Dad came home while we were gone, but you can get to it as an entity."

At that moment, they heard a door closing and footsteps downstairs.

"My Dad's back, but he can't see you. The Cargan's in his study locked in a safe behind a portrait of my mother. You can't miss it. It's the only room in the house with the doors closed."

A male voice called out. "Oriana, are you home?"

"Yes, Papa, I'll be right down." She turned to Josh. "See you soon." She left the room, and Josh looked after her for a while before starting his search for the study.

The house was huge, but as Oriana said, the study was obvious. A portrait of a middle-aged woman hung on the left wall. Josh studied it for a while before hunting for the Cargan. She was as beautiful as Oriana, except her hair was silver where Oriana's was coal black. He felt through the wall and found the safe, then through the metal to the Cargan. He hummed the activation note and vanished.

* * * * *

As usual, his room was like an icebox, but he opened his window to restore some warmth. Josh plopped down on his bed and thought of Oriana. *She's really hot, and there's no way we can ever be together except on Mythos. I'd better take good care of that Cargan.*

CHAPTER 15

The next day Roger's intercom buzzed, and Anita informed him Phil Bastin was on line one. Roger picked up immediately.

"Phil, how are you. Any news from the state legislature?"

"I'm fine, but I'm afraid the legislature's giving us some trouble," Phil said.

"Oh, how's that?" Roger asked.

"Old senator Mitchell heads the committee responsible for that kind of purchase, and he's raising hell about the sculptures and some other items in the mansion. He claims the state can't be responsible for any item it doesn't own. We'd have to give the state all the items on his list, and it's a pretty long one, or remove all the items in question from the property. The sculptures are worthless, but he's included all of the paintings, and some of those are valuable. I figure there's around three million in artwork they'd pick up if we left it in the house, and we don't want to do that. The sculptures belong to you, though. We'd need your approval to let the state have them."

Roger thought for a moment then remembered Wycham's offer. "A man named Wycham approached me the other day with a plan to build a museum in San Francisco to house the things. He really thinks they're great examples of modern art. It would take some money from me and some help from Bastin Mining, but I think that's what I want to do."

"You're kidding. Old man Wycham wants to build a museum to house Charley's sculptures?"

"Sure, he loves the things. He told me he's willing to give ten million to the project."

"I can't believe it. That old bastard's tight as the skin on a bean. I can't imagine him parting with that kind of money to build a museum. We've done business with his companies for years, and he screws us every chance he gets. We'd have dropped his stuff a long time back, but Charley insisted we buy from Wycham. John and I were thinking about ways to cut him off now that Charley's dead."

"I couldn't believe it either, but he seems to be sincere. What you've just told me makes me even more skeptical about it, though. He told me he's going to need a big tax write-off next year. Can you think of any other reason the guy would want to do this?"

"Well, he is very rich man a. It's a mystery to me otherwise. It can't be because he and Charlie were such great friends. Charlie hated him, and it looked to me like the feeling was mutual."

"I'm having my lawyer look over the paperwork for the deal. I'll let you know if he finds anything out of the ordinary there."

"Good idea. Get back to me after that, and we'll talk some more about this museum idea."

They hung up, and Roger made a note to call his attorney next week."

* * * * *

Roger's lawyer called on Monday.

"Roger, I can't find anything out of line in Wycham's

proposal. It's all very straightforward, and the costs seem to be in line with that type of project. If you want to do it, I'd say go ahead."

"Thanks, Tom. I don't know what I'm going to do yet. Wycham's put a lot of pressure on me by chipping in with $10 million of his own money, and anything near that amount would take a good part of my fortune."

"Depends on how much you want to spend on your grandfather's memory."

"That would be about $19.95. We were never close," Roger said.

Tom laughed but held it to a respectful chuckle, "It's up to you. I see no legal reason you should stay out of it."

"Thanks for the input. Send the papers back to me as soon as you can."

They hung up, and Roger was more perplexed than before. He'd been sure there was some fly in the contract ointment, and now he had to look elsewhere.

His next call was to Phil Bastin.

"Phil, have you found anything else that might motivate Wycham's zeal for setting up a museum for Charlie's art?"

"Not a thing. There's no possible way he could obtain any business advantage by the deal. His tax dodge explanation seems to be the only reasonable answer."

"Could there be anything valuable in the make-up of those things—gold, silver, anything?"

"We checked that out. The things are made of waste material from the old gold mine. We don't even work that mine any more. The gold and uranium played out years ago."

"I'm in a real bind here. I feel like I have to give something, but I can't match Wycham's contribution," Roger said.

"Well, if you put anything into it, Bastin Mining'll feel obligated to chip in also. After all, he was the founder of the company. Hey, I just had an idea. We have to take all the artwork out of Wanagiyata. Maybe it could go to the museum too. Do you think Wycham'd go for that?"

"I imagine he would if you threw in a couple million along with it," Roger said.

"I don't know if the board'll go for a Bastin Mining contribution to an art museum in San Francisco," Phil said.

"You and John control 51% of the stock, don't you? You can tell the board about Wycham's donation, and I'll agree to match whatever Bastin Mining gives. They can think of it as a matching grant. The foundation Wycham's set up's a 501(c)(3), so the money's all tax deductible."

"That's very generous of you," Phil said. "What does Evelyn say about that idea?"

"She'll jump at any deal that keeps those things out of the house. I can get her signature on the dotted line any time we want to go forward with this. Wycham's working on some grants for the rest of the money. He feels confident he can raise the cash."

"There's a board meeting next week, can you put together the proposal by then?"

"Sure, I'll put one of my people on it right away."

"That museum won't be up for two or three years. What'll you do with the sculptures in the meantime?"

"Wycham's offered to store them rent free in one of his warehouses until the museum's finished. I tell you, he's really nuts about 'em."

"I still can't believe old man Wycham's willing to part with ten million bucks for an art museum. Oh well, maybe he's gone senile or something?"

"He seems pretty normal to me, Phil. Can I count on your help with Bastin Mining?"

"Sure, sure, I'll get that done for you. We'll go ahead and sign the deal with the state minus the artwork and the sculptures. Call me as soon as you get a shipping address."

"Thanks a lot, Phil. I'll call you as soon as I can. Give my best to Nancy." Roger hung up and immediately called Wycham's office.

That night after dinner, Roger gave his family what he thought was welcome news.

"Evelyn, Josh, I've got some good news. I've found a permanent home for Charley's sculptures."

"Where?" Evelyn said.

"A guy named Wycham's going to build a modern art museum in San Francisco. Isn't that great?"

Evelyn sighed in relief. "I won't have to have them in my house, and we can get rid of the one Josh seems so fond of."

"Dad, I can't give up my Carg... er sculpture. It's my musical inspiration!"

Roger stroked his chin thoughtfully before responding to his son's plea. "Well Evelyn, it is *his* sculpture, after all, and he keeps it in his room. What's the harm?"

Evelyn sighed heavily. "I don't know why you always side with the boy, but I guess it'll be okay as long as he keeps it out of sight."

"I'll even put it in my closet when I'm not using it for inspiration," Josh offered in an effort to ameliorate the crisis.

"Very well, you can keep it, but I'll hold you to that idea of keeping it in the closet," Evelyn said.

* * * * *

Bastin Mining came through with $2 million, and Roger matched it. Wycham secured a bridge loan until the grants were finalized, and design work began. Two weeks later, the State of South Dakota owned Wanagiyata, and the Cargans were on their way to Miami except for the Mythos unit permanently ensconced in Josh's closet.

CHAPTER 16

Mark Wycham counted the boxes as they came off the truck. They were short by one. He accounted for the Mythos unit which was of no consequence to him, but there was still one missing.

"Jergens, you idiot, I told you how many there were. Didn't you count them when you loaded?" The burly man in overalls cringed instinctively though he towered over the older Wycham.

"Sure, Mr. Wycham; but that's all there were, I swear it. We couldn't find any more in the whole place. Their guy even helped us look. He didn't know where it was, and we never found it." The man seemed to be very sincere, but it would not surprise Wycham to learn Jergens held one out for later sale. Wycham nodded to someone Jergens could not see, and Manjahba possessed the man.

"Now, tell me again that all of the sculptures at Wanagiyata are here," Wycham asked.

"Like I already said, that's all there were," Jergens insisted.

"He's telling the truth, Wycham. This is it," Manjahba answered and left Jergens' body.

Jergens shuddered a bit but put it down to the drafts in the warehouse. "Honest, Mr. Wycham. We wouldn't cheat you. You pay too well, and we know you'd get even for any double crosses."

"I'm sure you did your best," Wycham figured he didn't need any disgruntled employees. "Here's the bonus I promised you for safe delivery."

Wycham handed the man a check.

Jergens inspected the check and folded it once before putting it away in a pocket of his overalls. "It's always a pleasure doing business with you, Mr. Wycham."

Wycham and Manjahba admired their newfound resources. The boys had done an excellent job of crating them up, and there was no damage as a result of the move. A crew of Ulan entities arranged the Cargans on the floor of the old warehouse in the exact positions they occupied at Wanagiyata. A freshly painted compass rose covered the floor area just south of the collection, and a huge map of Earth adorned the far wall. Wycham even installed a computerized system for locating all the key cities and tourist attractions of his planet even though he knew entities would not be capable of using it directly due to the lack of force field technology on Earth. This is where Manjahba and his Ulans would prove helpful.

A crew of six Ulans would be on duty at the improvised terminal to help entity travelers find their way. They could manipulate the computer without using a force field, but their real purpose was far removed from service to fellow entity travelers. They were the key element in Manjahba's plan to dominate first Mica then several other planets including Earth. Control of the terminal on Earth was the final piece in the complex structure.

"Is the transfer room set up and working?" Manjahba asked.

"So far, it all checks out perfectly. We'll have to use a real subject to be sure, but your people say they're confident it will perform as expected," Wycham said.

"How about the remaining Cargan, and this man Smith?" Manjahba spoke the name with a note of disgust in his voice.

"I don't care about the Mythos Cargan, Charley was the only one who used it. Smith may know where the Gira unit is, and you can leave him to me. He knows all the Cargans need to be here to comply with the provisions of Bastin's will. He'll help us out."

"I don't trust him," Manjahba said. "He's too intelligent, and he has too much money. If he should find out what we're doing here, it could mean big trouble with the Grand Council."

"Smith doesn't even know they're Cargans, and even if he did, who would tip him off? Nobody in the universe suspects us at this point. The only other person who could even guess what we're up to would be Charles Bastin, and he's dead."

"Just the same, I won't feel comfortable until all the Cargans are under our control, and our operation is in full swing. We need that Gira Cargan."

"I'll take care of that. It has to be in the nursing home if it isn't at Wanagiyata. After we have all the Cargans, how long will it be until we start seeing the full rewards of our enterprise?" Wycham asked.

"I would say less than one of your Earth years once we're in full operation–perhaps less."

"Just remember my part of the spoils," Wycham reminded the Ulan. There was no guarantee Wycham would not meet the same fate as others who stood in the way of the Ulan scheme.

"You will get all I have promised, and more," Manjahba said as a smile spread across the usually grim, round face. "Providing, that is, you manage to obtain the remaining Cargan."

Wycham's sense of dread returned, but he had no choice other than to go along with whatever the Ulan wanted. He was in too deeply now.

CHAPTER 17

Two days later, Roger entered his office, and Anita handed him his phone messages. He noticed one from Phil Bastin and passed it back to her.

"Would you get Phil on the phone for me, please," he asked then went into his office. A short time later she announced the call was ready.

Roger picked up. "Hello, Phil, what's new."

"Roger, I've found the missing sculpture," Phil said.

"Where was it?"

"You remember the shipping people told the staff at Wanagiyata they were one short. I remembered Charley was holding one when he died, and I called the nursing home. They said they'd shipped it to me. Turns out, it was packed in a box with a bunch of Charley's personal stuff they'd shipped to my house. Nancy found it yesterday. She was going through his things to see if there was anything valuable before giving the whole box to Goodwill. It was wrapped up in his underwear. We called the nursing home in case he'd wanted them to have it, but they said it's the one Charley was holding when he died. Nancy shipped it to your house by UPS."

"That's fine, Phil. Josh seems to like them, and there's no hurry to get it to Wycham. Josh'll be really happy to get another of Charley's sculptures. He seems to think they help him write rock music."

"They're ugly enough to do that. Take care, Roger."

Roger smiled as he hung up the phone. Evelyn would have a cow, but he'd let his son play with it for a day or two before sending it on to Wycham.

* * * * *

Roger had a late meeting that day that included dinner. He arrived home that evening to find Evelyn baking brownies. "Mmmm, smells good in here," he said as he put down his briefcase and enfolded her in his arms.

"Roger! I'm baking," she protested feebly.

"My second favorite dessert," he said, nodding toward the brownies.

"And, what's your favorite?" she asked coyly.

"You know what that is." He kissed her gently, but she pushed him away quickly.

"Not now. I have to get these brownies in the oven." She returned to her baking while Roger sat down in a kitchen chair.

"Phil called today. They found the missing sculpture."

"I didn't know one was missing," Evelyn closed the oven door and set the timer on the stove before sitting down opposite her husband.

"Phil said Wycham's people claimed one was missing when they picked the rest up at Wanagiyata. It's the one Charley was holding when he died. Nancy shipped it here, but I'll get it on to Wycham as soon as Josh has a look at it."

"Roger! You know how I feel about those things. I don't think they're a good influence on our son. Right after we got home from South Dakota I went into his room to check on him and found him sitting there with that thing in his lap. I thought he'd just gone to sleep holding on to it, but he was more like in some kind of trance. I had to really shake him to wake him up, but he seemed to be okay."

"Anything else?"

"Yes, the room was very cold, but he had his window open too far."

"Is that all? I've gone to sleep holding a book or listening to the stereo."

"No, one other time I looked in on him after dinner. He was doing his homework, as usual, but when I checked back before going to bed, he was sitting with that thing again, and he was rigid just like the other time. This time I decided to just let him come out of it by himself, thinking maybe that would teach him a lesson when he woke up all stiff and sore in the morning."

"I see. Was he all right in the morning?"

"Yes, he didn't seem to have any ill effects from the experience."

"Well, I can't see any harm in them. I'll get rid of this new one as soon as I can. Where is he now?"

"He went to band practice. He won't be home until later."

"Well then, that leaves us some time to enjoy his absence." Roger reached for her hand, but Evelyn pulled back quickly.

"Roger, I have to wait 'til these brownies are done. They're for the Women's Charity Guild bake sale tomorrow, and I have a hair appointment in the morning."

"Okay, but when that oven timer dings, it's 'ring-a-ding, ding for us."

* * * * *

The next morning at breakfast Roger informed Josh of the expected package from South Dakota. "Your uncle Phil called me yesterday at work and said they'd found another sculpture.

It's the one your great grandfather had at the nursing home."

"Oh yeah. Didn't somebody say he was holding one when he died?" Josh asked.

"This is the one. It should arrive here today by UPS. Your mother has her volunteer day today, so be sure and check the front porch for a package when you come home from school."

"Okay, Dad, but can I open it up and check out the new car... er sculpture?"

"What did you call it?" Evelyn asked.

"Sorry, I was thinking about cars and it just slipped out." *Josh you idiot! You almost blew the whole deal. Be more careful.*

"Yes, you can keep it for a day, or so, but I have to send it on to Mr. Wycham by the end of the week," Roger said.

"Ugh, I hate the idea of having two of them around." Evelyn said.

"It's only for a day or two, dear. After all, Josh says they help him write music, and we should encourage his creative talents."

"It goes before Tuesday, and that's final," Evelyn said.

"That's okay, I'll check to see if this one's haunted. It probably isn't, and in that case, we can send it out right away," Josh agreed.

* * * * *

That afternoon Josh ran up the large circular drive to the front of his house hoping to find another Cargan. He was not disappointed. A large box sat next to the door, and on close inspection it proved to be from Bastin Mining Company. He unlocked the front door and carried it inside.

It was not heavy, but his backpack full of school books added to his delay climbing the stairs to his room. Dumping the backpack, he tore into the package and pulled a small

Cargan from the plastic peanuts. It was only slightly larger than the Mythos Cargan, but every bit as ugly. He set it down on his credenza and turned on his keyboard. A quick run of the scales showed this unit responding to F#.

I wonder where this one goes. I bet great grandpa used it to escape from the nursing home. I wonder why he didn't take the Mythos Cargan? That would have been my choice. He must have had some reason for keeping this one with him. Oh well, there's only one way to find out.

Josh grasped the worn locations and hummed F#. He soon found himself in a totally dark terminal.

He let his eyes become accustomed to the dark and realized this particular terminal was closed for the night. He was about to return home when a voice from the public address system caused him to jump. The voice spoke in Giran, but it sounded familiar in some way.

"I'm sorry, our terminal is closed during hours of darkness on this side of the planet. You may wait inside the terminal or come back in two Giran hours."

I know that voice. It sounds a lot like great grandpa, but it can't be. He's dead. I think I'll try the helper door and see if they've seen anything peculiar lately.

He moved to the green door and pressed the button. The door opened on a ghostly figure of Charles Bastin.

"Great Grandpa? Are you a ghost or an entity?" Josh blurted out in English.

The apparition seemed to be as shocked as Josh. "Josh, Roger's Josh?" Charley said.

"Yeah, it's me, great grandpa. We found the Cargan you had at the nursing home, and I had to try it out to see where it went. Are you a ghost?"

"In a way. My corporeal body's dead, but my entity escaped it before I died. Come on inside and tell me how you found out about Cargans."

Inside the helper room, Josh presented his cheek to Charley.

"Oh, I see you know how t' greet a entity. I hope yer ready fer this." He touched Josh's cheek with his and smiled as the boy pulled back automatically.

"Wow! That's not like any other entity I've ever greeted," Josh said.

Charley laughed at his great grandson's reaction. "Don't worry 'bout that. All us entities that've lost our bodies come across that way. It is good to see you even though I don't know how you ever found out it was a Cargan. Sit down and tell me 'bout it."

They both sat down and Josh told Charley how he discovered the sculpture's true character.

"I always thought your house was haunted, and I figured the Cargans had something to do with the ghosts. When I was there for your funeral, I got a funny feeling when I looked at the Mythos Cargan, so I was really glad you left it to me."

"That funny feelin' was me, Josh. I came back to see who'd come t' my funeral and hear all the nice things people'd say 'bout me. I always thought it'd be great to be able t' attend yer own funeral, but some o' them relatives was only interested in my money. I saw you lookin' at the Cargans, and I thought I'd give ya a hint about Mythos. I knew a young man like you'd appreciate what goes on there. I remember when I was your age. I couldn't wait to 'get intimate' with a girl," Charley tried to skirt around a delicate subject.

"Things haven't changed that much," Josh assured him.

"I knew you'd have the most fun with it, that is, if ya ever figured out what it was." He gave Josh a knowing wink. "You been there yet?"

Josh blushed and looked down at the floor. "Yeah, a couple of times. I even met a girl there."

Charley beamed his pride. "Tell me 'bout her."

"She's from Brem, and her name's Oriana. She's really hot, too."

Charley laughed merrily. "I loved Mythos, 'specially after I got older. Do your parents know about the Cargans?"

"Oh no, they don't have a clue, and I don't want them to know. That'd spoil all the fun."

"Well, I don't think it'll hurt ya none, but you'll have t' be really careful t' keep our secret. By the way, what's happened to the Cargans and Wanagiyata? I figured John'd sell everything as soon as the will was probated."

"Dad says Wanagiyata was donated to the state as a resort, but the state won't take the paintings or the Cargans. Dad and some guy named Wycham are building a museum of some kind for them. Isn't that great news?"

Charlie did not seem to be thrilled. His expression sobered, and his voice took on a deeper tone. "I figured Wycham'd make a play for the Cargans, but I didn't expect it so soon. He knows what they are, 'cause he wheedled one out o' me a few year's back."

Josh interrupted. "You mean he's doing entity travel too?"

"Yup! It's a long story 'bout how he got me t' give him one, and I'll tell ya all about it some other time. Wycham's why I left 'em to your daddy. I knew he was astute enough to keep from making a big mistake with 'em. I wanted to warn him 'bout Wycham, but I lost my ability to communicate before I got the chance to do that. I didn't figure he'd ever consider 'em more than just ugly sculptures. Has he found the electronics inside 'em yet?"

"No, I looked at the circuit board, but I figured I'd better not let Dad find out about it."

"Good boy! He'd be sure t' dig inta that side o' the things, and he might be able t' figur' it all out, what with him bein' th' top dog at that big electronics company."

"Why are you worried about Wycham if he's doing entity travel too? He wouldn't want anyone else to find out about it either, would he?"

"I'm not so sure. I did business with that weasel for a long time, and he screwed me every chance he got. We got t' be sure we know what's in it for him afore this museum deal goes too far. Where's he got th' Cargans now?"

"Some warehouse in Miami."

Charley went pensive for a moment. "Hmmm, I'd love t' check that warehouse out, but he'd recognize me right off. 'Sides, I have a rough time getting away from this terminal."

"I could check it out for you," Josh volunteered.

"You'd have t' go as a entity so's you could get inta places he's got locked up."

Josh answered quickly. "Hey! I could go from here to another planet with an Earth Cargan, then to Earth as an entity, couldn't I?"

"Sure, that'd be th' way t' do it, all right. Come on! I'll find ya a route."   Charley led Josh into another room full of computers and sat down at one featuring a funny looking keyboard. "This here computer has a device that lets me punch th' keys. Can't work any o' them others." Charley waved a ghostly hand toward the rest of the devices. After a few commands he smiled broadly.

"Yeah, here it is. Ya goes t' Xemba then t' Earth." He entered more commands then indicated the display to Josh. "This here's th' Xemba Cargan. It's 'bout this high." He held his hand above the floor to indicate the height. "Better'n that, I'll show it to ya." He rose to leave, but Josh spoke.

"Before we do that, would you tell me how you found out about Cargans in the first place?"

Charley smiled at his great grandson. "Okay, sit down. It'll take me a while."

They resumed their positions in the helper room, and Charley began. "It was right after my Pa died. I'd gone down to inspect his mine along with Mike Maloney, a buddy of mine who was supposed to know somethin' about gold mines. Dad was never able to make the mine pay, but I figured there might be some way of getting' more gold out o' it with modern methods."

"While we were lookin' 'round I kept seein' somethin' out o' the corner o' my eye, but Mike never saw nothin'. That night your great grandma woke me up sayin' she'd seed a ghost."

"She was scared as hell, and I'd 'bout got her calmed down when she screamed that some man just walked right through the bedroom wall. She could only sob and point to where he was supposed to be standin'. I couldn't see a thing, but she swore he was there tryin' ta talk to her. I humored her along figurin' I'd call the men in the little white coats in the mornin'. I thought she'd gone off her rocker completely when she said it was comin' for me. I told her, 'Sure, sure...' but then I felt it. It was like somebody grabbed hold o' my insides with icy hands. I thought I was havin' a heart attack, at first, but I'd always heard heart attacks was painful, so I figured this weren't one of 'em. She told me the ghost walked right into me."

"I blacked out, and when I woke up, she told me I'd said to take the hall mirror down to the mine where I'd been that afternoon. She said I'd told her we'd be able to see and hear it there. We got dressed and drove over in my pickup truck with the hall mirror in the back."

"We set up the mirror in the tunnel, and there he was as plain as the nose on your face. He was a tall fellow in funny clothes, and he had long, blonde hair. I could see him in the mirror, but I couldn't see anything makin' the reflection. Your grandma could see him, though, and hear him talk too. She had me put my hand where the ghost was, and I got that cold feeling again. After a minute or so I could hear him. He said he was from a planet named Gira and his name was Mullu. He'd been stranded here on Earth about six months back when somethin' he called his Cargan screwed up. Course, I had no idea what he was talkin' 'bout then."

"He asked me if I'd build one for him so's could get home before he decomposed. He said all the stuff I'd need was here in the mine, and he'd show me how to build the electrical gear."

"Now I was suspicious about this thing; so I asked him how he knew English if he was from some other planet. He told me he'd picked it up by listenin' to people and watching our television. He figured that since he was stranded here he'd have to be able to communicate with somebody on Earth to have any chance of gettin' back home. We took him back to the house where he had the wife get a pencil and paper, and he dictated how to make a Cargan."

"Your great grandma wasn't much of a technical person, but she was good at shorthand. I understood some of it, but a lot of the stuff was just plain over my head. The hardest part was the electrical dohickeys. Neither she nor I knew anything 'bout that. We just drew what he said to draw and made notes as he dictated them. We were there all night that night and most of the next two days takin' down information and makin' sketches before he said we had enough."

"I took the stuff to Bob Townsend, our mining engineer, and he understood the mechanical parts; but the electrical stuff was a mystery to him. That's when I got Motorola involved. They assigned Ransom Milton to the project. Milton was amazed at the stuff Mullu gave me, but he said it'd never work, and that I'd be wastin' my money on a special chip. When he told me how much it'd cost, I agreed with him."

"I went back home and told Mullu I didn't have the money to make the electrical stuff he needed, but he said that'd soon be no problem. He told me 'bout the uranium, and within a year I was makin' a ton of money minin' that stuff 'stead of gold. I went back to Milton and told him I didn't care if he thought it'd work or not–just build the damned things."

"It took a while to get everything together, and Mullu lived with us during that time. He was an interestin' guy. He told us all about Gira and how beautiful it was. He was mighty homesick, and we tried to cheer him up as much as we could."

"Didn't anyone ever come looking for him?" Josh asked.

"I asked him if they'd send out a search party, or somethin'. He said he was too far from home for them guys to find him.

Seems he was tryin' to get to someplace called Gorgon 4 when he wound up on Earth. He figured some disturbance in our galaxy caused him to drift off course."

"How did he know how to make a Gira Cargan if he was way off course?" Josh asked.

"He didn't. He said he was guessin' a lot 'bout the antenna design, but thought it'd be close enough for him to make it home. He said he'd done some spyin' at NASA, and worked out some rough coordinates for the Earth/Gira route. I asked him to come back if it wasn't right and make corrections so I could go to Gira if I wanted to. He was pretty hesitant 'bout doing that, but I told him I had somethin' comin' for helpin' him get back home. Turns out, he was right on the money, but I'm ahead of myself."

"It took several months to assemble everything we needed, and a bright young college kid working over the summer for me helped my engineer put it all together."

"I imagine lots of the ghost stories people tell are really sightings of entity travelers, eh great grandpa?"

"I reckon so. Th' funny thing was, once I got that Cargan built, those 'ghosts' came flocking into our house by the boatload. We only had one Cargan, but they said it was their ticket home. Your great grandma was having a field day. They were givin' her inside information on the stock market out of gratitude, and she started makin' a killin'. They also gave me a lot more information on the Cargans. That's when I started buildin' more of them."

"How did Wycham get a Cargan?" Josh asked.

"I bought a lot of equipment from one of Wycham's companies. One night at a party he'd thrown for his customers,

I got a little too drunk and blabbed about the ghosts. Wycham wanted to see them, so the next time he came to our place I took him into the conservatory and tried to introduce him to one figurin' he'd never see or hear 'em anyway. I was really surprised when he started talkin' with one right off. The entity traveler figured Wycham was in on the Cargan secret and let the cat out of the bag. Once he knew what they did, Wycham hounded me 'til I gave him one."

"Which one did you give him?"

"I figured he didn't know one planet from another one, so I gave him th' Ula Cargan. I'd been there once and didn't like it a bit. I certainly didn't want t' go back. It's a cold, barren place with some scary folks on it. Ulans can do things as entities other people can't. They use 'em fer police in the business o' entity travel. I'll introduce ya t' one sometime."

"I still think he'd want to keep our secret."

"Don't count on it. Wycham's got some scheme up his sleeve, I'd bet on it."

"Does anybody else on Earth have a Cargan?"

"I gave one to a college kid we had for a summer hire. I made it for a guy from Phobos 3, but I went there once and didn't like the place, so I gave it to him. Another one was stolen from the house, and I can't tell ya where that un went."

"So, why did you choose this particular planet?" Josh asked.

"Gira's one of the most beautiful planets in the universe. If you can stay a while I'll show ya 'round. Besides bein' incredibly beautiful, the people are so advanced. It's a real paradise. Only problem is they're real religious folks with a lot o' superstitions, particularly 'bout entities." Charley glanced at the large clock. "It's almost dawn now. My shift's over then, and I'll take you around a bit after I show ya th' Xemba Cargan. You do know how to do entity transportation don't ya?"

"Sure, no problem, but you said your shift was up. Do you work here?"

"On a part time basis. The terminal is normally closed from sundown to sun up, but some people still don't know about it and come in anyway. The Girans are superstitious 'bout the dark, and they don't like entities movin' around at night. If someone comes in who's not aware of that, I help them figure out if they want to wait around 'til daylight or go back home. You see, the whole terminal's surrounded by one-way entity shields that come on at dark. You couldn't've left if you'd wanted to. They gave me the job so's I'd stay put at night."

"Wow," was all Josh could manage. "So you're immortal now."

"The Girans told me I won't last. They give me fifty years to live, if you can call it that."

Charley looked out the window to see the sky beginning to brighten. "Come over to the window. The sunrise is real pretty from here.

Josh glided to the window and watched as the sky turned from a dull gray to pink then into a brilliant orange. Long ropes of black clouds formed across the horizon in a vain attempt to bind the dazzling, golden circle just beginning to show above the snow-capped mountains. The huge ball shrank to manageable size as it shook loose from its bonds, and the sky applauded its escape by assuming a deep blue green hue shredding the clouds into wisps of white cotton. He'd never seen anything like it.

"Man! That's cool," he managed. "Why is the sky that

color?"

"They got some gases in their atmosphere that give it that greenish tint. The Girans perform their most sacred ritual every day at sunrise. The whole planet gets up for it. Soon this place'll be teemin' with people doing entity travel. My replacement should be here any minute."

As he spoke the door opened and a small green man appeared. "Good morning, Charley Earth. I see we have a guest today," the small man nodded at Josh as he offered his cheek.

"This is my great grandson, Josh Smith. Josh, this here's Mister Winble."

Josh brushed the little man's cheek and felt a very warm sensation. "It's a pleasure to meet you."

"And I you, Mister Smith." Winble thought for a moment while he deciphered the English term 'great grandson.' "Ah yes. You are the son of one of Charley Earth's grandchildren. I love the Earth English way of naming relatives. Do you plan to stay long on Gira?"

"No, great grandpa's going to show me around a bit then I'll go home."

"Well, Charley will make sure you know about all of the peculiar customs on this planet concerning entities and keep you out of trouble. Enjoy your stay. By the way, Charley, I just received a special notice about the Earth terminal. Perhaps Mr. Smith should know about it before he returns home?"

"What's it say? You know I don't read Giran that well," Charlie said.

Winble produced a small, hand held computer from his briefcase and punched up some text on its screen. "It says there have been two entity disappearances on Earth in the last two days.   One was a Senator from Ula and the other was a businessman from Grava III. The Council is sending a Marshal to check into it, but it will be several days before we know any more."

"What do you mean, sir? Earth doesn't have a terminal," Josh said.

Winble gave him a puzzled look then turned to Charley for an explanation to his great grandson.

"Since I had all those Cargans, people used t' use my conservatory for a terminal. I didn't have none o' the gear like you seen here, but the Grand Council okayed my place as a provisional terminal. Everybody else in th' galaxy thinks it's a terminal."

"Oh, I see, now Wycham's warehouse in Miami is the terminal," Josh said.

"I suppose that's what he's done. This changes our plans 'bout you goin' there. Since the Marshals are gonna check it out, there's no need for you t' go. If anything funny's goin' on, they'll find it."

"Will I be okay using my Cargans?" Josh asked.

"I think you'll be okay. It's probably somethin' wrong with those two Cargans. They might'a been damaged in shipment," Charlie said.

"Thanks for the warning Mr. Winble," Josh said as he extended his cheek to the small green man.

"Only doing my job, Mr. Smith. You and Charley have a good time seeing Gira."

With that, Charley led Josh out of the room and into the terminal now busy with Giran entities departing and arriving. They moved to the compass rose and waited their turn to depart.

"I can't get over the fact I'm talking to you after you're dead," Josh said. He was too interested in hearing Charley's story to bring up this awkward subject before.

"You think you've got a problem? I'm the one what's dead." Charley seemed a bit indignant.

"I'm sorry. I didn't mean to be a jerk," Josh apologized.

"It's all right," Charley seemed apologetic himself. "It's just that the only way you can ever feel or smell or taste anythin' is through someone else. The only thing you can do for yourself is look, and that's not much of a life no matter how beautiful the scenery is."

It finally came their turn to move out, and Charley led Josh through lush river valleys, over majestic mountains, past thundering waterfalls and into beautiful caves. They saw the ruins of Gira's ancient civilizations and watched plays being performed. Charley was glad Josh spoke Giran, though he did have to translate for Josh in one or two spots. They enjoyed native dances at several small villages, but as the sun began to set, Charley led Josh back to the terminal.

"You'll wanna get back before sunset. Gira's no fun for an entity after the sun goes down," Charley reminded him.

"It's just been so good to see you, Great Grandpa," Josh smiled as they landed back at the compass rose.

"I guess you know all of my stories were true, now," Charley said with an impish grin.

"I think I always suspected they were," Josh said as he gripped the Cargan and hummed F#.

CHAPTER 18

Back home, Josh placed the Gira Cargan next to the Mythos unit in his closet. He sat down in his computer chair and reflected on his experience. The time he'd spent on Gira probably exceeded all the time he'd ever spent with his great grandfather in the past, and it was the most valuable time of all. *Jeez, I wish I'd known about this entity travel stuff a long time ago, but I can see why he didn't tell us kids about it. He doesn't trust this Wycham character, and now there are problems with the Earth Cargans. Seems like too much of a coincidence to me, but he thinks the Marshals, whoever they are, can take care of it, so who am I to worry about it? Just think, I'm one of only three people who's ever used a Cargan here on Earth. What a rush!*

Oh well, better get down to business here. The band's got another gig at that teen club in three weeks, and Mr. Karrasnik thinks we need a female singer. Sounds like a good idea to me. Who could we ask? I got it! We'll audition for the job. I'll bet there's tons of girls who'd like to do it.

* * * * *

Evelyn noticed the empty box in the kitchen and called Josh on the house intercom. "Did that other sculpture come today, Josh?"

"Yeah Mom, I got it in my bedroom."

"Just be sure you keep it there, and remember, it has to go to

Miami next week."

"Oh Mom! I really like this one. Can't I keep it?"

"You'll have to ask your father about that. He does have an obligation to Mr. Wycham, you know."

"I know, I'll ask him tonight."

* * * * *

That night over dinner, Josh informed his father of the new arrival. "That other sculpture arrived today. It's really cool. Can I keep it."

"I told you you could keep it for a few days," Roger replied.

"I want to keep it with my other one for musical inspiration, Dad," Josh said.

Roger set down his fork and looked at his wife. "What do you say? You're the one who doesn't want any of Charley's work in the house."

"I told Josh you had an obligation to the will and to Mr. Wycham to keep the collection together. Isn't that correct?"

"I do, and Wycham's called me specifically inquiring about the missing sculpture. I told him we'd get it to him as soon as we found it. I guess you'll have to give it up, Josh, sorry."

"Dad! It's not like the collection's on display someplace, or anything like that. Can't I keep it until the museum's finished?"

Roger thought for a moment and shrugged his shoulders. "You have a point there, son. I'll let you keep it until I talk to Mr. Wycham again, that is, if it's okay with your mother." He turned to Evelyn for her comments.

"I guess you can keep it 'til then, but the rules are the same for it as the other one. Keep it in your room."

"Sure, Mom." *I sure hope Mr. Wycham doesn't want the Gira Cargan right away. He's got that warehouse like a terminal, though.*

The only way I could convince Dad to let me keep it is if I tell him about great grandpa, but then he'd probably want me to give up the Mythos Cargan too. This really sucks.

* * * * *

The band agreed with the idea of a female singer and Josh's plan to audition for the job. Each member had several suggestions, but they decided to see who would respond to the call in the school newsletter.

The notice came out on Wednesday and by Friday Josh had four candidates for the job. Auditions were set for Rodney Barnes' place on Saturday night. The girls each agreed to bring an outfit they would likely wear while they performed and furnished Josh with the music they would use for their audition.

Saturday night came, and Rodney's mother served as chaperone while the girls changed in the bathroom of the carriage house. As they emerged, it was obvious Mrs. Barnes did not think much of the costumes, but she held her tongue knowing they were no worse than some of the music videos she'd been exposed to.

The first girl was Nancy Goodall, a brunette with dreamy gray eyes and a rather full figure. She wore black tights with silver knee boots and a skirt so short the boys were salivating. Her sleeveless black sequined top was bare at the midriff and cut low down the front invoking more fountains of saliva. Heavy gothic makeup topped off the image.

Josh spoke to her. "We've got a two bar lead in, and you come in here." He pointed to a spot on her sheet music, and she nodded her understanding.

The band blared the lead in for "Firework", and Nancy came in right on time.

Her voice was on the husky side, but it only accentuated her gothic image. She finished in a flourish, and the band relaxed.

"That was great, Nancy," Josh complimented. "You can go change now, and we'll let you know on Monday."

"Okay, Josh. You've got my number, and I expect to hear from you no later than Monday night, okay?"

"Sure, I'll call you before then," Josh said. "Who's next?"

"Me." Angie Richards, a freckled redhead built like a beanpole with almost nothing in the way of a bosom, stepped forward. She wore a long-sleeved, green sheath dress down to her knees but slit up the front nearly to her crotch and cut down the front to her waist. The slit was wasted on her skinny legs, but Josh knew she had an excellent voice.

"Hi Angie," Josh greeted her. "You ready?"

"I'm ready. You got my music?"

"Yeah, you come in here, okay?" Josh pointed out the spot on her copy.

"That's right," she agreed.

The band began, and Angie crooned out "Dog Days Are Over" in a manner compelling every ear in the room to listen. The end of her song elicited spontaneous applause from the band as well as the other girls and Mrs. Barnes.

"Wow! Terrific Angie," Josh said. "Same thing. I'll call you before Monday night."

"Okay, Josh." Angie left the room to change.

"Next!" Josh commanded.

"I'm next." Marilyn Morgan stepped forward wearing a black fur vest over a gold bra and gold lame short shorts. Mesh stockings ended in gold calf high boots. The platinum blonde hair and heavy makeup gave the impression of an old-time movie star. Gold painted fingernails topped off the ensemble.

"I know where to come in, Josh—just get going." She struck a provocative pose and waited for the band. It took Josh a moment to divert their attention from her very long and shapely legs, but they hit the song "Animal" with gusto. Marilyn continued her sensual activities during the song, and the band was sweating a bit before the last note sounded.

"Oh boy, that was hot!" Josh said.

"I get the job, right?" Marilyn said.

"I'll let you know Monday," Josh managed after clearing his throat. "I guess you're last Julia."

Julia Kidwell stepped forward wearing blue jeans almost too low on her hips to be possible, and a blue butterfly tattoo peeked provocatively out of the waist band. A white blouse tied high on her waist revealed a tantalizing amount of her ample breasts. Silver platform heels raised her above Josh by several inches. Her raven black hair hung loosely past her shoulders, and her makeup was subdued for stage purposes. The girl next door look almost made Josh melt, and he was hoping she sang as good as she looked.

"I'm ready when you are, Josh," she said.

The band began to play, and Julia came in right on cue for "Teenage Dreamer." Her voice was very soft, but she seduced the microphone in a manner designed to drive a teenaged boy crazy. It certainly succeeded with Josh. He almost missed a chord near the end of the piece. He was glad to finish the song without suffering from tight pants.

"Good job, Julie. Call you Monday, okay?"

"Sure Josh, talk to you then." She left the room to change.

The band began to shut down, and Josh made sure the last

girl was on her way home before he called for a meeting. "Okay, guys, which one do you like?"

"God! That Marilyn Morgan is hot! She'd be quite an attraction on stage. How about those legs?" Rodney Barnes offered.

"I don't know, her voice isn't that hot. Angie's a better singer," Bill Thompson said.

"Yeah, but she's too skinny. We need somebody with some sex appeal," Willie Jenkins protested.

"That leaves out Nancy. I don't care how much skin she shows, it ain't worth looking at." Rodney Barnes' comment invoked ribald laughter from the boys.

"What about Julie? She's good looking and she sings very well, I thought," Josh said.

"Julie's pretty enough, but she sings very softly," Bill Thompson said. "Can she belt one out if she has to?"

"I heard her sing a lot stronger than tonight in the a cappella choir," Willie Jenkins said.

"I think she's the best we saw tonight, all things considered," Rodney agreed.

"Okay, I'll call Julie and tell her she's got the job. Remember, practice next Tuesday night, same time, okay?" Josh said.

"I don't envy you having to tell the other girls they didn't make it," Bill Thompson said as he packed his drumsticks.

"All part of the job," Josh said. "Can you give me a ride home Will?"

"I'll take you home, Josh," the female voice startled the boys. They turned to see Julie Kidwell in the doorway holding a small suitcase.

"Julie! Were you listening to all this?" Josh asked.

"Don't worry, I won't tell the other girls about your Chauvinistic remarks. Thanks for letting me be your singer, guys."

A flurry of subdued, almost unintelligible acknowledgements followed her statement, but she only smiled in response.

Josh unplugged his guitar, placed it in its case and turned to his band. "See you guys on Tuesday." He didn't wait for their response. He was too busy making sure he kept up with Julie.

She led him to a dark colored Toyota and punched the key fob to open the trunk. She put her suitcase inside and turned to Josh. "You can put your guitar in the trunk."

He stowed the instrument then took a seat on the passenger side as she buckled in and started the car. "I'm really glad the guys liked you. I was hoping they would."

She pulled away from the Barnes house and turned on the road toward Josh's house. "I've been waiting for you to ask me for a date, but you didn't seem interested in me. I thought auditioning for your band might urge you along a bit."

He was glad the darkness hid his blush. "Yeah, I've been meaning to ask you out, but just haven't found the right time. I wanted it to be special." *God, Josh, what a dumb ass you are! She likes you, and you never had the courage to ask her out.*

She changed the subject. "Your band sounds great. Have you got any gigs lined up?"

"Just one, at that same teen club we did a while back. The manager there called me a while back, but he said he'd like for us to have a female vocalist. That's why we set up the audition."

"Great! Are they paying you?"

"Not much, only $100, but it's a start."

An awkward silence followed, but Josh's mind was racing

for a proper subject of conversation. *Think, idiot! What do you say to convince her you're really interested in her?* His best answer was, "I really liked your costume tonight." *God! How lame!*

"Thanks Josh, did you notice my tattoo?"

Oh boy did I! I'd love to see where that butterfly's coming from, but how do I make a tasteful comment about it? That's it!. "I thought it was very tasteful."

"Good, I'll paint it back on for the gig. My parents won't let me get a tattoo, so I have to do the temporary kind."

Phew! Dodged a bullet there. "Me too. Dad's really strict about that. He says I'll only regret having one after I turn thirty."

"I'd never have one where it could be seen by anybody I didn't want to see it." She turned her attention from the road for a moment to smile warmly at Josh.

He felt his hormones getting the better of him and changed the subject. "You know where my house is, don't you?"

"Sure, next road on the left, right?"

"Yeah, the gate code's 429."

They pulled up to the gate for Josh's house, and passed through the gate to the front of the house. Julie got out with him and stood by as Josh retrieved his guitar from the trunk. Julie's next move surprised him. She threw her arms around his neck and kissed him. It was not what anyone would call a passionate kiss, but it was a bit too hard and lasted a bit too long for a friendly goodnight.

"Goodnight, Josh. I'll see you Tuesday." She almost ran to the driver's door and was inside before Josh could respond. As the car pulled away, Josh mumbled, "Goodnight Julie."

* * * * *

Tuesday night Julie picked Josh up as arranged that day at school. Josh loaded his guitar into the trunk and approached the passenger side door with some misgivings. *What do I say to her? What if she wants to kiss me again? Stupid ass! Act like a man. What would Johnny Depp do? He'd be cool. He'd act like nothing happened, wouldn't he? Maybe she'll make the first move again? No, she'll be waiting for me to do something, but what? I have to acknowledge that kiss some way.* He opened the door and sat down. "I'm glad you're picking me up tonight. I could really get used to your kisses." *What did I just say? I can't believe I said that. That's cool?*

Julie smiled at him and nodded her head to one side. "How romantic, Josh. I feel the same way, but tonight is band practice." She started the car and pulled away.

Say something else, you nerd—something more normal. "You look nice tonight."

"Thank you. I didn't think I should wear my performance costume for practice."

"Right! I don't think the guys'd be able to concentrate on the music looking at you in those clothes."

"Thank you, again, I think. I hope it wasn't too revealing."

"Oh no, it was just what I'd have asked for." The air conditioning blower wafted the aroma of her perfume toward his side of the car for a moment, and he thought his head might explode from the scent. He sniffed audibly. "Nice perfume."

"Do you like it? It's a new one I'm trying. If you like it, I'll be sure to wear it whenever we're out together."

"I love it."

"Good, I'm glad you do." She took her eyes off the road and

smiled at him in a way that conjured up images of them together naked in Josh's mind.

I'd better change the subject quick. It's getting pretty hot in here. "Did you pick out some songs you want to sing at our gig?"

"Yeah, the list is in my purse. Take a look at it and see if you approve."

Now Josh knew a woman's purse was forbidden territory for any man. "That's okay, you can show it to me when we get there."

"Go ahead, silly. Nothing in there'll bite you." She laughed merrily at his embarrassment.

"Okay." Josh opened the black leather bag and noticed the usual female equipment for hair and makeup. A folded paper sat in the middle of the tubes and plastic boxes. He picked it up and froze immediately. Underneath the paper was a small, rectangular foil package with a raised circular ridge. It was unmistakably a condom. He closed the purse quickly, almost trapping the paper and his fingers in the process. Trying to act nonchalant, he opened the paper and studied the titles. "Hey, these look great. We'll see which ones the boys feel most comfortable with."

"And the ones I do best," she offered. The poorly disguised smirk told him she knew of his discovery in the sacred confines of her handbag, but she said nothing.

He was glad Rodney's house was close by. He made a pretense of studying her song selections until they pulled up at the carriage house.

Practice went well, and Josh declared the group ready for their performance that Saturday. As he packed up, he was looking forward to the ride home with Julie and the possibility of another kiss, or more.

As they pulled away from the carriage house, Julie said, "Are you any good at math, Josh?"

"Sure, I get good grades in math, why?"

"I've got a math test tomorrow, and I'm really stumped on some things the test will cover. Would you be willing to tutor me a bit?"

"Sure, when do you want to do it?"

"How about tonight?"

Wow! This is great, but it's kinda late. I'd better call Mom. She'll probably think it's okay since I'm helping someone out with school work. "Sure, I need to call my Mom and let her know where I'll be, though."

"Naturally," Julie responded.

Josh dialed his mother on his cell phone and got permission easily. He gave her Julie's number and hung up elated at the prospect of spending time alone with Julie. They drove to her house.

Julie parked the car in one of the four garages adjoining the Kidwell home and led Josh through an empty house to her bedroom.

"Where's your parents?" Josh asked.

"They're out for a late evening. They won't be back until well after midnight." She moved to her backpack and pulled out a math book. "Sit down here, Josh." She indicated one end of a couch and took her place next to him. She opened the book to a section on quadratic equations. "This is the part I'm having trouble with."

Josh moved closer and looked at the page. "Oh, this isn't so bad. See, all you have to do is either factor it or use the quadratic equation. Look at this one." He used several of the textbook examples to drive his point home while he resisted the urge to smother her in his arms brought on by the heat from her body and the aroma of her perfume.

She closed the book abruptly. "You're so intelligent. I think I understand it now. Let's work on something else." She dropped the book on the floor and threw her arms around him, pulling him close for a passionate kiss. He responded with vigor, and they began a very hot session of heavy petting.

Oh man! Is this the night? She's really hot, and I don't think I can stand much more of this. I'm sure glad I had those sessions on Mythos with Oriana. At least I have some idea of how to go about this. He was about ready to take the next step when Julie pushed him away and sat up.

"I'm sorry, Josh. I'm not ready to have sex with you yet. Besides, I don't know if I can do that with any boy." She began to straighten out her clothing.

"Why not?" Josh was still breathing heavily, but he was recovering.

"It's too dangerous. I'd die if I got pregnant, and what if we're really not right for each other?"

"I'll use a condom, but how long will it take before you decide one way or the other about us?"

"The condom's no problem. My Mom makes me carry one with me all the time in case I get into a situation I can't get out of. Thank God I've never had to use it." She clapped one hand over her mouth as if trying to hold back the words.

Josh sensed the problem. "It's okay, I'm a virgin too."

Julie relaxed and fell back on the couch, obviously relieved. "Do I flirt too much for a virgin?"

"No, no, you're not a teaser, or anything like that. You never gave me the wrong impression." He lied, but what else could he say. Suddenly, a solution hit him.

"If I let you in on a big secret, could you keep it to yourself?"

She looked at him with a quizzical expression. "I guess so. It depends on what it is."

"I mean, this is really, really top secret stuff. If it ever got beyond you and me, it could be a real disaster."

"Josh, you're scaring me. Are you a vampire, or something?"

"It's nothing like that. This is the real thing. It's a way for us to have sex with no complications, but it involves some really heady stuff. I'd have to be sure you'd keep quiet about it."

She looked at him with an incredulous expression now. "I don't know any way to have sex without complications. What are you trying to tell me?"

I'll have to trust her a little bit, but maybe I could tell her about Mythos indirectly? "Okay, look. Suppose you could go someplace where you weren't really you—someplace where you could have sex with someone, but it wasn't really you having the sex?"

"What are you talking about? Do you mean on some kind of drug, or something?"

"No, no, no drugs or anything like that. It's all perfectly normal, in a sense, and you wouldn't lose your virginity either. Would you be willing to do something like that?"

"Okay, since this is purely hypothetical, I'll go along with it for a while. I guess I would be willing to have sex under those conditions. Tell me the details."

"Here's where the top secret part comes in. Promise you'll

never tell anyone what I'm going to tell you. You have to give me your most sacred promise."

Julie looked at him as if he were crazy, but said, "I promise on my hope of heaven. Tell me what you're talking about."

"Okay, you go to another planet as an entity, then you possess people there and have sex through them."

She began to laugh. "Oh Josh, that's ridiculous. You mean we steal a spaceship from some alien and travel years and years to some other planet?"

"You don't need a spaceship. All you need is a Cargan, and I've got two of them. I've been to four planets; Mythos, Brem, Regulus and Gira. Mythos is where you have sex. If you want, I'll show you how to do it."

"This is unbelievable. You don't have to worry about me telling anyone about that. They'd think I was nuts. If you believe what you just told me, I'm not so sure about your sanity."

"Look, I'll prove it to you, but we'll have to wait until my parents are out of the house to do it. Would you be willing to try it?"

"I can't believe your parents don't know about something this serious. If it's true, it's the discovery of the ages. It's better than men on the Moon."

"It's real, but if my parents knew about it, they'd put a stop to it right away and my Dad would turn it over to the government. That's why my great grandpa kept it a secret all his life."

"Your great grandfather did this too?"

"Yeah, he had over thirty Cargans. He's been all over the universe."

"I still think this is some sort of scheme to get me in bed with you, but I like you, and I really don't think you're crazy. You let me know when we can do this 'Cargan' thing, and I'll do it."

"Hey, that's great! I'll let you know as soon as my parents have a late night out."

Their mood was interrupted by the sound of doors closing downstairs.

"Julie, are you home?" a female voice called.

"Upstairs, Mom. Josh is helping me with my homework. We'll be right down." She turned to Josh. "They're home early. How do I look?"

"I think you need to run a comb through your hair," he answered.

Julie moved to her dresser and fluffed her hair before checking her general appearance in the mirror. "Come on down and meet my parents."

Josh followed her downstairs and went through the obligatory ceremony of meeting Julie's parents before she drove him to his house. As he retrieved his guitar from her trunk, she moved close to him and presented her lips for a goodnight kiss. Josh obliged her willingly and said, "I'll call you when we can do the Cargan trip."

"I'm really looking forward to that. It's got to be one of the most unique come-ons anyone's ever tried. Goodnight, Josh."

CHAPTER 19

The next morning Roger dialed Wycham's office in Miami. The secretary put him through immediately.

"Roger, I was just going to call you. I got a grant for the art museum from the Brinkley Foundation for $3 million. Isn't that great?"

"Yes, that's good, but I was calling you about the missing sculpture. I've got it at my house. Phil found it in with Charley's things from the nursing home."

"Good, I would hate to have lost one of them," Wycham replied. *Very good! Now we have the final piece in the puzzle. I'm glad Smith has no idea what they really are.* "Send it down when you can—no rush."

"We may keep it a while. My son's using it right now as musical inspiration."

"As I said, no rush. Send it down to Miami when he's finished with it." The phone went quiet for a moment, and Roger could hear Wycham speaking to someone in the background. "Roger, I have an important call waiting. Talk to you later."

"No problem, goodbye Mark." Roger hung up making a mental note to visit Miami in the near future to check on how Wycham was storing the sculptures.

* * * * *

Wycham hung up and turned to the spectral Manjahba. "Smith's found the Giran Cargan. His son wants to keep it a few more days, but I don't think he suspects anything."

"Good. If he gets too nosy we could always replace him."

"Let's leave that as a final option for right now."

"Still, you need to keep a close watch on him. He's much too rich and much too intelligent."

CHAPTER 20

Thursday night, Josh felt Oriana in his room.

"Hey, is that you, Oriana?"

"Hi, Josh. I found a great place for us to go on a date."

He had to smile at her outfit. It was a combination of Earth gothic and some kind of Star Trek look-alike. This time her hair was shocking pink. She moved toward the desk and noticed the second Cargan. "Oh, you have a Gira Cargan now. Where did you get it?"

"It was my great grandfather's. He's living as an entity on Gira."

Oriana shuddered. "How spooky, but now that you have a Gira Cargan, I don't have to steal Dad's Mythos Cargan anymore. I can come here by way of Gira."

Josh looked downcast. "We can still go to Mythos every now and then, can't we?"

"Sure, any time you want. I was always afraid my Dad would catch me with the Mythos Cargan sometime and ground me for good. Now I don't have to worry about it. We can go now if you like."

"That's okay, I just had to be sure you still wanted to go there with me."

Oriana laughed merrily. "Don't be silly. I love going to Mythos with you. In fact, if you were a real boy on Brem, I might even be tempted to let you do it with me in the flesh."

Josh's face brightened with that news. "Boy! I sure wish I were a real guy on your planet. I can't think of anybody I'd rather do it with the first time for real."

It was Oriana's turn to blush, and she was glad Josh couldn't see her face that well. "That's very sweet of you, Josh."

What am I saying? I'd rather have Julie as a first time lover, but that just popped into my mind. Josh changed the subject quickly. "Hey, I told you I'd play some rock and roll for you next time. Want to hear it?"

"Yeah, play something for me."

Josh hooked up his guitar and ran off a hit tune. "What did you think?"

"Awfully noisy, isn't it?"

Josh put his guitar away and turned on his stereo. "I'm not really a pro yet. I'll play you some cool stuff."

The latest rock hit blared from the speakers as Josh sat tapping his foot in rhythm. When it ended, he paused the CD. "Want to hear some more?"

"I don't think so. It would never catch on back on Brem. Want to go to Agam Valeem now?"

"Sure, lead the way."

"We'll use your Gira Cargan, it's shorter."

Josh felt the room grow warmer as Oriana left. He grasped the Cargan and followed. Oriana was waiting for him.

"Now we have to use the Archa Cargan. This way." She led Josh to another Cargan, and they soon found themselves in the Archa terminal.

"I've got to find Ava in the helper room. She's going to show us around the ruins. This way."

They glided to the green door where Oriana pushed the

button. A woman only slightly older than the teenagers answered. She wore an orange jump suit with several embroidered patches. She recognized Oriana immediately, and they brushed cheeks.

"Oriana, I was expecting you a bit earlier. Welcome to Archa."

"This is Josh from Earth. He's the reason I'm late. He wanted to play some of his music for me."

Ava turned to Josh and offered her cheek. Josh brushed it with his and felt a very sensual presence.

"Welcome, Josh. I'm pleased to meet you."

"Same here, Ava."

Ava turned to Oriana. "Is his music good?"

"I don't know. I've never heard anything like it. It has a good beat, and it's loud, that's about all I can say about it."

The girls laughed, and Josh blushed a bit.

"You guys ready to go?" Ava asked.

"After you," Oriana replied.

"I'll be right back. I have to become an entity, like you. I'll be at that Cargan over there." She pointed to a Cargan like the universal Cargan on Brem.

Oriana and Josh moved to it, and Ava soon appeared in ghostly form. "This way."

Ava led her charges to a compass rose and oriented them. She took off through the window, and Oriana and Josh followed her out of the city toward the setting sun. "Agam Valeem is this way," she said as she pointed the way.

A large mountain range stood directly in their path, and Josh was looking forward to traveling through the rock. He was surprised when Ava started to climb over them.

"Why don't we just go right on through?" he asked.

"That wouldn't be advisable, Josh. Going through solid rock is hard on entities. You could even get stuck inside under the wrong conditions. A short trip may be fine, but you'll pay for it with aching muscles and joints for several days. Besides, the terminal can't track your entity when it's inside rock. It's much safer to go over."

They passed over the mountains, but it was still several minutes before they arrived at an extensive complex of ruins, reminding Josh of ancient Egypt. There were no pyramids, but even from a hundred feet in the air he could see broad boulevards running in orthogonal patterns as far as the eye could see. Ruins of great palaces and temples bordered each street. What were once tall columns littered the ground like children's blocks scattered about a playroom floor. It was something to rival anything he ever saw on Earth.

"This is Agam Valeem," Ava announced. "The ancient capital of the Magraan Empire. It's over ten thousand of our years old. The Magraan's ruled most of this quadrant of Archa for more than four thousand years before the river dried up."

"What caused that?" Oriana asked.

"Our scientists think a huge solar storm transformed our planet from a green paradise to what you see today. The way they coped with a dwindling water supply is one of the marvels of the universe. Our first stop will be that modern building on the left, the one with the large windows. Do you see it?"

"Yes," Oriana and Josh said in unison.

"That's the museum. I can show you some of the things we've learned about the Magraans. Follow me."

They made it through the walls of the museum with Josh

only getting lost once. The people in the building did not seem to notice them, and they could see several other entities milling about. A local guide led one large tour group of regular people past them, and Josh felt privileged to have a private tour guide so well versed in the history of the site.

Ava led them to a large map of the complex on one wall of the museum's main room. "This gives you a general layout of the city. Just outside the South door of the museum is the imperial palace. We'll start there; then we'll head up this avenue, which was called 'the street to heaven' in their language. They gave it that name because the emperor was considered to be a god, the son of their main deity, Ashraa."

"Ashraa was the mother of all things, and each emperor must be born in her womb. Every year at the harvest festival, the Emperor coupled with the statue of the goddess; and six months later, the statue would produce a child. If a suitable male heir already existed the child would be a girl to be raised as a priestess of Ashraa. If there was no male heir, or if the current male heir was deemed unsuitable, the child would be a boy."

"How did they determine the current heir was a no good?" Josh asked.

"That was the easy part. Each heir received extensive education from the best minds in the empire in all phases of science and politics. The mentors would meet twice each year to determine if Ashraa should have another son. If the present heir was not measuring up to their expectations, or if he showed any physical defects or health problems, the annual coupling of the emperor with Ashraa would produce another son. The birth of a male child automatically signaled the existing heir was unacceptable to Ashraa, and he would be sacrificed immediately."

"They weren't going to have any dud emperors, were they?" Josh said.

"The Magraan system wasn't entirely foolproof," Ava added. "They had a few 'duds', but they also had a good system for correcting that problem. If the emperor's coupling with the goddess produced no offspring, male or female, the emperor was deemed impotent; and he was sacrificed to the goddess. A regency of the advisory council ruled until the successor child was considered competent to take over."

"Sounds foolproof," Josh said. "But, how did they get a statue to have a child?"

"That was the easy part. The statue of the goddess is hollow, of course. One of the priestesses entered it during the annual coupling ritual, and the emperor had intercourse with her through the statue. The belly of the statue was moveable to give the appearance it was pregnant. The priestess would have her baby and it would be pushed through the statue's vagina to be 'born'."

"Wait a minute, you can't tell me a people sophisticated enough to build these structures believed such stuff," Oriana scoffed.

"Only the common people had to believe. The elite knew exactly what was happening, but they accepted it as the best system they could contrive to insure the peaceful succession of a competent ruler. You have to admit it worked well since they survived for over 4,000 years without a civil war."

"What if the priestess didn't get pregnant?" Josh asked.

"Part of the monthly worship ritual included the ceremonial

coupling of the high priest with several of the priestesses. Only the emperor coupled with the idol, but since none of the ruling elite knew which priestess was in the idol at the time, any one of them could claim her child was the heir. There was always a good supply of pregnant priestesses to choose from," Ava explained.

"You said the goddess gave birth in six months. That seems like a pretty short time." Josh said.

"Our normal gestation period is only five months. We have very small children, and they must be carefully cared for until they are several months old. Supposedly, the extra month was put in for the goddess because she was carrying the next emperor. The real reason was to be sure a baby would be available at the right time."

"They sure had it all figured out," Josh was amazed at the sophistication of such an ancient people.

"From the palace, we'll go past some of the residences of the nobles and wind up at the temple of Ashraa. On the way, I'll explain some of the writings you'll see on the walls of the public buildings. They used these walls as their history books, and children learned about their heritage by visiting these places. They not only learned history, they also found out how their society worked. Clever, eh?" Ava said.

Ava was a wonderful guide. Oriana and Josh marveled at the works of the Magraans. They learned the Magraans had iron, but most things in their homes were made of brass or fired clay. Only their weapons and armor were iron.

The temple of Ashraa was impressive all by itself. The mosaic floors survived almost intact, and showed fantastic craftsmanship. Ava explained that the columns of the temple had once been faced with gold, but it had been looted over the centuries until the site was preserved as a monument. The statue of Ashraa was the most impressive part of the display.

A beautiful, golden woman with ample breasts and protruding stomach sat in a marble chair with her legs spread to reveal her female parts. She was somewhat larger than life size, but not grotesque as she smiled down upon the visitors from her pedestal three meters above the temple floor. A black stone stairway led up to her from either side adorned with golden banisters containing silver decorations of leaves, vegetables and flowers. Animals in gold and silver with precious stones for eyes capered between the balusters holding up the railings. At the top of the stairs, censures burned incense, filling the temple with a sickly sweet aroma.

A large pit directly in front of the platform holding the goddess contained ashes and partially burned bones. Ava explained that sacrifices to Ashraa were burned there. During worship ceremonies, a large fire blazed before the goddess while animals were thrown into it alive, along with unacceptable emperors or defective heirs.

"You mean all of this stuff is here from that long ago?" Josh said.

Ava laughed. "Oh no, we've reconstructed most of it from their tomb inscriptions and some surviving documents. The bones are fakes."

They joined another entity group for the demonstration of the statue's special features. A non-entity guide explained how the priestess entered the statue for the coupling ritual. A woman dressed in the fashion of the ancient priestesses demonstrated the process. Josh watched in eager anticipation, but she remained modest at all times. The guide showed how the stomach moved to simulate pregnancy, and Josh was impressed with the design. The statue even featured stretch marks as a means of hiding some of the seams.

The script of the Magraans was quite advanced and much more easily readable than Egyptian hieroglyphics. With help from Ava and a little practice Josh was able to begin pronouncing some of the words, though he had no idea of their meaning.

Josh suddenly stopped. "I'd better be getting back. I wouldn't want Mom to find me attached to that Cargan. She'd ask too many questions.""

"We can go back now, if you like. You've really seen all there is to see here," Ava said.

The trio flew back to the terminal where Oriana and Josh thanked Ava for the tour before heading for Gira.

Oriana spoke after they materialized inside the Giran terminal. "I'll just go back home from here, Josh." She offered her cheek.

Josh brushed it with his. "You sure we can't make a stop at Mythos?"

Oriana laughed. "Not this time, Josh. Next time we can do that. Goodbye." She drifted off toward another Cargan, waving to Josh as she did.

Josh watched her vanish and moved to the Cargan for his home, wishing the next time would be soon.

CHAPTER 21

The band set up at the teen club just as the last time except Julie changed in a small dressing room behind the stage. The DJ announced them, and the curtain opened to Julie in the same outfit she wore for the audition. The crowd responded with wild cheers as the band broke into a popular rock song with Julie belting out the lyrics and gyrating seductively.

No one was dancing. The assembled adolescents gathered around the stage and bounced in time to the music. Fortunately, Karrasnik's security people were already in place between Julie and several overeager boys. As the song ended in a wild crescendo of drums and guitar wails, the applause overwhelmed Julie and the boys. She turned to Josh with a big smile, and he responded by blowing her a kiss. Julie turned back to the crowd and waved her appreciation before moving to the rear of the platform.

Josh took the microphone and spoke, "That was Julie Kidwell, give her a big hand." Once more the crowd cheered and whistled with shouts of "More!" intermingled. "She'll be back later. We're the Spacing Guild, and we hope you like our band enough to want us back in the future. Right now we'd like to play some music to dance to." They started an instrumental number, and the teens gradually dispersed back to the dance floor.

The evening passed quickly as the band played the planned songs and two encores before the curtains closed. Karrasnik appeared as the applause died down and the DJ resumed his patter. "You guys were great, and you're fabulous," he addressed the remark to Julie.

Josh responded, "Thank you, Mr. Karrasnik. I'm glad they liked our stuff."

"I told you a female singer would do the trick. Here's your money." He handed Josh five twenty-dollar bills. "Look, I'd like to have you on twice a month, same deal, okay?"

"Well, I don't know," Josh said. "How much do you charge for admission when you have a live band?"

Karrasnik looked at Josh with a wary gaze. "Wait a minute, I get lots of bands wanting to play here, and I don't pay any of them more than $100. You can take it or leave it."

"I estimate you had about 500 kids out there tonight, and your sign said the cover was $5.00 when a live band played. That's $2,500 gross. I figure it takes about half of that to keep the doors open and the lights on, so you net $1,250, not counting concessions. Let's say half of that goes for taxes, insurance, etc. That leaves $625 pure profit in your pocket. We'll settle for only 40% of that which comes to $250. I think that's fair. If you don't think so, I guess we'll leave it." Josh saw the crestfallen looks of his fellow band members, but paid no attention to them. He saw the crowd's reaction to Julie and more contemporary music, and he felt sure Karrasnik could easily afford his price.

The manager thought for a moment before responding. "How about $150, and that's my final offer?"

Josh could feel the band urging him to accept mentally, though they said nothing. "I'll do this. We'll play for $2.00 for every kid over 300 who's here on the nights we play. That means you could owe us as much as $400. I saw you with a counter in your hand at the doorway. If we can't bring you more of a crowd than 300, we'll play for nothing."

Rodney Barnes moved closer to Josh and whispered, "Josh, take the $150. I need the extra money and so do the rest of the guys."

"Leave this to me, Rod. I know what I'm doing," Josh whispered.

Karrasnik was quiet for a moment but his eyes seemed to light up just before he answered. "Deal! You get $2.00 for every kid over 300, but you take my count."

"Deal!" Josh said, and he shook hands with Karrasnik.

"Okay, how about Saturday two weeks from now?" Karrasnik said.

Josh looked at the band and Julie and received four nods. "Okay, you got it."

The boys packed up the gear and left, but Josh waited for Julie to change. She emerged from the dressing room in normal clothes and joined Josh. "You did a good job negotiating with Karrasnik, but you missed one thing."

"What's that?" Josh was non-pulsed.

"See that sign over there?" she pointed at a small sign on the wall next to the door.

Josh moved closer in order to read the notice. It was the standard fire marshal's posting for a public place, and it listed the maximum capacity for the teen club as 400.

"Hey, I know he had more than that in here tonight!" Josh said.

"He probably did, but I'll bet that counter never goes above

400," Julie said.

They drove to Josh's house while Julie did her best to lift him out of his anger over being bested by Karrasnik. Shortly before they got there Josh's cell phone rang.

"It's my Mom," Josh said as he checked the caller ID. His face brightened considerably after the conversation. "Hey, guess what? My parents are going to be out late tonight. We could do Mythos if you still want to."

"I guess you won't be happy until I try this, so we might as well."

At the house, Josh showed her to his room and produced the Cargans from his closet. He set them on his computer credenza. "There they are," he said, waving a hand past the pair.

"God! They're ugly enough." Julie inspected the items with a skeptical expression. "Are you trying to tell me you can go to other planets using these things?"

"You don't go in person, you go as an entity. You're like a ghost when you get there. Your body stays here."

"Sure, sure, now tell me how this is supposed to work."

"Hey, I just thought of something. I don't know if two people can use the same Cargan."

"Now's a bad time to think of that," Julie said.

Josh thought for a moment then snapped his fingers. "I know, you can use the Mythos Cargan, and I'll go to Gira then to Brem, use Oriana's Cargan there and meet you on Mythos."

"Who's Oriana?" Julie's expression turned somber.

Oh, oh, you screwed up there, Josh. Think fast. "She's a friend I met on Gira. She told me her father has a Mythos Cargan."

"How good a 'friend'?"

"Just a friend, that's all. She's nothing for you to worry

about. She lives on another planet anyway."

"Hmmm, I'd like to meet her sometime," Julie said.

"You'd have to go to Gira, but we can do that after we see Mythos." He pulled a chair up to the Mythos Cargan and indicated Julie should sit down. "Now, put one hand here and one hand here." He pointed out the grip locations on the Cargan. "I'll give you the activation note in a minute. Remember, don't panic. You'll be a ghost with your arms inside a tree when you get there. Just stay close to that tree, and I'll find you. If for some reason I don't show up, just hum the same note, and you'll be right back here. Got it?"

"I got it. Give me the note."

Josh plugged in his keyboard and hit G#. Julie hummed the note, and her eyes popped wide open as she lapsed into a catatonic state. Josh gripped the Gira Cargan and soon found himself inside the terminal. It was day on Gira, so he didn't bother to look up his great grandfather. He found the Brem Cargan and materialized inside that terminal. There was a small line at the universal Cargan, and he joined it. *What was her code? Let's see. It was two consecutive numbers. I think it was 5859.* When his turn came he punched in the number and soon found himself inside Oriana's house. It seemed to be empty, and he was glad he didn't have to dodge people who might be able to see him. He put his arms into the safe and found the Cargan. Humming the note, he reached Mythos at the beech tree he and Oriana used before.

I forgot, the last time we were here we were unicorns. I think my tree's that way. Josh sped off in that direction and lifted a bit above the treetops in order to spot his clearing and the sycamore tree. It took a few circles, but he soon spotted Julie standing next to the tree with a dazed expression. He landed beside her.

"Hey, it's okay. I'm here now," he said.

"Wh, wh, wh, where are we?" Julie stuttered.

"You're on Mythos, the place I told you about. Come on, I have to find that tree where you get the nymphs and satyrs."

He started off, and Julie followed wide-eyed. "It looks a lot like Earth," she said.

"Yeah, but it sure is different in a lot of ways," Josh said.

"Especially those funny-looking trees," Julie said. She pointed to several trees where large, green globes similar to grapefruits dangled from the branches. "What are they?"

"Some stuff the creatures here eat," he replied.

Julie reached out to touch one, and Josh cautioned her, "Don't touch 'em, they're really icky."

Her hand passed through the globular goo, and she swiped at the fruit several times in a natural reaction to her failure to make contact.

"Why can't I grab it?" she asked.

"You can't touch things when you're an entity. I was warning you for later."

"What 'later'?"

"You'll find out in a little while."

He led her to the clearing where he and Oriana made love and reached inside several trees before he found a small keyboard. There were only four buttons, but he had no idea what ones to press for a nymph and satyr. He tried each button individually with no results. *Hmmm, must be a two digit code* He pushed the first two buttons, and was surprised to see two dragons appear. Julie jumped and screamed.

"It's okay, they're tame, I think," Josh assured her. *Never thought about dragons. I guess they do it in mid-air. Might be nice, but I think I'd better stick to something more familiar.* He tried buttons one and three, and they produced two Centaurs pawing the ground next to the dragons. *I wonder how you tell these things to go away?* He pushed three then one, and the centaurs galloped off. *Okay, you just do it backwards.* After two and one, the dragons flew off, and he tried two and three. To his great relief, a satyr and nymph appeared.

"Okay, all you do now is possess the nymph while I possess the satyr, and we can have sex."

"How do I do that?" Julie asked as she stared at the woman.

"Just melt into them, like this." Josh possessed the satyr and spoke. "See?" It was obvious Julie didn't understand him. *Of course, the satyr's speaking his language, dummy.* Josh left the satyr and said, "See?"

Julie giggled. "She's a bit on the plump side, isn't she? Do you really want to have sex with her?"

"Sure, why not?"

"I don't know about having sex with that." She pointed to the satyr.

"Would you rather do it as centaurs?"

Julie screwed her face into a disgusted mask. "God no! Did you see the organ on that guy?"

"Come on. What have you got to lose?" Josh possessed the satyr and motioned for her to possess the nymph. Julie moved tentatively inside the female's body.

"See, that was easy," Josh said.

"I can understand you now. This is really weird." She moved a hand to her mouth quickly. "Josh! Oh my god. Look at you." She pointed to his crotch.

The satyr was aroused, and Josh moved to embrace Julie. "Now we can do it with no problems."

She pulled back instinctively. "Is the nymph a virgin?"

"I don't know. Check her mind out and see."

Julie seemed pensive for a moment. "Oh lord no, she's had hundreds of men, I mean satyrs, including this one a dozen or so times." She seemed to compose herself. "Where do we go?"

"Right here. There aren't any bedrooms that I know of."

"On the grass?"

"Sure, lay down."

"This seems so, so, commercial. Where's the passion?" She lay down on the grass, and Josh lay down beside her.

"Just relax and get into the mood. The passion'll come." He kissed her gently, and felt her relax a bit. *I guess I'd better take this slow and easy.*

Afterwards they lay together, but Julie seemed troubled. "What's wrong?" Josh asked.

"Nothing, it's just I never thought I'd enjoy being chubby and making love to a goat-man. It was very nice, and you were very gentle. I can just imagine what it must be like to do it as us. I guess we really have had sex together in a sense, haven't we?"

"Well, in one way we did, I guess, but I didn't get to see you naked nor you me."

"That is true." She rolled over and stroked the satyr's beard. "I'm much better looking without clothes than this nymph, though."

"I'm sure you are, and I don't have what this satyr has either."

Julie laughed. "I hope not. It was all this gal could do to

handle you. God! Listen to me. I'm talking like a whore."

"How else would you talk about it?

Julie suddenly sat up. "Wow! We'd better get back before your parents come home. We've been here over and hour, I'd guess."

"Don't worry. Time slows down back on Earth while you're here. If we went back now, you'd see we've only been gone a few minutes."

Julie lay down again. "I can't believe this is anything but a dream, but we're dreaming it together, and that's nice."

"It's not a dream. I'll take you someplace else next time, but I have to find out if two people can use the same Cargan. Dad says I have to ship the Gira Cargan down to Miami pretty soon."

"Well, I hope we can do this again. What a great way to learn how to make love. It doesn't matter if you screw up, and nobody's upset if you do. You can tell me what boys like, and I can tell you what girls like, and we can get to be great lovers without all the heartburn."

"See, I told you so."

She rolled on her elbow and smacked Josh on the thigh. "Don't be a smarty. I just had no idea anything like this was possible. I hope I don't go back and find you've just seduced me while I was asleep." She suddenly turned serious. "Wait a minute. I just realized you've been here before. Who was it with?"

"On my first trip to Mythos I met a girl who was looking for someone to have sex with. I never saw her before or since, honest."

"What about that *Oriana*?"

"I told you, she's just a friend I met on Gira."

Julie rolled on her back again. "This is so peaceful. I hate to leave."

"We can go back now, if you want to, or we could do it again," Josh prompted.

Julie rolled on top of the satyr. "Okay goat-boy, do your stuff."

* * * * *

Julie awoke holding what she now knew was a Cargan and turned to see Josh still rigid and holding the Gira unit. She checked herself over to make sure she hadn't done anything she shouldn't and found no change from when she first sat down. The clock on Josh's desk showed only twenty minutes had elapsed. She finally noticed the room was like ice, and was looking for a thermostat when Josh came to life.

"What did you think?" he asked.

"That was a blast, but it's awfully cold in here."

"Yeah, that happens." Josh turned up the thermostat.

"Do you see why you can't tell anybody about the Cargans?"

"I sure do. I certainly can't tell anybody about Mythos and what I did there."

Josh gave her a knowing smile, and Julie turned serious. "Don't get any ideas about doing that stuff here, Josh. I have no intention of getting that involved with you at this stage of our relationship."

Josh held his hands up imploringly. "Did I say anything?"

CHAPTER 22

Monday at school Rodney Barnes sat down next to Josh at lunch. "Hey, was that a great gig or what? They loved us."

"Yeah, they loved us, but I really screwed up." Josh took a desultory bite from his pizza.

"What do you mean? I thought you really screwed that Karrasnik guy."

"No, he screwed me. The fire marshal limit for that place is 400, and I agreed to use his counter."

"He must have had nearly 500 in there last Saturday."

"I know, but he won't show any more than 400 on his books in case he gets checked. I'm sorry, I should have known."

"Don't worry about it. We each got $20 for one night, and we'll get $40 from here on out." Rodney's tray was loaded down with food, and he dove into it with gusto. Between bites he said, "Hey, you and Julie seem to be hitting it off pretty well."

"Nothing serious. She's not interested in sex."

"Too bad, she's really hot." Rod returned to his food and remained silent.

Willie Jenkins parked his tray across from Josh. "Hey Josh, how's Julie? I noticed she's been taking you home instead of me."

"Nothing there, Will. She just gives me lifts, that's all," Josh replied.

"I think I'll ask her out. Man! Those tits of hers are first class."

Josh felt anger rising in his stomach, but he suppressed it with some difficulty. "She doesn't impress me as the loose type."

"Hey, have you struck out with her? Is that it?" Willie chided.

"I've only seen her twice riding home in her car, for God's sake. I think that's a little too early to start groping around on her."

"Not me, I check 'em out quick. Why waste your time with the ones who won't play around?"

"Lots of luck. You have my permission to try," Josh said.

* * * * *

That night the familiar warm glow of Oriana flooded into Josh's mind just before he was ready to climb into bed.

"Hey Josh! Ooops, sorry. I didn't know you went to bed this early."

Once more Oriana's appearance almost elicited laughter. The garishly sequined black halter top exposed bare midriff above blaze orange short shorts. For the first time her legs were bare, and several tattoos created an interesting pattern on the inside of both thighs. Black sandals showed gold-painted toenails. The hair was now silver.

"It's okay. What's up?"

"One of my girlfriends just got back from a field trip to Gira, and she said they've got some beautiful botanical gardens there. Want to go on a date?"

"Not tonight, I have school tomorrow, and it's already late."

Oriana laughed. "Not tonight, silly. I thought we might go

four of your Earth days from now. We'd have to go about this time, though. The gardens are only open to entities during the day there."

"Sure, that would be a Friday here, and I wouldn't have school the next day. I could sleep in."

"Okay, now that you have a Giran Cargan, I'll just meet you there. This same time in four days, okay?"

"Yeah, see you then."

The warm feeling vanished, but Josh couldn't go to sleep right away. *I sure hope she'll want to go back to Mythos soon.*

* * * * *

Four days later, Josh arrived on Gira well ahead of Oriana. Josh knew his great grandfather was the helper during the night hours, and planned to get there well before daylight. He wanted to see if two people could use the same Cargan and check for any further news on the Earth terminal. He pushed the green button before Charley could announce his usual warning.

"Josh! Good t' see ya again, boy. Come on in."

"Hi Great Grandpa! I got a date on Gira today, and I came early to ask you a question."

"A date, eh. Some girl from Earth?"

"No, the girl from Brem I told you about before."

"Oh yeah, I remember. You gonna introduce her to me?"

"Sure, but first I want to know if two people can use the same Cargan."

"No problem as long as they're both entities."

"No, I mean two real people."

"Oh, that *can* be a problem. One of 'em might wind up in the wrong spot. I never tried it, and nobody's ever asked that question before. Most folks've got their personal Cargans. You know 'bout them?"

"Yeah, Oriana has one on Brem. I really need to know about this because I've got a girl on Earth I want to take to Mythos. She doesn't want to have sex on Earth, but I took her to Mythos, and I think she kinda liked it. I want to take her back again."

"Well, how'd ya do it that time?"

"She used the Mythos Cargan and I went to Brem through Gira and used Oriana's father's Mythos Cargan. I'm afraid Dad's going to make me send the Gira Cargan down to Miami with the rest of them, and I won't be able to do that anymore."

"I see. This Oriana, is she the girl you got a date with today?"

"Yeah, she'll be here in a few minutes, but I don't want her to know about the Earth girl. You know what I mean?"

Charley laughed merrily. "I used t' juggle four or five gals from different planets, I sure do know what you mean. Let me check the computer."

Charley turned to a computer with a special keypad and entered commands. He searched for several minutes before he found something.

"Yup, says here you can do it long as both parties kin get at least half o' th' grip locations." He scratched his head a moment. "As I remember the Mythos Cargan, there ain't much room fer doin' that. Also, the grip points ain't very well marked on my Cargans since I was th' only one usin' 'em. I think it'd be pretty risky tryin' that on yours."

Josh slumped in his chair and frowned. "Damn, I was hoping it'd work. If Dad makes me give up the Gira Cargan, my sex life is in the toilet."

"What about this gal from Brem?"

"She's hot and all that, but it's not the same thing. Know what I mean?"

"Yup, sure do. Tell you what. Winble'll be here pretty soon. He may know some way t' do it. We'll ask him." Charley sat back in his chair and beamed at Josh. "You got the makings of a fine man 'bout ya, Josh. What do you wanna do when you finish school?"

"I haven't decided yet. I like music a lot, and I've got a rock band that's just getting started. Maybe I'll stay with that."

"Well, my advice to any young man is to do the thing he loves and damn the money. If you work hard at anything the money'll come, but it's hard to put that much effort into somethin' ya hate. Stay with the music if that's what you love. I can't say I ever thought much of your generation's musical tastes, but I understand there's lots o' money in it for the top people."

"Sure is! Millions, if you hit the market right." Josh was surprised that an adult would accept the idea of a career in rock music. "The other thing I wanted to ask you about was the Earth terminal. Is everything okay there now?"

"Nope, th' Marshal checked it out, but he couldn't find nothin'. I'm sure Wycham's got some scheme goin', but it wouldn't do for me t' try lookin' into it. Wycham'd spot me right off and do his best t' get rid o' me."

"But, you're already dead."

Charley laughed. "You kin kill entities too, but it takes a special machine. Wycham'd have access to one if he's doin' somethin' criminal, that's fer sure."

"I could do it for you. Just tell me what to look for."

"Nope, too dangerous. I'm tryin' t' get th' Marshals t' do another check, but it'd take a Grand Council order now, and that means some hard evidence."

"What's a Grand Council?"

"That's th' governin' body for entity travel. It's kinda like a supreme court back home. Don't you worry none 'bout it. I'll get'er done. You just work on getting' yer gal back t' Mythos."

Charley leaned back in his chair, and his eyes took on a dreamy look. "Ah Mythos you don't have to worry about possessin' people on that planet."

"Oriana told me about possession being illegal. Why is it okay on Mythos?" Josh asked.

"All the critters there are androids. They ain't people, so it's no problem."

"Do you go there a lot now?" Josh asked.

"Sure do. It's the only thing that keeps me goin' these days." After your great grandma died, I decided not to remarry. I could'a had all the women I wanted, I was rich enough; but I decided to use Mythos instead. I could possess a satyr or a centaur on Mythos and have the time of my life without spendin' a nickel. You get all the sensations of a corporeal body without any of the consequences. It's great. It's also the only way two entities can have sex. One of you possesses the male and the other the female. It really doesn't matter much who does who."

"I tried it both ways, and I really don't like being the female."

Charley laughed merrily. "Well, it's all what ya like and don't like. You're lucky, your gal has a good attitude toward it."

"We haven't been back for a long time now. I'm hoping we can go there after our visit to Gira today." Josh checked the window and saw it was still dark. "While we've got some time, tell me more about the Marshals."

"Marshalls are the cops of entity travel. Don't ever mess with one. Want to meet one?"

"Sure, why not?"

Charley pushed a button on one of the consoles and a large man in a dark blue uniform entered the room. He looked like a football player to Josh.

"Did you need me, Charley?" the Marshall asked in Giran.

"I'd like you to meet my great grandson Josh, Machma. Josh, this here's Marshall Machma."

Josh presented his cheek, but the Marshall only nodded his way.

"Marshalls don't rub cheeks, Josh," Charley explained.

"Oh."

"Machma here's an Ulan. Most o' the Marshalls are Ulans cause they can control entities and handle real stuff while they're entities. Show 'im what I mean, Machma."

The Ulan raised a hand, and Josh felt himself being lifted off the sofa and moved toward the wall. His back crashed against the wall instead of passing through it, and he felt pain for the first time as an entity.

"Wow! That's awesome."

Machma moved Josh back to the sofa and set him down gently.

"See what I mean. Don't mess with these guys. Every terminal has some Marshalls assigned to it. If you ever have any trouble, go to a helper and they'll get you a Marshall if you need one."

"Do they all speak Giran?" Josh asked.

"Yeah, most of 'em. They all wear translator helmets when they're on duty, just in case."

A light blinked on a control panel, and Charley checked a computer screen. "I think your date just arrived, Josh. Why don't you go get her and bring her in to meet me?"

The Marshall went back through the door after bidding Josh goodbye. Josh left the helper room and greeted Oriana. "Good to see you again," he said as they touched cheeks and Josh felt that same warm sensation.

Oriana's appearance was more subdued than he'd ever seen before. Her hair was tastefully blonde, and a light blue knit top covered everything. Darker blue slacks ended at the ankle above normal navy blue low heeled shoes.

"You look great today," Josh said.

"Thanks, you have to be pretty conservative when you go to Gira. You got here early. I was thinking I might get here before you did," Oriana teased.

"My great grandpa is the night helper here. You know, the guy who made my Cargans. Would you like to say 'hello'?" Josh asked.

"He's the one that's dead, isn't he?" Oriana's voice betrayed her apprehension.

"Yeah, but he's a neat guy. Come on in." Josh pushed the button.

The helper room door opened, and Charley beamed at Oriana. "Welcome to Gira, lovely lady."

Oriana presented her cheek but flinched a bit as she felt the cold sting of the dead man's entity.

"I'm sorry," she apologized. "I wasn't prepared for that."

"Few people are, my dear. Don't let it bother ya none. I've growed used to th' reaction by now. You ain't offended me."

"Thank you; you're very kind." Oriana blushed in spite of Charlie's assurances.

The windows of the helper room began to brighten as the sun rose on the terminal. Charley looked at the clock and turned back to the two teenagers. "It'll be light soon, and you can leave. Do you know where to go on Gira?"

"No, which way to the gardens?" Josh said.

"First, you have to understand the special rules here on Gira," Charley said. "You may not leave the daylight part of the planet at any time. Girans are not that comfortable with entities in the first place, and they don't want you around after dark. Also, you must always announce yourselves when you encounter them. Don't assume they can see and hear you, and never try to possess a Giran. You probably wouldn't be able to do it anyway, but they'll have you thrown off the planet if you even try it. Do you both understand all that?"

"Yes, sir." they answered in unison.

Mr. Winble entered at that moment. "Mr. Josh, how good to see you again, and who is the beautiful young lady with you?"

"Hi, Mr. Winble, this is Oriana, she's from Brem."

Oriana brushed cheeks with Mr. Winble followed by Josh.

"I have many good friends on Brem. In fact, I was helper there for several years, but that was well before you were being born, Miss Oriana."

"Hey Winble, I got a question for ya. Can two people use the same Cargan as corporeals?" Charley asked.

Winble thought for a moment before responding. "That is

not recommended, but in an emergency, both people can grasp the Cargan as long as they have some portion of their hand on the grip area."

"Then it don't have t' be the whole hand?" Charley asked.

"No, no, one finger is sufficient."

"That answer yer question, Josh?" Charley said.

"Sure, thanks, Mr. Winble."

"You are entirely welcome. Will you and Oriana be spending some time on Gira today?"

"Yeah, Great Grandpa was just going to show us how to get to the botanical gardens."

"Oh, a truly impressive place and very beautiful. Have a good time."

"Now, let's go out to the big map so I can show you how to get there," Charley said.

He led them out to the map wall and pointed out the formal gardens at the capital city. They found the correct bearing and headed for the compass rose.

As they traveled to the capital, Josh filled Oriana in on his great grandfather.

"He does sound like a neat guy," she said.

"Yeah, would you believe he still goes to Mythos?"

"Why not? An old man like your great grandfather could still enjoy himself even though he might not be capable of doing it in the flesh, so to speak. By the way, what was behind that question about two people using a Cargan?" Oriana gave Josh a suspicious look.

"Oh, ah, I, ah was just curious in case, ah, I wanted to take my parents to Gira. We don't have personal Cargans on Earth."

"Josh, are you sure it wasn't because you wanted to take

some Earth girl to Mythos?"

Busted, but I can't let her know she's right. "No, no, I wouldn't want anyone but my parents to know about Cargans. They're a big secret on Earth. Mythos is just for you and me." *Good job, I hope she believes it. I don't think there's much chance of her ever meeting Julie.*

"Okay, as long as you keep it that way." She moved closer to Josh and brushed her body against his. Josh felt the warmth of her affection and nearly fainted.

The sprawling capital of Gira soon appeared before them. It was a large city but not as large as Los Angeles or San Francisco by any means. The broad streets were crowded with vehicles, but they all looked the same. They were even the same color. Periodically, one would pull to the curb and the occupants would get out apparently leaving the vehicle empty. Josh was surprised when the thing continued on with no driver.

The Girans reminded Josh of the Amish people on Earth. They wore their hair cut at shoulder length–male and female. Their loose fitting gowns went all the way to the ground, and bell sleeves hid their hands. Josh was wondering how they told the sexes apart when he noticed all of the men wore beards neatly trimmed to about seven centimeters in length. Their pale skin almost blended in with the white of their robes, while soft, blue eyes shone brightly from under heavy lids. He understood now why Charley was so emphatic in his warnings about them. They must be a race of monks.

"There are the gardens," Oriana pointed to an expanse of green behind a large building with a golden dome.

"We'd better check in someplace," Josh advised and looked about for some kind of office.

"I think that's the place, over there," Oriana pointed to a small kiosk where Girans were filing through a turnstile.

The two descended to the kiosk and stood in front of the window in an attempt to catch the attention of the Giran woman greeting people as they came through. Apparently, there was no sort of admission charge, as no one was offering money or credit cards.

Josh cleared his throat several times with no hint of recognition, but one of the young Giran children tugged at her mother's robe and pointed their way. The mother spoke to the kiosk attendant in Giran, and she nodded in acknowledgment. Looking directly at Josh and Oriana for a moment she finally smiled and waved them inside after making an announcement over the garden's public address system.

"She just told everyone we're here," Oriana said.

"Charley said the Girans aren't really that comfortable with entities," Josh suggested.

The gardens were every bit as beautiful as Charley said they would be. Exotic plants held clusters of brilliant flowers. Josh bent to smell them and pulled back in surprise.

"I can't smell them. It seems like I've smelled flowers on other trips. Why not these?" Josh asked.

Oriana laughed. "Silly, entities can't smell with their noses. You smell like this."

She bent close to a flower and brushed her cheek against it. "Mmmm, this one smells great."

Josh followed her example, and a sensation of smell coupled with a warm, earthy glow was his reward.

"It's just like smelling them, only more so. I must have touched the flowers I smelled on other trips. This is wonderful."   Josh literally flew from one plant to another advising Oriana of each new sensation.

"Do this one, Josh.   It's like eating a chocolate sundae." Oriana pointed out the flower to Josh then flitted like a honeybee to the next blossom.

Josh barely scented Oriana's 'ice cream' flower when she called again. "I wish I had some perfume like this one. Smell it."

He bent to the plant and felt an overwhelming urge to take Oriana in his arms. The sensation from that plant was pure erotica. He didn't recognize the flower, and the Giran name appeared to be even stranger than the light pink blossom spreading in a graceful fan from its stem. A voice from behind caused him to turn.

"That one can be almost addictive, young man."   It was a male Giran of middle age. He was rather short compared to the others of his race, and his eyes radiated kindness.

"What plant is this?" Josh asked him.

"It's scientific name is Immaculata Garensis, but we call it the Bora Flower," the Giran replied. "My name is Xulan; and I am the overseer of the gardens. What planet are you two from?"

"I'm from Earth, and she's from Brem."

"I know Brem, but I've only heard of Earth. One of your people is a helper in our terminal, isn't he?"

"Yes, sir, he's my great grandfather."

"He's an interesting fellow. He tells me Earth is a lush green planet. Is that true?"

"Mostly it is. There's some places that are desert, but it's mostly green."

"We have an Earth Cargan in our terminal. I'll have to go there some day. What are your names?"

"I'm Josh, Josh Smith; and this is Oriana, a friend of mine," Josh said.

"Welcome to Gira. Is there anything you'd like to ask me?"

Josh and Oriana spent the rest of the day with Xulan learning about the phenomenal variety of plants the Girans managed to bring together in one place.

"These gardens are wonderful, Mr. Xulan," Oriana complimented.

"Thank you. We Girans don't like to travel, and our gardens let us enjoy the vast variety of the universe without the inconvenience of leaving home."

"I think we'd better get back to the terminal, Josh, I told my parents I wouldn't be away long," Oriana prompted.

Josh agreed. "Thank you, Mr. Xulan. It was nice of you to spend so much time with us."

"Yes, thank you very much," Oriana added.

"Entirely my pleasure. I hope you will come back and see us again soon."

Josh and Oriana bid Xulan goodbye and headed for the terminal.

As they approached the Giran terminal Josh asked Oriana, "Do you have time to go to Mythos?"

"Sure, I'd like that. Why do you think I made up that lame excuse about my parents looking for me?" Oriana smiled warmly. She touched Josh's hand and the surge of sensual desire was overwhelming.

* * * * *

Saturday morning Roger informed Josh he had to send the

Gira Cargan to Miami on Monday.

"Aw Dad, I really need that one for our next gig at the teen club. I'm in the middle of composing a song based on that sculpture."

"Mr. Wycham is really impatient to have all the sculptures together. I told him I'd send it Monday."

"If I can keep it another week, the band'll be finished with the next gig. All I need is one more week, please?"

Roger sighed and pushed his hair back from his forehead. "Josh, why do you always have to make an argument out of everything we ask you to do? I've stood up for you against your mother on those things, but I promised Mr. Wycham I'd send it down to him as soon as we found it, and that was two weeks ago. I think I've gone the extra mile on this one. It goes back Monday, and that's final."

"Okay Dad." Josh sulked back to his room and retrieved the Gira Cargan from his closet. He held it on his lap and studied the strange sculpture while he contemplated the problem. *I can't send this one to Miami right now. I really need to stay in touch with Great Grandpa now that there's trouble with the Earth terminal. He said he'd need hard evidence for the Grand Council, but he couldn't risk investigating himself. He doesn't want me to go there, but who else could do it? I think it's time I looked into the situation myself. What better witness could he have than somebody with no axe to grind—somebody who could only say what they saw without putting any spin on the subject? If I've only got two days, I'll make the most of them, starting tonight.*

CHAPTER 23

It was nearly midnight when he rose from the bed, slipped his feet into sheepskin slippers and moved to the Giran Cargan. He hummed the proper note and soon found himself in the terminal. It was still day on the planet, and he knew Charley would not be there, but he quickly found the green door and pushed the button. Mr. Winble answered.

"Hi, Mr. Winble, can you tell me where the Xemba Cargan is?" Josh blurted out before the little man could open his mouth.

"Xemba, why would you want to go to that planet, Mr. Great Grandson Josh?"

"Great Grandpa said that's the place I need to go to find an Earth Cargan, and I need to check out the Earth terminal." Josh shifted from one foot to the other impatiently, and Mr. Winble picked up on the clue.

"You seem to be in quite a rush. What's the hurry? I'm sure there are other paths to the Earth terminal."

"Great Grandpa said that's the quickest route, and I need to get back here as soon as possible so I can tell him what I found."

"Very well, it's this way." Winble led Josh to a medium-sized Cargan.

"The activation tone is this." Winble hummed a note, and Josh hummed it back.

"Okay, D above middle C," Josh said.

"Whatever that means in your world. Charley Earth seems

to be very concerned about the Earth terminal, so be careful."
Winble said.

"I will, Mr. Winble. See you soon." Josh hummed the note and found himself in a dark terminal with only dim lighting above each Cargan. Entities with large, round eyes moved about the room, conversing in a series of shrill whistles. The noise nearly gave Josh a headache before he found the Earth Cargan. He suspected it must be some kin to the sonic language of dolphins or the radar of bats. He quickly hummed the proper note to escape the pain, and materialized inside Wycham's warehouse.

This is no warehouse, this is a real terminal, Josh thought. He was the only entity in the place, and he wandered around the room, carefully noting the position of the Xemba Cargan for the return trip. Each Cargan now sat on a pedestal featuring a nameplate in the Giran language. He saw the compass floor and the wall map, but he was not prepared for the appearance of the two huge entities materializing from the wall map.

Their skin was pale gray, and their baldheads shone as brightly as if they were polished. Each wore a loose fitting robe of deep blue covering their enormous frames, and the heavy gold chains draped across their shoulders glittered in the dim light. Josh figured as real persons the men would weigh in excess of 300 pounds, but they did not appear to be fat. Their features were sharp with craggy chins and hooked noses protruding slightly from their chiseled faces. Deep, black eyes stared from under heavy lids. They had no eyebrows, and protruding foreheads overhung the dark orbs like forbidding cliffs. They were definitely not to be trifled with.

The shorter one spoke in a language Josh did not

understand. He shook his head to indicate that fact. "Please speak Giran," Josh said.

The two entities conferred for a moment, then, the taller one spoke in a deep bass voice with a heavy accent. "May we help you, young man?"

Josh figured they were some kind of security Wycham had arranged, and decided he should identify himself.

"I'm Josh Smith, Roger Smith's son. I've just come to check out the terminal. We had reports some of the Cargans may have been damaged in the move."

"We have performed a thorough inspection on all of the Cargans, and I can assure you that none of them were damaged," the large man said.

"I was on Gira the other day, and the helper there said there were reports of entity disappearances on Earth. The helper figured they were caused by damaged Cargans." Josh felt his story was credible, but he was beginning to feel uncomfortable around the two hulks. His instincts told him he should find some way of ending the conversation as quickly as possible.

"The entities in question have been found and safely returned to their home planets. It was only a minor technical problem resulting from the primitive nature of the Earth Cargans. Fortunately, we were able to correct the problem, and we have advised the Grand Council accordingly."

"Well, that's all I needed to know. Thanks for the information," Josh said as he backed toward the Xemba Cargan smiling profusely at the two somber entities.

The entities watched him until he gripped the Cargan then vanished through the map wall. Josh decided he needed to find out more about this new Earth terminal and slipped out through the wall of the warehouse instead of using the Cargan.

He hovered above the building noting the high fence topped with barbed wire all around it. At two entrances, armed guards stood inside gatehouses, and floodlights turned the night around the building into day. Wycham was certainly taking the security of the Cargans seriously. He made one trip around the warehouse and noticed nothing out of the ordinary, except that it was much larger than the space taken up by the terminal.

Curious about what other things Wycham might have stored inside, Josh dipped down through the roof over the end opposite the Cargan room. Skids full of boxes stretched from floor to ceiling, and a forklift truck sat idle in the middle of one aisle. One end of the large room held what Josh figured was a loading dock with several overhead doors large enough to accommodate semi-trailers.

I wonder what's in these boxes, Josh thought. He passed through several skids of what looked to be auto parts but stopped in his tracks at a solid metal wall inside a wooden crate near the center of the stacks.

That's funny, I passed through all kinds of metal until this. What is this stuff? He tried several approaches to the crate and each attempt failed. He found a dozen other crates just like it scattered about the warehouse intermixed with normal items. *What are these things,* he thought, but he put it down to his lack of knowledge about many items of a technical nature.

Josh continued through the warehouse finding only normal items until he reached the wall that should have separated the regular warehouse from the terminal. As he passed through that wall, he encountered strange looking machines resting still and cold in the dark room. They were like nothing he had ever seen before, and he could not deduce anything about them from his own experience. *Dad would know what this stuff is*, Josh reasoned. His thoughts were interrupted by the appearance of the same two huge entities he saw in the terminal. They glided toward him with purposeful expressions, and Josh knew it was time to leave.

He flew straight up and out of the warehouse with the two entities close behind him. He imagined himself as a supersonic jet fighter and saw he was outdistancing them for a moment, but they soon regained the ground. Josh looked about for a possible way to lose them, but only the row of hotels on the Miami shoreline presented hope of escape. Josh figured he could use them just like an airplane would use clouds and made straight for the nearest one.

He barely beat the closest entity inside and abruptly turned left and back out into the night again. He glanced behind and saw no one, but a quick look overhead disclosed the second entity swooping down on him from above. Josh turned back into the building and dove down into the lobby before exiting through another wall. This time, the first entity appeared around the corner of the building and headed straight for him.

Josh wracked his brain for an answer while he flew into the next hotel with the entity in close pursuit. Going up would not help him as the other entity was surely watching for him to exit from above. Down was the only logical option. Josh dove for the hotel basement.

Josh remembered Ava's caution against penetrating solid rock, and he hoped she was overstating the problem. His only chance of escape was to travel underground far enough to lose the pursuers. He'd have to risk it.

He dove into the concrete floor of the basement only to find another basement. He continued on into the hard compacted sand under the hotel until he reached rock and turned in the direction he thought was west. Glancing behind, he could only see rock. There was no visibility beyond his immediate presence, and he breathed a sigh of relief, though he did not slow down.

A dull pain began to penetrate his entire body, and he calculated this was the danger Ava warned him about. The pain grew sharper as he traveled, and when he felt he couldn't stand any more, he turned straight up.

It took only a few seconds for him to burst from the ground and into the clear night sky. He strained his eyes to spot any pursuers and found none. Josh shook his limbs to relieve the pain, but it was only temporary. *I can't go back the way I came now*, he thought. *Those creeps will be looking for me for sure.* Spotting a large city to his right, he headed for the airport. *I'll just find a flight going to San Francisco and follow that.*

Josh entered the terminal and found a flight for San Francisco leaving in a few minutes. He waited like a passenger observing the people around him. None of them seemed to notice his presence, but a small dog in a travel cage kept yapping at him.

The plane loaded and taxied out with Josh hovering just above it. "This is fun," he said as the plane accelerated down the runway with Josh keeping pace. He followed the big bird to where he could see the lights of a huge city. He descended and entered the big airport terminal.

Okay, this is St. Louis. I have to find another San Francisco flight. Soon he was on his way again. The jet liners were slow by entity standards, so he left that plane once he sighted the next city. He descended to the airport and found it was Denver. He used this same method all the way to San Francisco. He left the airplane at that point and corrected his course to intercept the freeway system on the south side of the sprawling metropolitan complex.

Luckily, Josh remembered which highway led home. He descended to pavement level to read the exit signs. He was startled by the first truck passing through him, but soon got used to the sensation. He raised himself above the traffic level once he knew he was on the right path. Taking the exit for his neighborhood, he found he was not sure which of the streets led to his home.

The string of estates looked the same to him, but he finally recognized Rodney Barnes's house. He smiled wickedly as it occurred to him that he should pay Rodney a visit to see if his friend was sensitive to entities. He swooped down to the window level of the big house and tried to remember which room was Rodney's. He had been in the house several times, but seeing it from the outside was different. Suddenly, he kicked himself mentally for not realizing he could just go through the walls.

Josh passed through the outside wall and found himself in a closet. It must have been Rodney's father's closet by the number of suits and white shirts. He passed through the closet door and into a bedroom where Mister and Misses Barnes were sleeping soundly. Feeling like a peeping Tom, Josh quickly passed through their door into a familiar hallway and down to the room he knew was Rodney's.

There on the bed snoring away like a chain saw, was his bass player. Josh moved next to the bed and assumed what he figured was a scary pose.

"Rodney Baaaaaarnes," he wailed in his best imitation of Marley's ghost.

Rodney didn't budge, but Josh remembered the flowers on Gira and the cold sensation entities produce. He put his hand on the boy's forehead and waited. Rodney just pulled the covers up around his neck and turned away from Josh's hand.

He felt that, Josh reasoned as he reached his hand through the covers and placed it where he figured Rodney's behind should be. This time the boy's eyes popped open.

Rodney sat up in bed and surveyed his room. "That was a weird dream," he whispered to himself. "Just like somebody hit me in the ass with a cold towel."

"Rooooodney Baaaarneees!" Josh howled again with no more effect than the first try.

Rodney looked at the clock and lay back down. "Better get some more sleep. That damned alarm'll go off too soon anyway," he mumbled as he closed his eyes.

Josh stood there half mad at the fact he couldn't get any more of a rise out of his friend than that. It was then he noticed a pair of slippers sticking out from under the bed. The heads of two pink bunnies smiled softly at him. "Rodney Barnes wears bunny slippers!" Josh laughed out loud at the embarrassing discovery.

"Who's there?" Rodney was bolt upright in bed again.

Well, it seems emotions are more effective than words, Josh surmised. *Maybe we can have some fun after all.*

Josh visualized vampires, flying bats, and blood seeping from fresh fang marks on a woman's neck. Rodney shivered, and a look of fear began to creep across his face.

"This is spooky," Rodney whispered. "I wasn't dreaming about vampires, but it seems like I was." He rubbed his eyes and sat on the edge of his bed, his feet searching for the pink bunnies.

Josh moved to the slippers and tried to put them on his hands.

"Damn," Josh swore as his hand moved through the slippers just as it had when he'd tried to pick up a stick to help the woman on Mythos. He thought to make them walk by themselves, but that plot failed.

Rodney found his footwear and walked to the window. He surveyed the sky and the landscape in the moonlight then checked his closet and under his bed.

"Jeeez," Josh snickered. "He thinks there's monsters under his bed."

Satisfied he was safe, Rodney resumed his sleeping position, though his eyes were wide open and periodically scanning the room for any unwanted intruders.

Josh began to feel a bit sheepish. He knew if someone did the same thing to him he would be just as frightened. He decided Rodney had enough, but it was good to know about the bunny slippers in case he ever needed some leverage in the future. He passed through the wall and out into the night.

From Rodney's house, it was a simple matter to find his own. Soon, the familiar shape appeared; and he felt a sensation of relief that only comes with knowing you are almost home. He sailed through the walls to his own room to find his body still glued to the Cargan. He guessed that all he needed to do was to merge his entity with the physical shape before him. He settled down into the same posture and felt familiar warmth he had not noticed was missing while he traveled. The process of combining his body and his entity snapped him out of his sleep almost immediately.

He checked himself over just to be sure he was not damaged by the ordeal, and was soon satisfied he was truly back to his old self again.

Josh climbed into bed and lay awake figuring out how to tell his great grandfather about the warehouse and the funny crates he couldn't penetrate.

The pains in his joints eased somewhat since he assumed his normal condition, but he knew he would not be interested in gym class at school on Monday.

CHAPTER 24

"Wake up, Josh. You're going to be late for church." Evelyn shook her son heavily to rouse him from a sleep so sound he had not even heard his own alarm clock buzzing.

The pain induced in his joints by his mother's forceful prodding brought Josh back to the world of the conscious with agonizing abruptness.

"Ouch! Geez, Mom, not so hard."

Evelyn stood back from the bed a bit. "Your alarm clock was buzzing its head off, and you were sound asleep. Are you feeling okay?"

Josh tried to sit up, but his muscles protested so painfully he fell back onto the bed immediately. "I had a rough night last night. I didn't sleep good."

"Probably too much pizza. Get up and get ready. You can have some cereal before we go if you hurry." She left the room once she saw he was vertical.

Josh hurried through his morning routine and gulped down a bowl of Cheerios before piling into the family car.

As they pulled out of the driveway, Evelyn said, "We have a function at the country club after church. Do you want to join us, or would you rather we take you home first?"

Josh needed no time to consider this question. "I'd rather you take me home, Mom."

"Are you sure? It's a birthday party for Mrs. Blanton, and both of her daughters will be there."   Evelyn knew Josh appreciated the Blanton's younger daughter after watching him ogle her at the club pool all summer.

"I'm dating Julie Kidwell now. I'd just as soon get some extra studying done."

Evelyn raised an eyebrow at this remark. She glanced at Roger, who only shrugged. "Okay, we'll drop you off on our way to the club."

* * * * *

Wycham sat behind his large desk apparently speaking to empty space, but actually holding a conversation with his partner in crime, Manjahba.

"The Smith boy was at the terminal last night. That means he knows about Cargans. I think it's time we did some substituting here on Earth," Wycham said.

"I warned you about Smith. Do you think he's suspicious?" Manjahba said.

"He hasn't given me any indication he's aware of the sculptures' true nature. They only have the Mythos and Gira Cargans, and Smith's agreed to send the Gira Cargan to me. He wouldn't do that if he knew what they were. I think the boy's discovered Mythos by some quirk of fate, and he's keeping it a secret from his parents."

"Given you Earth peoples' puritanical attitude toward sex, I'm not surprised the boy is keeping Mythos a secret, but if he gets caught, he may be forced to divulge the true nature of the sculptures. We'd better do something about this quickly."

"I think I can lure Smith here on some pretense, and we can substitute for him. The best way to control the boy is through his father. I don't think his son is a problem as long as he can keep the Mythos secret, and if he does get caught, it would be best for us if his father were on our side. Besides, I could use an ally at Theta Industries. I'm thinking of expanding my business empire into electronics."

"I agree. Let's get Smith out of the way as soon as possible." Manjahba rose and moved away from Wycham's desk. "I'll speak with you again next week." He vanished through the bookcase wall.

* * * * *

Josh sat impatiently through church and the ride back home. He bounded up the stairs and made a beeline for the Gira Cargan. What he wasn't expecting was Oriana possessing his mind.

"What are you doing here now? I thought you could only come at night."

"No school today on Brem, and my parents are off on business trips. I thought we could go somewhere here on Earth. You did promise to show me around."

"I know, but I've got something really important to do right now. Can't we do it some other time?"

He finally focused on her image and had to suppress his reaction. Her hair was purple, and her outfit spoke rebellion from every seam.

"Josh! I don't get days like this very often. Why can't we go today? We can go to Mythos later if you want."

Oh boy! I sure didn't need this today. I might as well bring her in on the problem. Maybe she'll understand. "It's like this. My great grandpa suspects there's something funny going on at the Earth terminal, so I went there last night and got chased out by two goons. I have to get back to him and tell him what I found."

Oriana didn't seem to be impressed. "What did you find that's so suspicious?"

"They had some crates in the warehouse part that I couldn't get into as an entity and there were some funny-looking machines in the room next to the terminal. Don't you see? I have to tell him about all that so he can go to the Grand Council and have them check it out."

"Josh, you don't know anything about terminal equipment. Why do you think that stuff is anything more than the normal gear?"

"Great Grandpa doesn't trust the guy who's got the Cargans now. He thinks something fishy's going on there. They had some entity disappearances lately, but the Marshals checked it out and couldn't find anything wrong."

"See, that proves I'm right. Now, let's go someplace cool on Earth."

Hey, I'd have to be an entity to take her someplace, and that means I'd have to go to Gira then come back to Earth like I did yesterday. If Oriana went with me, she could see the stuff in that warehouse for herself, and that should convince her. "Okay, we'll go to the Grand Canyon, but we'll go to Gira together then back to Earth so I can show you what I'm talking about at the Earth terminal."

"Fine with me. Let's go."

At that moment Josh's cell phone blared out Julie's ring tone.

"What's that?" Oriana asked.

"It's my cell phone. Don't you have cell phones on Brem?"

"Sure, but they don't make that funny noise."

Julie seemed to be in an exuberant mood. "Hi, Josh. My folks are with yours at the Blanton's party. How about we go to

Mythos today?"

Oh my God! I didn't need this on top of everything else. "Oh, hi Julie. Gee, I'm sorry, I've got a lot of work to do around the house today before Mom and Dad get home. You know, clean my room and all that kind of stuff."

Oriana whispered in Josh's ear. "Who's that? You sound funny."

Josh waved a hand toward Oriana's entity in an impatient gesture.

"You sound funny. Is someone there with you, Josh?" Julie asked.

"No, no that's just the TV. Hey, can I call you later? Maybe I can get these chores done early." Josh felt Oriana penetrating his mind, but he couldn't keep her out. He tried to think of anything besides he and Julie on Mythos.

"Okay, but don't make it too late. I'm really looking forward to another trip to that planet. Bye."

"What planet?" Oriana asked as she left Josh's mind.

"Oh, Gira. She wants to go back to Gira again."

Oriana thought for a moment before her next statement. "You only have one Gira Cargan, and two people using the same Cargan is not recommended. How did you take her to Gira?"

"Easy, she went directly to Gira and met my Great Grandpa while I used the Mythos Cargan to go there through Brem."

Oriana gave him a quizzical look, but seemed to accept the explanation.

"Okay, let's get going."

He felt Oriana leave him then picked up the Gira Cargan. In a few moments he stood next to her in the Gira terminal.

"Where to now?" she asked.

"Over here, we go by way of Xemba." Josh led the way to that Cargan, but Oriana held back.

"Xemba? That's a really weird place. I always feel spooky going there."

"We won't be there long, the Earth Cargan's real close."

Josh stopped at the Xemba Cargan and hummed the note for Oriana. He went first at her insistence.

Josh stood in the dim terminal trying to keep the high-pitched singing of the Xembans out of his head. Oriana appeared holding her ears, and Josh led her to the Earth Cargan. She only uncovered her ears long enough to hear the tone.

They arrived in Miami, and Josh led her to the wall map.

"This looks like a regular terminal," Oriana said as she surveyed the scene.

"The strange stuff's on the other side of that wall." Josh pointed the way. "The goons chased me out when I went in to check it."

"That's not right, Josh. The terminal people love to show off their gear. You must have done something wrong. Let me have a look." Oriana glided toward the wall and a green door. Josh sped ahead of her.

"Wait! Just peek in through the wall. If those goons are in there I don't want them chasing us."

"Oh all right. I'll just peek." Oriana melted into the wall with most of her body remaining on Josh's side. He noted she had a very nice bottom. She quickly pulled back with a startled expression.

"Josh, that's not the normal terminal stuff. I've been in a lot of control rooms, and this one doesn't look like any I've ever seen. Something funny's going on here."

"Come on, let's get out of here. We can talk about it on the way to the Grand Canyon." Josh glided to the compass rose and took off in a westerly direction. Once they were outside the terminal, he spoke, "Now you've convinced me things aren't right here. I need to get to Great Grandpa and tell him. Will you come with me?"

"Sure, after we see the Grand Canyon. Is it a long way?"

"Yeah, a long way from Miami."

"Then we shouldn't be dawdling." Oriana took off at what Josh thought must be supersonic speed. He strained to catch her.

"Not so fast, you'll pass it up," Josh called.

"It can't be so 'grand' if I can pass it up from this altitude." Oriana looked back at Josh with an impish grin. "Come on, keep up." She sped off at even greater speed.

Josh barely managed to keep her in sight. They flew for what seemed an hour before he spotted the Mississippi River. He called to Oriana. "That's the biggest river in my country."

She slowed a bit and looked down at it. "Impressive. What's that big city on our left?"

"That's New Orleans. I've heard it's quite lively at night, but I guess it's not much during the day."

"Then, I'll come back at night sometime." Oriana laughed and flew on over the Texas plains and the New Mexico desert.

"We're getting close now. Keep an eye out for a big canyon," Josh yelled.

Oriana stopped and hovered over a section of desert. "What's that?" She pointed to rows and rows of airplanes stretching for miles.

Josh hovered beside her. "I don't know. They're warplanes, but they must be old ones. Some kind of junk yard for fighters, I guess."

"God, Josh, how many war planes does your country need?"

"I don't know. If these are the clunkers, we must have thousands and thousands of the good ones."

"Thousands and thousands? Do you people still fight wars?" She gave Josh an incredulous look.

"We haven't had a big one in years and years, but there's all kinds of little ones going on all the time."

"Ugh, how barbaric," she said.

A sudden flash of recognition hit Josh. "I know where we are now. I saw a TV show about this place once. The Grand Canyon's that way." He pointed north. "We're too far south."

The pair turned, and it was only a few moments before Oriana gasped at the sight of flat-topped mountains with blazing layers of color rising from the deep bed of a small, muddy river barely visible from the rim.

"Wow! You weren't kidding when you said 'grand'. This is bigger than anything I've ever seen." Oriana zoomed down through the gorge and marveled at the rock formations. She flew to the rim near the lodge and stopped. Josh joined her.

"Really something to see, isn't it?" Josh asked.

"I'm so glad you brought me here. Let's go in there and see what's going on." She pointed to a building where a lot of people were coming and going. They passed through the walls and spent some time looking at the displays before gliding back to the center of the canyon. Oriana flitted back and forth taking in all the sights.

"Look at that, Josh! Those people are riding some kind of

animal into the canyon."

Josh followed her finger to a mule train traversing a wall of the canyon. "That's one of the mule rides. My family went on one when we were here two years ago. I was always afraid my mule would stumble and throw me into the canyon, but it didn't."

Oriana laughed and gave the mule ride a closer look before hovering over the river.

"Josh this is wonderful. It's really very romantic too. Let's possess some people and make love."

"What? Doing it on Mythos is one thing, but doing it here?"

"Why not? I saw several lodges up on the rim. We could check out the rooms."

"It's the middle of the afternoon! Everybody's out looking at the canyon. Don't be silly."

"Well, if you don't think it's a good idea. Why don't we go to Mythos, then?"

"Sounds good to me, but you gotta tell great grandpa about the funny stuff in the Earth terminal. This way back to Miami." Josh turned back East.

"Which is closer, your house or Miami?" Oriana asked.

"My house, but don't we have to go back the way we came?"

"No, silly. We can go to your house, and then I can use your Gira Cargan ahead of you."

Josh suddenly remembered his escape from Miami. "Oh yeah, you're right. All I have to do is possess myself. I did it once before when had to get away from those goons."

"You got it. Now, which way to your house?"

Josh thought for a minute. He wasn't sure what bearing to

take for home. "We go to the ocean and turn right. That's the only way I know to get there. This way." Josh headed off toward the declining sun with Oriana close behind.

Josh was quite surprised when they hit the Pacific just south of San Francisco. He thought he'd be much farther South.

"Right over there." He pointed toward Santa Cruz and followed the freeways home. They passed through the walls and up to Josh's room where his body sat glued to the Gira Cargan.

"Okay, just possess yourself and you're home again. Then we can take off for Gira."

Josh did as she suggested and found everything seemed perfectly normal. "Okay, I'm ready to go." He reached toward the Gira Cargan.

"Wait for me to go first," Oriana said. She moved to the Gira Cargan and vanished. Josh resumed his seat and hummed the activation note.

He was pleased to see it was night on Gira. Charley would be on duty. He and Oriana glided to the green door and pushed the button. Charley was there to greet them.

"Well, what brings you two back t' Gira?"

"I have to tell you about what we found at the Earth terminal. I think it may be enough to convince the Grand Council to look into it further," Josh said.

"Well, come on in and tell me 'bout it." They entered the helper room, and Josh and Oriana related their adventures in the Earth terminal. When they'd finished, Charley seemed worried.

"I wish I could get there and have a look. It sounds like they got an entity replacement operation goin' there, but the Grand

Council'd need more proof than you two got to take action. I'll try 'em though. Maybe they'll at least send another Marshall to look at the stuff behind that wall. I'll come t' your place and let you know if they decide t' do that, Josh."

"One thing, Great Grandpa. Dad's going to ship the Gira Cargan off to Miami tomorrow. You'll have to find another way to get to me."

Charley thought for a moment. "I got lots o' ways t' get t' your place 'sides usin' the Gira Cargan. Don't worry 'bout that. You two go on home, and I'll let you know what the Council decides."

Josh and Oriana left the helper room, and Oriana spoke, "If your Dad makes you get rid of the Gira Cargan, I'll have to steal my father's Mythos Cargan again. I really don't like doing that too much, but if I have to, I will."

"Thanks, I wouldn't want to give up on our trips to Mythos."

"Well, I did offer to go there with you today," Oriana said.

Josh smiled broadly as they reached the Earth Cargan and vanished to his room as a stopping point on the way to Mythos.

* * * * *

Josh awoke at the Mythos Cargan and remembered his promise to call Julie. The trip to the Grand Canyon and the visits to Gira and Mythos only occupied two hours of the afternoon due to the reverse time compression factor. He wondered how long his parents might be at the party, and figured it was already too late for a trip with Julie. He hesitated over the phone just long enough for it to ring before he could pick it up.

"Smith residence," he answered as his mother demanded.

"Josh, this is your mother. Do you want to have Sunday dinner with the Blantons and us at the club?"

What a break! She knows I don't like eating at the club. "I'd rather not, Mom. I've really got a lot of studying to do."

"Will you find something to eat?"

"Sure, I'll nuke something. I'm not really that hungry."

"Okay, we should be home around five, or so."

"Sure, Mom. No problem. See you later."

Josh hung up and punched the air with his fist. "Yes! Now to call Julie."

Julie was elated, and Josh was on cloud 9. *Wow! Two girls in one day. I don't care if it is on Mythos, this is great!* He went into his bathroom and doused himself with his favorite cologne.

Josh only had to wait a short time for Julie's arrival. He escorted her up the stairs.

"I'm ready if you are," she said.

Josh used the same procedure as last time for their rendezvous on Mythos. This time, he passed Oriana in the hallway on his way to her father's Cargan. He hoped she hadn't sensed his presence, and he was relieved to see her pass on down the hall without turning. He found Julie waiting at the sycamore tree. Without words they glided to the clearing and called for a nymph and satyr. This time, Julie needed no prompting, and they fell into sexual bliss immediately.

Back in Josh's room another entity emerged from Josh's body. It was Oriana, and she was quite shocked to see the situation. *Aha! I thought I felt him a while ago. He's used my Dad's Mythos Cargan again.* She moved to Julie and inspected her closely. *So this is my competition. I have to admit she is attractive, but that dirty little rat lied to me. He's having sex with her right now,*

I'll bet. Why else would she be glued to the Mythos Cargan? I could kill him.

Oriana started to return to Brem when an idea popped into her mind. *I think this gal needs to know all about our mutual lover. I'll just join them on Mythos.* She moved to the Mythos Cargan and vanished.

At the sycamore tree, Oriana studied the situation for a moment. *They need to go to a summoning tree, and I'll bet they don't go far beyond that before they have at it. Should I go as an entity or as another nymph? I think a nymph would be best.*

She found the summoning tree with Josh and Julie busy nearby.

"Oh, that's disgusting. He makes me sick, but I can't do much about it as an entity.

Neither of them noticed her reach inside the tree and summon a nymph. Fortunately, the female arrived from behind Oriana, and she was able to possess it without disturbing the busy couple.

I know just what this jerk needs. She walked back to the stand of energy trees she'd seen walking to the summoning tree. *A couple of these things should get his attention.* She carefully plucked two of the soft, sticky globes and carried them back to the still-busy lovers. She stepped from behind a tree with a sinister gleam in her eyes.

"Want to make it a threesome, Josh," Oriana said as she hurled one of the blobs at him.

It squashed on impact and spread green goo over the goat-man's body.

"Ow, that hurt."

The satyr's head jerked up abruptly, and the nymph

screamed before pushing the goat-man away and curling up in a pitiful attempt to cover her private parts.

"Who are you?" he asked as he brushed green glop from his face and beard.

"Yes, who is this, Josh?" Julie asked.

"Just 'the girl you'd most like to do it with for real the first time'," Oriana responded

"Oh my God, it's Oriana," Josh said as he scrambled to his feet.

"Who?" Julie persisted.

"A girl I met here before," Josh said in an aside to Julie as he moved toward Oriana. "I can explain everything, Oriana, just give me a chance."

"Have you and she ...?" Julie almost whispered, pointing to each one in turn.

Josh turned back to Julie. "It's not what you think, Julie."

"Oh yes it is, Julie," Oriana said. "This lying two-timer's been doing both of us and telling each of us we're the only ones."

"Wait, can't we discuss this less passionately?" Josh pleaded.

"Jo-osh! We're talking about sex here. You can't talk about that subject without passion," Julie said.

"But, this is Mythos. It's not real," Josh said.

"You big jerk, I gave myself to you, and even if it was through some alien woman, it was me inside. I can't believe you can be so casual about it," Julie screamed.

"She's right," Oriana shouted.

"You're the one who said people can have sex on Mythos without hang-ups," Josh said.

"I meant no diseases or pregnancies. I still expected you to be faithful to me," Oriana said.

"You're only an entity! I could never have sex with you in the flesh. I could never marry you or have children with you. This is ridiculous!" Josh said.

"Just an entity!? Is that all you think of me as, 'just an entity'?" Oriana said.

"What about me?" Julie said. "We could be a real couple, and here you are running off to have virtual sex with another girl."

"What's wrong with that? It isn't me, and it isn't real. Where's the harm?" Josh said.

Oriana turned to Julie. "He's hopeless, Julie. I think it's time to leave."

"You've got that right," Julie said. She started to leave her nymph, but Oriana held up a hand to stop her.

"What?" Julie said.

"Here, this one's yours," Oriana said as she handed the second glob to Julie's nymph.

"Thank you very much," Julie said as she splattered the gooey fruit on Josh's chest.

"I needed that," Julie said.

"Now we can go," Oriana said.

The girls left the nymphs and drifted off toward their respective trees, Julie to Earth's and Oriana to Brem's.

Josh called out to them, but neither girl was capable of understanding the satyr now. It took him a while to realize this, and by the time he left the satyr's body, it was too late. He retraced his path through Brem, but Oriana was not in the hallway, and the door to her room was closed. Josh felt the closed door was a sign he should let the situation cool off a bit.

He found the family's personal Cargan and was soon back in his room. Julie was gone, but the aroma of her perfume lingered in the air. He sat down to think about the experience.

What were they so upset about? I could see it if they were both Earth girls. Oriana surprises me most. I thought she was just in it for the fun. Why would she get serious about us? I hope Julie won't quit the band. I've got to find some way to square this with her, even if she doesn't want to go out with me again.

It took him a while to notice the Mythos Cargan was missing.

Oh no, she took it with her. Now I've lost both girls and my ticket for sex.

Josh picked up his guitar and began composing a sad song about his problem.

CHAPTER 25

Josh heard nothing from Charley the rest of Sunday, and his father confiscated the Gira Cargan before he left for work on Monday. Josh caught his bus for school somewhat down from the loss of easy access to his Great Grandfather and Mythos at the same time.

At lunch period, Josh sat alone in the cafeteria reliving his debacle with Julie and Oriana. Rodney Barnes's arrival caused him to rejoin the world of the living.

"Hey Josh!" Rodney hailed his fellow band member.

"Hi Rodney. Did you have a good weekend?" Josh couldn't resist the question.

"Funny you should ask about that." Rodney looked at Josh quizzically. "Saturday night I had this weird dream about vampires and a cold sensation, like somebody stepped on my grave."

"Stepped on your grave?" Josh reacted to the unfamiliar phrase.

"Yeah, my dad always says that when he gets a chill or a funny feeling."

Josh smiled knowingly and turned the conversation to other things.

While he spoke, Josh scanned the cafeteria for Julie. She finally came in with two other girls and sat down on the other side of the room.

"Excuse me, Rod. I have to talk to Julie about band practice and our next gig," Josh said. He rose and walked to Julie's table. "Hi Julie, can we talk for a while?"

Julie looked at him with an expression that would freeze the fires of hell. "I'm eating my lunch, Josh."

"It's about practice Tuesday and the next gig for our band."

Her expression softened only enough for polite conversation. "I'll be there, don't worry. I wouldn't let the other guys down."

"Thanks, that's what I wanted to know." Josh felt a compelling need to thaw out, but he had to find out about the Mythos Cargan.

"By the way, can I have my sculpture back?" Josh said.

Julie looked at him with anger building behind her eyes. "Get your tray and join me at that table." Julie indicated a vacant area and excused herself to her lunch friends.

Josh returned to Rodney.

"That was short," Rodney said.

"I just wanted to make sure she was going to be there tomorrow night and next Saturday. She's fine."

"I thought you two might be an item after the last time at the teen club," Rodney said.

"Naw, I don't think she thinks of me that way. See you at practice Tuesday, Rod."

He carried his tray over to Julie and sat down.

"I'll give it back to you at band practice, but you have to promise me not to use it with anyone but me," Julie said.

"Hey, I know how you feel, and I won't go with Oriana anymore, I promise," Josh said.

"I'm warning you. If I ever catch you with another girl on

Mythos again, I'll quit the band." She took a bite of her salad and glared at Josh over the fork.

"I really like you, Julie, and nobody wants you to quit the band. I'll behave." Suddenly Josh had no more stomach for lunch, but he picked at his pizza while Julie finished her meal in silence. She wiped her mouth with her napkin and spoke.

"I like you too, but I won't put up with you having sex with other girls, even if it isn't the real thing. Understand?"

"Yeah, I understand." Josh put on the sheepish look he usually reserved for his parents.

"Good, see you at practice." She rose and walked toward the tray turn-in area.

Josh waited until she'd dropped off her tray before following her. He left the cafeteria feeling only slightly warmer.

* * * * *

Roger stopped by the shipping department during his lunch break and sent the sculpture to Wycham. On the way back to his office he thought about the collection and how it seemed so fortuitous Wycham wanted to build the art museum. By the time he reached his office he'd shrugged it off as a stroke of luck. Anita spoke as he came in. "Mr. Wycham called for you while you were out. Do you want me to get him for you?"

"Yes, would you please?"

He sat down at his desk and picked up the phone when Anita buzzed him.

"Hello, Mark. What's new in Miami?"

"Thanks for returning my call so promptly, Roger. I have a possible donor for the museum, but he's giving me some trouble. He wants to talk to all of the principles involved in the project before he writes his check. Could you possibly come down to Miami sometime in the next two weeks?"

"How big a donation are we talking about? That might influence the speed of my response."

Wycham laughed. "He's talking about $5 million. He needs the tax write-off, but he wants to be sure this is a legitimate deal and not some scam."

Roger checked his calendar while Wycham spoke. "If I take the red-eye out Wednesday night, I can be there on Thursday before noon, but I'd have to get back to San Francisco on Friday. Is that okay?"

"No problem at all. I'll set up a meeting for Thursday afternoon. I'll let you know if plans change."

"Oh, by the way, the missing sculpture is on its way to you. I shipped it today."

"Good, good, thank you, Roger. I'll see you Thursday."

* * * * *

Tuesday night came, and Julie was right on time for band practice. They went through the numbers planned for Saturday with only a few corrections, and Josh cornered Julie before she could leave.

"Julie, please give me a ride home so I can talk to you about last Sunday."

"What's to talk about?" Julie continued to stuff her sheet music into a folder.

"I want to apologize for my actions, if you'll let me."

"Apology accepted. Now, I have to go."

"But, Julie, I want to try to make it up to you some way. Please, let's talk it over, even if it's just for the few minutes on the way home."

She turned to him and Josh seemed to think her expression

softened a bit. "Okay, I'll give you a ride. I promised to give your Cargan back anyway."

"Thanks." He followed her to her car and buckled into the passenger seat. They drove away in silence. Josh figured the ball was in his court.

"Julie, I met Oriana on Mythos my second time there. She taught me about the nymphs and satyrs, and we had a few entity dates. I never took her seriously since there could never be anything real between us. When you agreed to sing with the band, I was in heaven. I've wanted to date you for the longest time, but I was afraid to ask. You are a junior, after all, and I'm a sophomore, but when you said you liked me I fell crazy in love with you. I wanted us to have sex, but I understood when you didn't. Then I thought of Mythos, and I was ecstatic when you agreed to go there with me. I want us to be what we were again."

"What about Oriana?"

Julie's stern expression told Josh there was no room for negotiation on that subject. "That's all over. I was going to tell her the next time she came to see me, but that next time was Sunday while we were on Mythos. I never had the chance to break it off before that. After Sunday, I don't think she'll want to see me again anyway."

Julie pulled the car over into a driveway and stopped. "You need to tell her it's finished, Josh. I don't want there to be any doubt in our relationship. I thought it over, and I realize I was silly in being jealous of Oriana. I know there can never be anything real between you and her, but the thought of you two on Mythos makes me see red. I know boys have a different attitude toward sex, but if you and I are going to get serious, I can't tolerate the thought of you going off and having virtual sex whenever it suits you."

Don't blow it, Josh. This may be your only chance to make things right with Julie. Say the right thing. "I promise I'll break it off formally with Oriana, and I also promise never to go to Mythos again unless it's with you."

"That's what I wanted to hear." Julie leaned across the center console and kissed Josh passionately.

"Wow! Does that mean you forgive me?" Josh asked as she broke off the kiss.

"Yes, but don't ask me to go to Mythos again until you've settled things with **her**." The tone of voice left no doubt about Julie's feelings for Oriana.

"Does that mean you'd like to go to Mythos again sometime?"

"Maybe. I'll have to think about it a lot, but right now, I think I might." She turned back to the steering wheel, started the car and drove away. Josh felt himself floating an inch above the seat just as if he were an entity again.

* * * * *

Late that night Josh felt a cold sensation in his room. "Is that you, Oriana?" he called hopefully. The cold gripped his body, and Charley's voice echoed in his brain.

"Nope, tain't her, just me."

"What's up, Great Grandpa?"

"I had ta come here by way o' Mythos. What'd ya do with th' Gira Cargan?"

"Dad sent it to Wycham, and I didn't have time to warn you."

"That's okay. I knew somethin' wuz funny when I wound

up in a mailbag. Had to go back to Gira and take th' long way here."

Josh stifled a snicker as he imagined the old man inside a bag.

"Tain't funny. Th' Grand Council sent another Marshall, and he didn't report anything funny. He said they had some equipment there associated with a knowledge retention program, but Wycham explained it was just there for when Earth got full recognition. The Marshal bought it and so did th' Council."

"What's a knowledge retention program?"

"It's a way t' hold on ta some smart feller's knowledge after he's dead. The scientist, or whatever, lets part o' his entity be transferred to somebody else who picks up what he knows. Fer instance, we could'a saved Einstein's knowledge o' quantum physics if'n we'd had such a thing back then."

"Sounds logical to me. What do you think?"

"I think it's mighty suspicious, but I can't do nothin' 'bout it without the Council's okay. Keep your eyes and ears open for anything strange about those Cargans."

"I will. Hey, how did you get here if there's no Mythos Cargan on Gira?"

Charley laughed. "I know every terminal with a Mythos Cargan this side o' Korpin 3. They ain't many of 'em, but it's not too hard t' get here usin' one of 'em."

"If I want to come see you. How would I do that?"

"Well, ya just go t' Mythos and… Wait a minute. Come along and I'll show you how."

"Okay, you go first." Josh climbed out of bed and moved to the Cargan. He waited a moment to let Charley exit then hummed the activation note. Charley was waiting for him at the sycamore tree.

"You gotta pay good 'tention t' the next Cargan tree, Josh. It ain't easy t' spot. Follow me." Charley led Josh along the forest paths pointing out landmarks along the way.   Josh made extensive mental notes about the route. Charley stopped at a small tree among a grove of maples. "This here's th' tree, but they ain't no marker plaque on it. You can tell it's the right one by this funny lookin' knot here." He pointed out a grotesquely shaped knot resembling a hideous face.

"I think I can recognize that one all right. Where do you find the Cargan?"

"Right here." Charley put his hands into the tree just above the knot. "The activation notes like this." He hummed the note for Josh.

"Okay, B above middle C. I got it."

Charley vanished, and Josh followed. The next stop was a very busy terminal. Charley was waiting for him. "This is Hellos. The Gira Cargan's over there." He pointed to a row of Cargans near the large windows and glided off in that direction.

Go to Mythos, along the right hand path to the grove of maples, the Cargan's just above the funny-looking knot, B above middle C, this is Hellos. I gotta write all of this down when I get home.

Charley stopped at a very tall Cargan with six silver discs attached to the gray bars. Charley pointed to a plaque on the base. "Since you kin read Giran, you can see this here's the Gira Cargan, but the note symbol's in Hellan. It goes like this." Charley hummed the note, and Josh copied the sound.

"I got it, B flat." *Go to Mythos, go along the right hand path to the grove of maples, the Cargan's just above the funny-looking knot, B above middle C, this is Hellos, the tall Cargan with six silver discs, hum B flat.* Josh kept repeating the directions like a mantra until Charley vanished then followed after him.

Charley was waiting for him in the Gira terminal. "See, that was easy. Now look at the Cargan we just come in on."

Josh saw it was identical to the one on Hellos.

"Think ya kin make it back home?"

"Sure, no problem. Find the Hellos Cargan, hum B flat, and I'm on Hellos. Go to the Mythos Cargan, it's near the windows. Hum B above middle C. Go down the path to the left to the sycamore tree, then home."

"You got it. Stay in touch now, ya hear?"

"Sure, I'll let you know about any funny stuff right away." Josh gripped the Cargan and followed the path back home. Once there, he wrote down the instructions while they were still fresh in his mind.

* * * * *

Josh was sound asleep when a vision of Oriana crept into his dreams urging him to wake up. He lurched into consciousness with the warm feeling of Oriana flooding his mind.

"Is that you, Oriana?"

"Yes, Josh. I wanted to apologize for being an ass on Mythos the other day."

Once more Oriana dressed normally.

"Look, you don't have to apologize. I'm the one who took two girls there."

"Just the same, I'm sorry. Do you forgive me?"

"Sure, but I need to tell you I'm really serious about Julie, and she wants me to break it off with you, so I guess I'll have to."

"I really don't want that, Josh. I need to talk to her and try to make her understand. I know she's real and I'm not, and it's only natural for you to want someone from your own planet, but I still want us to be friends. Can't we be friends?"

"Sure, it's okay by me, but Julie needs to be sure we're not a thing anymore."

"Tell me where I can find her, and I'll go talk to her."

Josh thought for a moment and decided it might be an excellent idea to maintain friendship with Oriana. After all, if things didn't work out between he and Julie, he'd need to have someone to share Mythos with. "I'll draw you a map," he said as he jumped out of bed and moved to his desk.

CHAPTER 26

Roger rented a car at the Miami airport and set the GPS to the address for Wycham's office. It was a straightforward drive, and he arrived well ahead of schedule. He took advantage of the time by grabbing a quick lunch at a nearby Thai restaurant.

Just before one that afternoon, Roger walked into a plush office suite and up to a very attractive brunette secretary. The sign on her desk read, Ms. Burdsong.

"Good morning, Ms. Burdsong. I'm Roger Smith. I have an appointment with Mr. Wycham." Roger always felt it was good practice to address secretaries by name.

"Yes, Mr. Smith. He's expecting you. Please go on in." She buzzed the door open, and Roger entered. Wycham looked up from a computer screen and rose to meet him.

"Roger, how good to see you. Come in and sit down." He indicated a comfortable looking chair next to his desk.

"Good to be here. Where's our prospect?"

"Oh, he'll be along later. He's always late. Did you have a good flight in?"

"Well, if you can call a redeye a good flight, I..." Roger suddenly felt unseen hands gripping his arms and another invisible hand over his mouth. Wycham seemed to be taking all this in stride. He was even smiling.

"Don't bother to struggle, Roger. My Ulans have you quite

securely. Let me explain what's going to happen. You're going to take a little trip through the galaxy and back to the things you think are ugly sculptures your grandfather made. Oh, I see you're puzzled by that statement. Those things are Cargans, and they are quite useful for traveling through the universe, as you're about to find out." Wycham rose from his desk and moved to a bookcase. He manipulated some books, and the case swung outward to reveal a small room with a chaise and one of Charley's sculptures.

The Ulans moved Roger forcibly into the room and up to the sculpture placing his hands on two shiny parts of the object. He heard Wycham humming a note and felt himself growing cold. He fell through a tunnel of red and blue lights toward a bright light. Passing through the light he found himself in a room with several other sculptures. This time, he could see two ghostly, hulking figures who grasped him immediately.

"What's going on here? Where am I?" Roger asked, but the specters ignored him. As they pulled him toward another sculpture, Roger noticed he was also a ghostly apparition. "What's this all about?" Again, no reply from the large ghosts who forced his hands on another sculpture and hummed a low tone.

Once more he passed through the light tunnel to enter another room full of sculptures. This room was much more active than the previous location, but more of the same hulking images took control of him there. They whisked him off to another sculpture where the ritual was repeated. This time he found himself in a room full of Charley's sculptures facing Wycham and three of the same variety of ghosts he'd seen in the previous two stops.

"Welcome back to Earth, Roger. You might be interested to know that you've just traveled over 50 light years in a matter of moments."

"What's going on here, Mark? Am I dead? Is that why I'm a ghost and seeing ghosts?"

"No, Roger, you're not dead. You're an entity, and these Ulans are also entities. Your body is very much alive back in my office, just down the street over there." Wycham pointed toward one wall. "In fact, we're going that way now." Wycham broke into maniacal laughter as the two specters grabbed Roger and propelled him to the wall. Wycham passed through a door to the other side.

Roger moved through the wall and found himself in a spacious room with several large cabinets connected to desk-sized consoles. A flat panel display on each console showed only some sort of cursor blinking in slow, rhythmic fashion. A myriad of wires and tubes ran between the cabinets and the consoles, and the place reminded him of a modern-day Frankenstein's laboratory.

Roger felt himself grow rigid. He couldn't move or speak. He tried vainly to protest, but no sound came from his mouth. The larger entity raised one hand, and Roger felt himself moving through the room toward one of the cabinets. The door of the device opened to the wave of the entity's other hand, and he flung Roger inside.

"Well, Roger, it's time for us to make a change," Wycham said. The broad smile on the old man's face did not seem to convey any sense of pleasure in the meeting. Roger got the distinct impression it was more the smile of a man who just won the lottery or received some other unexpected gift.

"Wycham, what's going on? Tell your goons to turn me loose."

"Oh, I can't do that, Roger. You see, these goons, as you call them, are my security force for the terminal. Quite effective, don't you think?"

"Very effective, but a bit misguided. Tell them who I am."

"They know very well who you are. You see I've been planning to lure you into my trap here for some time now."

"What are you talking about, Wycham?" Roger's mind whirled to find an explanation for Wycham's attitude and his recent experiences.

"If you had any knowledge of entity travel at all, you'd know precisely what I'm talking about. I'm talking about power, Smith. Raw power on a universal scale."

"What does that have to do with me, and this room, and these thugs?"

"You are a big problem, Roger. You see your son is aware of the true nature of the sculptures, and I can't risk him blabbing the secret to you. Should you discover the secret of Charley's sculptures, you might get the government involved. Before you know it, the Earth could be a full-fledged partner in the Grand Council, and I can't have that."

"Grand Council, entity travel, you're making no sense."

"I don't expect you to understand, but as long as Earth is a primitive terminal, my Ulan friends and I can operate here with impunity. Once this facility is brought up to universal standards, we would not be able to put our own people into critical positions on key planets."

Roger's worst fears were fulfilled. Charley's sculptures were not just ugly art after all, and Wycham knew it. *What a fool I've been! I had no idea about these things being anything of importance. I can see why Josh was so fascinated with these sculptures. He knows what they are. Why didn't Charley ever tell me about them?* "What are you going to do, Wycham?"

"It's a simple substitution process. These cabinets, here," Wycham swung his arm around the room, "are used to meld two entities into one. One of you and one of them." Wycham indicated the smaller Ulan. "When the job is done correctly, the end result is two Roger Smith entities. One of them combines your thought processes and memories with, say, Achmah's here, and the other is a zombie-like Roger Smith entity who is only the shell of his former self. The combined entity returns to your corporeal body and helps further our plans. The zombie entity is destroyed to tidy up the loose ends."

"My God!" Roger blanched at the idea his body would soon be invaded by an entity half himself and half an Ulan. It was an ingenious scheme. Who would be able to tell the difference between the new Roger and the old one?

"Oh, He won't care much." Wycham chuckled derisively. "We already have quite a few people in place on Mica, and we have begun to invade several other planets. The only piece of the puzzle left is the machinery needed to dispose of the zombies. The material we need for that unit is not available on Earth. It must be shipped in from another planet, and the closest one is three light years away, but I estimate we will be in business within a few weeks. We ordered the stuff almost three years back when Manjahba first approached me for use of the Earth terminal."

"Manjahba?" Roger asked.

"Manjahba is a very powerful man on Ula, and a patriot.

His planet is no better than a slave farm for the other inhabited planet in his system, Mica. With the help of the Earth terminal, and myself, we are replacing the politicians on Mica with more agreeable Ulans. Soon, the government of Mica will be under Manjahba's control, and things will begin to change for Ula. The reward for my assistance is an interest in any planet I choose. My extensive travels have given me knowledge of several profitable ventures around the universe, and soon I will have control of billions of dollars in intergalactic trade while Manjahba rules both Ula and Mica. One hand washes the other, as you might say."

"How does that profit you here on Earth?" Roger said.

"Gold can be shipped by certain races. It's an expensive process, but there's still enough left to make me the richest man on Earth."

"You'll never get away with this Wycham." Roger shouted the first thing that came into his mind, and cursed himself for being so trite.

"I expected something more sophisticated from you, Roger. You disappoint me. Yes, we will get away with it as long as we can keep the Grand Council off Earth. Other terminals have safety features that thwart our plans, but Earth is different. It's primitive and backward, and the minor anomalies we create are always explained away on that basis. We've 'gotten away with it', as you say, for quite a while now."

Roger faced the inevitability of his death. There was no argument he could use to make Wycham change his course. The man was power mad, and bent on sacrificing anything to get what he wanted. He was a ruthless businessman on Earth, and not even a large amount of money would make him spare

Roger's life. He decided to face the end bravely.

"Go ahead and do what you want to do. I can't stop you now, but I swear, if there is any way for me to thwart your plans, I'll do it."

"An empty boast, Roger. As soon as the needed material arrives, you will cease to exist on any level. Unless you can act from Hell, your threat is meaningless. Proceed, Achmah. Goodbye, Roger. It was good knowing you." Wycham turned away laughing as the smaller entity forced him back into the cabinet and closed the door.

CHAPTER 27

Achma, now in the guise of Roger, walked through the door of the house and announced he was home. Evelyn and Josh came into the kitchen to welcome him, and Achma studied his new family. *The boy looks like all the rest of these Earth adolescents, but the mother is quite lovely. She may make this assignment worth the time.*

"Did you have a good trip, Dad?" Josh said.

"Yes, I did. We got a very large grant for the new museum."

"That's wonderful, darling." Evelyn kissed what she saw as her husband.

"Did you get to see the rest of the Car… er, sculptures?" Josh asked.

Achma stiffened, but composed himself quickly. *I forgot, this boy knows they're Cargans.* "Yes, he has them stored properly and well protected."

"That's good. Say, can the band practice here next Tuesday?"

Achma looked at Evelyn who gave a slight nod of approval. "I guess you do need to practice. Yes, your band may come here."

"Thanks, Dad," Josh said over his shoulder as he ran up the stairs to call the other band members.

* * * * *

Josh lay in bed that night thinking about his father's remarks. *What was Dad talking about? Obviously he hasn't seen the Earth terminal. I wonder what Wycham showed him? I really hope great grandpa can convince the Council something's fishy there. Oh well, nothing I can do about it right now.*

* * * * *

Achma followed Evelyn up to the bedroom and consulted Roger's memories for the proper routine. He undressed and donned pajamas then moved to the bathroom sink. *They use this stuff on their teeth. Ugh, looks like green bird stools. Hmm, doesn't taste bad. Very pleasant feeling, in fact. Now this blue stuff in the bottle, but I shouldn't swallow it, he says. Yech, tastes like some kind of medication, but I guess these Earthlings need it to stimulate their sex drive.*

Achma turned from the sink to see Evelyn undressing. *A very lovely woman for an Earthling. They don't shave their heads, but I think I might like this hair fascination they have. It's been too long since I've had any female attention. I think I'll see if she's in the mood tonight.* He moved to the bed as Evelyn took control of the bathroom sink to remove her make-up. While she was occupied, he took off his pajamas and crawled in bed naked.

He watched Evelyn's routine fascinated at the ritual of Earth women painting their faces in the morning then removing it every night. *What a waste of time. Don't they know we don't need that mask? I guess it's the difference between Ulans and Earthlings.*

Evelyn disposed of the last blackened cotton ball and climbed into bed. Achma felt her hand touch his bare thigh. "Roger!"

"I thought you might like to make love tonight, Darling.

How about it?" He rolled to face her and kissed her gently on the forehead.

"I don't see why not, but I just wasn't expecting it, that's all."

"The spontaneous ones are always the best." Achma kissed her passionately on the lips and they lost themselves in bliss.

CHAPTER 28

The next morning Achma was down for breakfast early. He gave Evelyn a playful pat on the behind as he passed the stove on his way to the table.

"How's the sexiest woman in Santa Cruz this morning?" Achma asked. *These Earth women do know how to make love, I'll give them that, even if they are a bit on the scrawny side.*

"Roger! Josh will be down any minute now. Behave yourself."

Achma picked up the paper and scanned the headlines while he sipped the glass of orange juice Evelyn pre-positioned on his placemat. He turned to the entertainment section and scanned the movie listings.

"Honey, that movie you've been wanting to see is on at the multiplex tonight. Maybe we should go see it."

"Did you forget, Roger? We have that retirement ceremony for Will Janick tonight."

"That's right, I nearly forgot it. I wouldn't want to miss that. Will's contributed so much to Theta, and we'll sure miss him. Isn't that a black tie affair?" *How did I miss that? I have to do a better job of probing his memories.*

"I got your tux from the cleaners yesterday," Evelyn said. "The banquet starts at eight, and it's in San Francisco, so don't be late coming home."

"I won't. I need to practice my speech some before we go

anyway."

The rest of the morning routine followed the usual script with Josh coming down late and nearly missing the school bus. Achma was off to Roger's office, and Evelyn prepared for a day as volunteer at the local well baby clinic.

CHAPTER 29

That evening, Achma and Evelyn drove into San Francisco. They had no trouble finding the large hotel hosting Will Janick's retirement party, but they needed the assistance of the desk clerk to find the "Jack London Room." They walked into the large banquet hall and found their place at the head table. As Executive Vice President, Roger was expected to deliver the usual retirement speech and present Janick with the all-expense paid trip to Hawaii for he and his wife, along with the large walnut and brass plaque commemorating over thirty-five years of service to Theta.

Dinner was the usual chicken in an unidentifiable sauce accompanied by boiled potatoes and the ubiquitous "vegetable medley." Evelyn was surprised by Roger's enthusiasm over the dinner.

Ah, real food for a change. It's been a long time since I had an R&R back on Ula. I see he likes the meat. Mmmm, very good. The vegetables are not to his liking, but these Earth twits don't know what's good and what isn't. The white stuff looks best. Hey, that's delicious.

"This stuff is really good," Achma said as he shoved a very large chunk of chicken into his mouth and washed it down with a glass of white wine.

"Roger, not such large bites, dear," Evelyn said.

"Oh, sorry." Achma cut his next bite in half before

consuming it.   He followed the chicken with a piece of cauliflower deftly selected from among its fellow medley members.

Evelyn watched almost in shock as Achma picked all of the cauliflower out of his vegetables then followed up with the carrots leaving only the zucchini and broccoli behind on the plate. "When did you start liking cauliflower?" she asked.

Achma looked down at his plate in surprise and wiped his mouth with the large, beige napkin before responding. "Well, I, ah, I guess it just tasted good to me tonight."

"I don't want to hear any complaints the next time I want some cauliflower for dinner," Evelyn said. The scolding tone in her voice was only half in jest.

The evening progressed in the usual fashion with endless tributes to Janick's service in Theta's cause. At last, the time came for Achma's speech, and he moved to the central podium while retrieving his notes from the breast pocket of his tuxedo coat. He spread the notes out on the dais and looked around at the assembled crowd.

"Friends, fellow Theta employees, Californians, lend me your ears. I have come to retire Will Janick, not to praise him."

A titter of laughter ran through the hall in appreciation of the Shakespearian reference.

"The good that Will has done will live long after he is gone, and the bad will be shredded along with his personal files."

The laughter was less subdued now that people were getting into the concept.

"Seriously, though, when I came to Theta twenty years ago, Will Janick was my model and my mentor. He taught me the electronics business from the ground up. He started me out as a gardener for the plants in his office."

The laughter was loud and merry now, since no one believed Roger Smith ever turned a shovel of dirt in his life.

Achma reached for the glass of water under the podium and found it empty. Evelyn noticed the problem and quickly reached for a pitcher of ice water to remedy the situation. She poured the water into the glass as Achma held it over his speech notes, but the angle was awkward for her. Before she could stop it, a large chunk of ice slid down to the spout of the pitcher and diverted the water's flow to the notes below the glass. Achma watched in horror as the words on the paper dissolved into blobs of black and gray liquid. Evelyn moved quickly to blot up the water with her napkin, but the damage was done. Two paragraphs of notes were now completely unreadable.

Oh Damn! What was that woman's name? It was hard to find it, and he always had to dig deep in his memory to get it right. It began with a 'J', I know that. Jane—that's it, it's Jane.

The crowd gasped in response to the situation, but Achma quickly regained control. "It's alright, folks. Fortunately, I don't need many notes to talk about Will and his lovely wife Jane."

A gasp spread out across the large room, causing Achma to consult his notes. He shuffled through three pages before Evelyn saved him.

"It's Jan," Evelyn said behind the screen of her raised napkin.

"I'm sorry, I meant to say Jan. I've only known them for twenty years. You have to make some allowance for our short acquaintanceship."

The speech was on track once more, and the rest of the

evening went smoothly. On the way home Evelyn berated Achma for his goof. "How could you forget Jan Janick's name? Honestly, Roger, that was a bit embarrassing."

"You know how easy it is to say Jane instead of Jan. You've heard people do it a hundred times around them."

"Yes, I have, but you know how mad Jan gets when people call her Jane. You know that's her sister's name, and her mother used to do the same thing. I can't imagine you making that mistake."

"I've had a lot on my mind lately. I apologized to her didn't I?"

"She took it rather well considering the fact that you, of all people, should know better."

The rest of the ride home was spent in normal conversation about who was wearing what and who looked older or fatter than the last gathering of Theta executives.

* * * * *

Saturday night came and the band played to 400 by Karrasnik's count. As they divided the $200 among the five of them, Rodney Barnes said, "I know there were more than 400 kids here tonight."

"It's like I said, Josh. His counter won't go above 400 because of the fire marshal's posting," Julie said.

"I know, but how do we prove him wrong?" Josh asked.

"We'd have to keep our own count some way," Will Jenkins said.

"I agreed to go by his count," Josh said.

"I'll bet he's got his counter rigged," Bill Thompson said. "If I could get hold of it, I could see how he's fixed it."

"Fat chance of that," Rodney Barnes said. "He never lets it out of his sight."

"He might if he was distracted," Julie said.

Josh's face took on a suspicious look. "What are you talking about?"

"I'm saying, I've seen him ogling the girls on the dance floor. I think he likes young girls," Julie replied.

"You mean he's a pedophile?" Thompson asked.

"He may be, but I think I could keep him busy long enough for one of you guys to switch counters on him," Julie said.

"I could get another counter just like it for the switch," Jenkins said.

"And, I could fix it so's he couldn't zero it out," Bill Thompson offered.

"Okay. Will, you get a counter and give it to Bill to fix up. You can pay for it with my share of the money." Josh handed his share to Jenkins. "He's booked us for next Saturday night. We'll have to pull the switch before he starts counting, though."

"No problem. We just get here before he opens up, like normal. I get him out of his office on some pretense, and Bill makes the swap. I'll wear something more provocative next time" Julie said.

"How do you improve on that?" Rodney Barnes whispered to Jenkins.

"I heard that, Rodney. Don't worry, I'll think of something," Julie said.

"I don't like the idea of you coming on to Karrasnik," Josh said.

"You'll be there to protect me, won't you?" Julie said as she blinked her eyes playfully at Josh.

The obvious mockery brought titters of laughter from the

band members.

"I'll be close by, and so will the rest of the guys," Josh assured her.

"All set then. We do the deed next week," Julie said.

The band packed up, and Josh rode home with Julie.

"I'm glad you're not mad at me anymore," Josh said as they drove.

"You know, I was just as mad at Oriana until the other night."

"How's that?" Josh thought he knew, but he had to act dumb.

"I had this funny dream about her. It was so real—almost like she was inside my head. She told me how she was sorry for coming between you and I, and that she wanted to be my friend. She told me she liked you, but you were no more than a friend to her now that you had a real girl on Earth."

"That's some dream." *Good girl, Oriana!*

"Yes, it was. I decided I shouldn't be so mad at either one of you. By the way, have you broken it off with her yet?"

"Yeah, she came to see me last week, and we agreed to end it on a friendly basis. I'm glad you two can be friends. I haven't seen any of Brem, and she could show us around, if I ever get another Cargan."

"What happened to the ones you had?"

"Dad sent the Gira Cargan down to Miami with the others. All I have now is the Mythos Cargan."

"Can't two people use the same Cargan?"

Josh thought he sensed a bit of disappointment in her voice. "Yeah, but it's not recommended. I'm going to try to talk Dad into letting me have the Gira Cargan back, but I don't know how much luck I'll have with that. He seems a bit different lately."

"Oh, how's that?"

"Well, he went down to Miami to work on a grant for the museum, and I asked him if he saw the other Cargans. He said Wycham had them stored, but I know he's got them set up like a terminal."

"I don't understand. Who's Wycham, what museum and what's a terminal?"

"I forgot, you've only been to Mythos, and there's no terminal there. I'll fill you in on the whole deal." Josh explained the situation fully.

"I see, that's really spooky about your great grandfather being dead but living as an entity."

"Oh, it's okay once you get used to it. I need to get back and see him though, so I can tell him about Dad."

"Can you get there from Mythos?"

"Yeah, he showed me how. I'll go this weekend."

They reached Josh's house, and Julie leaned over the console to kiss him. Josh obliged with pleasure.

"I hope you get another Cargan, Josh. I think I'd like to visit Mythos again."

"Great! I'll really work on that." Josh almost floated from the car to the house on that news.

CHAPTER 30

Tuesday night came, and the band assembled at Josh's house. Evelyn insisted that they practice in the basement game room, and conveniently remembered she had volunteered to help with the church newsletter. She left the house to the band and Roger, who was busy in his office tapping away on his computer keyboard.

The band launched into one of the more avant-garde rock pieces in their repertoire, and the walls began to vibrate in rhythm with Rodney Barnes' bass notes and the drum beats of Bill Thompson.

Upstairs, Achma felt the vibrations. *Oh, very nice. Some of that music these people call rock. I'll have to be sure to take this back to Ula. This fellow doesn't seem to like it very much, but what else would I expect? The boy has some real talent. Maybe we can meld him into an Ulan entity? I think I'll go down and listen for a while.*

Josh was surprised to see his father's head appear in the doorway of the game room. When the band stopped playing, they were rewarded with applause from the adult listener.

"That was very good," Achma said as he walked into the room. "I think you kids are getting much better."

The boys and Julie looked at each other in amazement. The usual adult reaction to their music was complete distaste and a request to play more quietly.

"Glad you liked it, Dad," Josh said. He glanced at the other band members noticing their puzzled faces.

"Yeah, thanks, Mr. Smith," Rodney added regaining his composure after the shock of a compliment from an adult.

"I didn't think adults liked that stuff," Willie Jenkins said.

"Oh, it has a certain appeal. In fact, I'd say it has the harmony of the spheres in it," Achma said.

Once more the group was surprised, but Josh thought it might be time to strike while his parent was in a receptive mood. "Want to hear one of my pieces, Dad?"

Achma's face lit up in a broad smile. "You've written music?"

"Yeah, Dad. You've heard my stuff before." Josh scratched his head in frustration. It was like his father was high on something or drunk. He couldn't believe what he was hearing or seeing.

"Please play one of your compositions for me," Achma asked as he assumed a seat on one of the large, leather upholstered poker chairs.

"Okay, guys, number four. Ah one, ah two, and…" The band broke into the cacophony passing for music in teen minds while Josh studied his father. Roger's eyes closed, and he leaned his head against the back of the leather chair while his fingers drummed in rhythm with the bass notes. Josh had only seen this reaction a few times before and only in response to classical music. He figured his father must have fortified himself with a lot of bourbon before coming downstairs. Either that, or this was some clever ruse to cause his band to stop playing out of sheer shock.

The number closed with a flourish of chords from Josh's electric guitar accompanied by a frenzy of beats from the drums. Achma broke into wild applause.

"That was wonderful. You kids should make a record. Your music captures the harmony of the spheres all right," Achma said.

"Thanks, Dad. Would you like to hear something else?" Josh asked.

"I'd like to hear the young lady sing something," Achma said.

"Sure, number 14 guys. That okay with you, Julie?"

"Yeah, that's fine, Josh," she replied.

Once more Achma lost himself in the music. He broke into loud applause as the band finished.

"Wonderful, wonderful! You have a great voice, er, I've forgotten your name."

"It's Julie, Julie Kidwell, Mr. Smith."

"Certainly, how could I forget such a lovely face."

"Want another one, Dad?" Josh asked.

"I'd love to, but I have to get back to work. I don't want to interrupt your practice session too much. You young people just go on as usual." Achma waved at the band as he disappeared up the stairway.

"What was that?" Willie Jenkins asked.

"Does your dad do coke?" Rodney Barnes added.

"He must have been high on something," Josh said. "I've never had him tell me anything about our music except to keep it quiet."

"Oh well, I'm glad he didn't come down to shut us up," Bill Thompson said.

"We might as well take advantage of it," Josh said as he leafed through the sheet music to find the next number for practice.

After the other band members left, Julie stayed to talk to Josh. "You seem worried tonight."

"It's Dad. He seems sort of absent minded lately. He knows who you are, he's met you before."

"Older people just do that kind of thing. Don't worry about it. Just try to get another Cargan real soon." She kissed him and headed for her car.

CHAPTER 31

Evelyn returned from the church just in time to see the boys loading their equipment into Willie Jenkins' van.

"Did you boys have a good practice tonight?" Evelyn asked.

"It was great, Mrs. Smith," Willie replied. "Your husband even liked it."

"Roger?" Evelyn stopped half way into the door. "Roger liked your music?"

"Yeah, he said it had 'the harmony of the spheres'. At least I think that's the way he put it," Bill Thompson said. His words induced a short burst of chuckles from the other boys.

"Well, I'm glad he liked it." Evelyn continued into the house and checked the office, but Roger was not there. She found Josh in the game room packing away his guitar. Julie spoke on her way out.

"Oh hi, Mrs. Smith. We had a great practice tonight. See you next time."

"Goodnight, Julie. Give your parents our best."

"Hi, Mom. Did you see the guys outside?" Josh asked.

"Yes, they told me about your father liking the music. I couldn't believe it. Were they joking?"

"No, Mom. He really liked it. He even asked me to play one of my pieces."

"Well, that's a first. Better get to bed, young man. You've got school tomorrow."

"Sure, Mom. I'll be right up."

Evelyn left Josh to complete his clean up and went upstairs to the master bedroom to find Roger in his pajamas.

"How was the church tonight, Evelyn?" he asked.

"The usual things. I swear, that Martha Mills is the biggest gossip. She couldn't stop talking about that new youth minister and her goings-on with the choir director. They're both young, single people, and I can't see any reason why anyone should object to their dating."

Roger moved up behind her as she stood at the sink and placed a hand on each of her breasts.

"Roger, are you taking Viagra, or something?" Evelyn asked.

"What's the matter? I thought you liked to make love."

"I do, it's just that you seem so amorous lately. You aren't taking any kind of aphrodisiac, are you?"

"No, you just turn me on lately, that's all. Come to bed now. You can do all that cleanup stuff later." Roger steered her toward the king-sized bed.

CHAPTER 32

The next day, Josh arrived home from school to find his mother in deep thought over a pitcher of martinis.

"What's up, Mom?" Josh said.

"Oh, Josh. I was just thinking about your father?"

"Is something wrong?"

"No, it's just that he hasn't seemed like his usual self lately."

"How do you mean, Mom?"

"Well, it's a lot of little things. He ate cauliflower at that retirement dinner the other night, and he called Jan Janick, Jane."

"That doesn't sound so bad. You're always after us to eat cauliflower, and the names are pretty close."

"I could understand that if it wasn't for the other things."

"What other things?"

"Nothing a boy your age should know about. Besides, it's a private thing between your father and I."

"You mean sex?" Josh blurted out.

"Josh! Don't be so blunt."

"Well, is that it?"

Evelyn eyed her son. He was really not a boy any more, and she was certain he had been exposed to some heavy petting, as her generation used to call it, but she was pretty sure he had not experienced sex with a woman. She hesitated to say anything more.

"Let's just leave it there, Josh. It's not something I can talk to you about."

"I understand, Mom. I've had a funny feeling about Dad too since he came back from Miami. I can't put my finger on it, but he's different. He even liked my music the other night."

"I hope he isn't coming down with something. He works so hard." Evelyn always tried to tag each of Roger's maladies with the same causal factor. She sincerely felt he put too much of himself into Theta Industries.

"He's probably okay, Mom. I'm sure we're just worrying for nothing."

"I'd feel much better if he'd take a little vacation," Evelyn said as she poured herself another martini.

CHAPTER 33

Over the next two weeks, Josh noticed his mother becoming more and more introspective, but he had not noticed any further changes in his father's personality. The band successfully completed another gig at Karrasnik's teen club, and practice sessions were back in the carriage house at Rodney Barnes' place. Another practice session was scheduled for Friday night, and Josh approached his father about a ride.

"Dad, can you run me over to Rodney Barnes' house? Mom said she'd pick me up."

Roger looked up from his computer screen and smiled at his son. "Sure, I want you to do well with your music. Can you wait a few minutes? I just have to finish this one paper."

"It's okay, Dad. I don't have to be there for another half hour yet."

Roger helped load his son's equipment in the family van and the pair headed for the Barnes estate. On the way, they encountered an unexpected bit of construction, and Josh braced himself for the usual onslaught of complaints about the inefficiency of the city staff from the mayor all the way down to the Hispanic man holding the sign with "Stop" on one side and "Slow" on the other. Remarkably, Roger only turned and smiled at his son.

"Always some kind of delay, isn't there?" Roger asked.

"Yeah, Dad." Josh could hardly believe his ears. This type

of situation was a sure way to drive his father over the edge. Normally a mild mannered gentleman, Roger would transform into a brooding hulk at the slightest traffic delay, but here he was, acting as cool as a cucumber. The pair reached Rodney's house without so much as one cross word.

After practice, Josh called his mother for pickup. She arrived in her Cadillac, and Josh had to leave his equipment behind until the next practice. On the way home, Josh brought up the incident with the construction earlier.

"You know how Dad always gets mad when there's construction, Mom?"

"I know that side of your father better than anyone else. He changes from Dr. Jeykell to Mr. Hyde when he encounters traffic delays. I noticed that roadwork on the way over here. I suppose he flew off the handle over that."

"That's the weird thing, Mom. He didn't."

"He didn't? Are you talking about my Roger, your father?"

"He didn't even swear at the guy with the sign, like he usually does. It was really strange."

"Josh, I really think there is something wrong with your father. It just adds to all the other things I've noticed lately. I think I'll ask him to go see Dr. Marchotti for a checkup."

Josh thought about the situation. Everything different could be traced back to the trip to Miami. Something happened there to change his father in subtle ways. Most of the changes were things to be welcomed, but they were totally out of character. *I think I should go talk to Great Grandpa Charley before we do anything. He's done a lot of entity travel, and there may be some simple explanation for all this.*

They drove home in silence, and Josh headed straight for his room and the Mythos Cargan. He sat down and hummed the proper note hoping it was night on Gira.

* * * * *

The dark terminal was a welcome sight to Josh. It meant Charley would be on duty behind the green door. He pushed the button and was relieved to see his great grandfather standing there.

"Josh! What brings you here?" Charley seemed to be genuinely glad to see his great grandson.

"I've got to talk to you about Dad." Josh's sober expression conveyed as much gravity as his words.

"What's the matter?"

"It's Dad. He's been acting strangely ever since he went to inspect the new terminal, and Mom and I are worried something may have happened to him there."

"Tell me about it," Charley said leading Josh into the helper room and indicating two large chairs.

Josh sat opposite the old man and related some of the minor changes he and his mother noticed lately. "There's also something else Mom won't talk about. I think it has something to do with sex."

"Has he said anything out o' character?" Charley asked.

"What do you mean?" Josh leaned closer to the old entity and scrunched his eyebrows together in an expression of puzzlement.

"Has he said anything your Dad wouldn't normally say, somethin' you didn't expect?"

"Yeah!" A light went on behind Josh's eyes. "When he was listening to my music, he said it had 'the harmony of the spheres', or something like that."

"Where've I heard that before?" The old man rubbed his chin thoughtfully and turned to consult a computer screen on the wall beside his chair. "Yep, here it is. That there's an Ulan expression. They use it for anything they like real well, 'specially musicians who perform good. It's kinda like when we say 'bravo'. Given the Ulan's taste for loud music, what you young folks call rock'd be right up their alley. I think I need to pay that new terminal a visit, Josh.

"Can I go with you, Great Grandpa?"

The old man studied the boy long and hard before answering. "You can go if you stay right beside me, and do exactly as I tell you. This could be very dangerous. Do you understand?"

Josh nodded his head. "Yes, Sir."

"Good! I'm off duty here in another hour. We can go then. Did I ever tell you 'bout the time I went desert cat huntin' on Archa?" Charley launched into one of his tall tales to help the time pass more quickly.

Before Josh knew it, the sky outside the terminal windows began to stage the spectacular show that was sunrise on Gira. A small, green man appeared through the helper door and greeted Josh. "Mr. Great Grandson Josh, good to see you. Are you visiting your great grandfather again?"

Charley responded for them. "This is pretty serious, Winble. Josh here's been tellin' me 'bout how his father's changed since going to the Earth terminal. Seems he's actin' a lot like an Ulan lately. It all has a foul odor to me."

Mr. Winble's face changed from the usual cheery smile to a somber frown. "Are you sure you don't want a Marshal along on this trip?"

"I don't think so. It might be nothin', and I'll need more evidence to get a warrant from the Grand Council anyway." Charley said.

"What route are you taking?" Winble asked.

"We're goin' through Xemba to Earth. If we're not back in a half hour, send some Marshals to the terminal to check on us."

"Great Grandpa won't those goons catch us if we go to the Earth terminal?" Josh said.

"They ain't got no entity detection stuff on Earth, so they won't be able t' see us commin'. As soon as ya git there, go straight through the roof. I'll find ya outside. Okay?"

"Okay, I'm ready Great Grandpa."

"Okay, let's go." Charley moved toward the green door with Josh close behind.

"Be careful, you two," Winble called after them.

Josh soon joined Charley in the air above the warehouse.

"Hold it here. I don't think they spotted us, but we'd better lay low a minute t' be sure," Charley said. "Down behind that there building." He indicated a larger building across the street from the terminal.

Charley and Josh dropped behind the building.

"Where did you say them funny lookin' machines was?" Charley asked.

"They're in the middle of the building, in back of the terminal."

"Okay, here's what we'll do. We'll come in from street level. You tell me where to go in, but stay behind in case they spot me. If I don't come out in five minutes, go back and get Winble and the Marshals."

"Can't I go in with you?"

"No, you're my safety net. Those Ulans'll shoot first and ask questions later when they see it's me."

"I didn't see any guns, Great Grandpa."

"It's just an expression, Josh. They don't need no guns. Did you ever see any o' them there martial arts movies?"

"Sure, lots of them."

"Well, that's the way the Ulans work. They don't need weapons to kill ya, they do it with brain power."

"Cool!" Josh was truly impressed by beings that could really do the things he had only seen in movies. "But, you're already dead, Great Grandpa."

"Just my corporeal body, Josh. These guys can kill entities. Now do like I ask, okay?"

"Sure, Great Grandpa." Josh resigned himself to being a watchdog and stood by patiently while Charley entered the warehouse at the point Josh indicated. He had no idea how to tell when five minutes passed, so he counted what he thought were seconds in his mind. He had only reached two minutes and fifty-three seconds when Charley reappeared.

The look on the old man's face told Josh things inside the warehouse were very serious indeed.

"You were right, Josh. They got an entity transfer operation goin' on in there. I seen it once afore on Garga 3. We've got to get back and get the Grand Council movin' on this one."

"What's 'entity transfer'? Is Dad okay?" Josh asked.

"I'll tell ya all about it later. Let's get goin' afore those thugs find us. We'll head on back t' your house, and I'll git back t' Gira from there." Charley led the way back to Santa Cruz, but Josh had to find the house once they got in the general vicinity. The pair descended into the house and found themselves in

Roger's office. Josh was about to lead Charley to his room when he noticed his great grandfather perusing the many certificates and plaques hanging on the walls of his father's office.

"My grandson's done right well for hisself." Charley said.

"I'm pretty proud of him," Josh said. "I hope I can be as successful as he is."

"Success is all in your mind, Josh. Money's no measure o' success. Remember that."

"Yes, Sir." Josh responded with an air of deference to the old man's extensive experience. "My room's this way."

He led Charley up to his bedroom and was a bit surprised to find himself glued to the Mythos Cargan. Charley spoke first.

"I'm goin' back t' Gira. You stay here, and I'll be in touch as soon as possible. You act like nothin's happened. We don't want to tip off the entity what's invaded your father. I'm going to get the Grand Council on this right away. They may want your testimony also. If they do, I'll come to your house and possess you, but keep this all hush-hush until we're ready to act."

"What about Dad? Have they done something to him?" A tear streamed down Josh's cheek in spite of his efforts to hold it back.

Charley turned to his great grandson, and the sadness in the old man's eyes told Josh he should expect the worst.

"Your Dad's been melded with someone else, probably an Ulan from what you've told me. There may still be time to save him, but we got to act quick before they can destroy the remainder entities," Charley said.

"What're you talking about, Great Grandpa? What's a remainder entity?" Josh tried vainly to grasp the old entity's arm but only felt the coldness of the grave. The sensation invoked even more tears.

"Easy, Josh. I'll try to explain it to you. You see, there's ways of takin' two entities and mergin' 'em into one. The process is used to keep hold of the knowledge of great scientists or philosophers who are near death. The older man's entity is merged into a younger person with similar trainin'. That way the older man can die satisfied his knowledge is not lost to the universe. What's left o' the older man's entity is called a remainder. The older guy's entity can either be returned to his corporeal body or destroyed. Most people choose destruction since they wouldn't be no better'n vegetables if they went back to their old body."

"A few years back, they found a case where some crooks like our Mafia back on Earth were hijackin' entities and replacin' 'em with those of 'scaped criminals. The criminal assumed a new life safe from the law while the hijacked entity was destroyed. The police found the corporeal body of the crook and assumed he'd just been lost in space using a bad Cargan. It worked pretty well for a while, but they were eventually caught."

"You mean, Dad isn't Dad?" Josh asked.

"Nope, he's part your Dad and part Ulan. The rest of him's probably in one of them boxes you couldn't get into in the warehouse side of the buildin'. They haven't destroyed any of 'em yet 'cause they need a special alloy for that machine, and it ain't available on Earth. Like I said, you just act normal, and I'll git back to ya as soon as I can."

"Is it alright if I tell my Mom?" Josh asked.

"No, 'specially not your mother. She couldn't help but give

it away. This'll just be 'tween you and me 'til it's all over. Got that?"

"Sure, Great Grandpa. I'll be waiting for you."

"Now you just melt inta yer body there, and I'll leave as soon as you're off the Cargan."

Josh possessed his body and lifted his hands from the Cargan. He felt a cold wind pass through him before the room began to heat up again.

Josh walked back down to his father's office. He picked up a picture of he and his father standing on a pier next to two large marlins.   He brushed the tears from his cheeks as he remembered how proud his father was of him landing the fish, and how much he loved his father. It was not just the fantastic vacations and the huge home. Those things were meaningless next to the love flowing between father and son. Money could only buy nice things, but his father's love was beyond all value. The creature upstairs in bed next to his mother was something alien, and he felt invaded. It was like a science fiction movie, and he was playing a leading role.

Dad, I never realized how much I'd miss you if you were gone, Josh thought as the tears began to flow again.

I've got to get over this. I've got to put on the best acting job of my life to pull this off, but can I do it? I know what he is, but I have to pretend he's my father. Josh put the picture back in its place and returned to his bedroom.

* * * * *

Charley materialized in the Gira terminal in front of a relieved Mr. Winble.

"I am so very glad to see you back safely and soundly, as you Earth people say." Winble's smile was so broad it almost seemed it would burst his face.

"We got a real problem there, Winble. Wycham and whoever he's working with from Ula have an entity transfer operation goin'."

"What?" Winble sucked in his breath and his eyes widened in shock. "That is very serious indeed. We must report it to the Grand Council at once."

"I'll let you take care of that," Charley said. "I'm pretty sure they ain't destroyed th' remainders yet. The stuff they need fer that machine don't exist on Earth."

Winble broke in again. "The closest planet for that alloy would be Sirianna, about three light years from Earth."

"Evidently, the stuff ain't got there yet 'cause I didn't see a destruction machine anywhere in the place," Charley said.

"I will call an emergency session of the Grand Council right away," Winble said. He moved to another console to begin the process.

CHAPTER 34

The next morning Josh went down to breakfast to find his mother kissing his father goodbye as he left for work. The sight of this intimacy nearly made his stomach turn, but the thought of what was happening in their bedroom brought a red haze of rage to his brain. He fought back the urge to attack whatever it was inside his father, and greeted them in his usual manner.

"Morning, Mom, Dad. What's for breakfast?"

"Good morning, Josh." His mother pulled herself away from Roger and moved to the stove. "We've got pancakes this morning, if you want any."

"Hey, Josh." His father moved to Josh and wrapped an arm around his shoulders. "Winter vacation's coming up. I was thinking we could go to Aspen for some skiing. Would you like that?"

Josh used all of his energy to avoid recoiling from his father's touch. He calculated what his response would be if this were his father before he said anything. "That'd be great, Dad."

"Good! It's settled then. I was just discussing it with your mother when you came down. I'll have Annita make the arrangements." Roger blew a kiss to Evelyn. "I won't be late tonight, Dear."

"Call me if you are. I'm having egg foo young, and it's no good warmed over." Evelyn returned Roger's blown kiss as she stacked pancakes on a plate for her son.

* * * * *

Josh went through the motions of school that day. The image of some alien creature inside his father's body kept creeping into his thoughts. He was not even pleased when Rodney Barnes sat down next to him at lunch.

"When are we going to practice again?" Rodney asked.

"I don't know, Rod. I've got a lot on my mind lately, and I don't feel much like practicing."

"But winter break's coming, and I could use the extra money."

"So could I, but we'll have to cool it until after the break. Something more important's come up for me."

"Jeez, Josh. What's more important than making some extra money for the spring break trip?" Suddenly Rodney's eyes brightened. "Oh, I remember, that secret project for your Dad. Is that it?"

Josh silently thanked Rodney for reminding him. "Yeah, you guessed it. I can't talk about it right now, Rod. I just need some space, that's all. Things should work out in a couple of weeks, then we can get back to normal."

"Okay, but if you can't tell a band buddy, who can you tell?"

Josh knew the last person he could confide in would be Rodney Barnes. Rodney had a bad habit of blabbing every secret he knew at the drop of a hat. It wasn't that he was a deliberate gossip, Rodney just had a hard time remembering he wasn't supposed to say certain things.

They spent the remainder of lunch period discussing the virtues of several girls at the next table.

CHAPTER 35

Mark Wycham put down the phone thoroughly pleased with the success of Roger Smith's replacement. Things were going smoothly, and soon they would be able to wrap up the loose ends consisting of several special crates in the other side of the warehouse.

"What did he have to say?" The hulking specter of Manjahba loomed before Wycham's desk.

"Neither the wife nor the boy are suspicious, and he thinks Theta has the technology to build whatever we need. He'll send the Mythos Cargan as soon as he can to stop the boy's travels, but he thinks it would arouse too much suspicion if he sent it now. What's the latest estimate on the arrival of the materials we need for the destructor unit?"

"One of my entities found the probe about three day's journey from Earth. It is programmed to land just off your private island in the Caribbean."

"Is it properly masked?" Wycham asked.

"Yes, it will look just like a meteorite to your Earth sensors, but won't that bring a flock of scientists looking for the thing?"

"The water is very deep near that island. They'll know it's useless. I just hope the recovery system works as planned." Wycham rubbed his hands together in a worrying motion.

"They've done this kind of thing many times before, Wycham. As soon as we can calculate an exact time of arrival,

I'll give you the information."

"I still won't feel comfortable until we can eliminate those remainder entities. The anomalies they produce in the entity signals are getting harder to explain every day. We should have waited until everything was in place before we began working so close to the Cargans."

"There are risks to everything, Wycham. We've managed to satisfy the Marshals so far, haven't we? No more targets are due in until next month, and we'll have the destruction unit finished by then. You worry too much, Wycham. What have you got to lose?"

"Several million dollars of investment in that phony art museum if this whole thing falls through, and what if the Grand Council should choose to close this terminal?"

"They won't do that without a proper hearing, and my lawyers are confident we can find enough loopholes to prevent that. I run all the risks here. The Council can ban me from entity travel for life, and the Mican government could have me thrown in prison for what we're doing. The Council would only give you a short term ban on travel at the worst, and you've broken no Earth laws."

"Don't forget, entity travel provides a great deal of technology for my companies. I wouldn't want to lose access to that."

"You have enough information to make you twice as rich as you are already. Let me do the worrying for both of us."

Wycham sat back in his large, leather swivel chair and stared at his spectral partner. "Just be sure you have all the bases covered."

CHAPTER 36

It was two days before Josh felt the cold aura of Charley on the back of his neck. He sat up in bed and spoke to the empty room. "Is that you, Great Grandpa? If it is go ahead and possess me."

He felt the cold sensation envelop his body as his mind filled with images of decaying bodies, zombies and other horror story creatures.

"Damnit Josh! It ain't like that at all. Quit conjurin' up all that goulish stuff. It's just me."

"Sorry, Great Grandpa. What's happening with the Grand Council?"

"We got a hearing at two AM your time tomorrow morning on Gira. Mr. Winble says he'll prob'ly need your testimony. Can you make it?"

Josh answered without pausing to think about it. "I sure can. The sooner we get this settled, the sooner we can get Dad back."

"Okay, if you have any problems, find some way to let me know so's we can postpone the hearin'."

"Got it, Great Grandpa. I'll be there." Josh felt the room grow warmer and lay back in bed.

CHAPTER 37

Josh couldn't go back to sleep. He dressed in clothes he thought appropriate for the Grand Council and passed the time with a computer game.

He didn't know anything about the Grand Council, but he felt it must be something like the Supreme Court. He tried to visualize himself on the witness stand, and kept seeing judges in white wigs and black robes. He shook off that image only to have it replaced with every science fiction character he had ever seen in a movie or a TV program.

Shortly before the appointed time, Josh felt a cold chill in the room and Charley's voice filled his mind.

"You ready t' go, young man?"

"Sure, Great Grandpa, but you have to go first." Josh waited for the room to warm a bit then grasped the Mythos Cargan. He hummed the proper note and followed the circuitous path the Gira. Charley and Mr. Winble met him there in entity form.

"Good evening, Mr. Josh," Winble said as he offered his cheek in greeting.

Josh brushed the green man's cheek and felt that same pleasant sensation he felt with every Sellan he ever greeted.

"Hi, Mr. Winble. Where's the courthouse?" Josh said.

Winble laughed at Josh's eagerness. "It's this way, Mr. Josh. I hope you are just as eager after you meet the Grand Council."

"Are they scary, or something?" Josh asked.

"Don't pay no 'tention ta Winble," Charley said. "The Council's just like any other court. Keep your mouth shut when it ain't your turn ta talk and tell the truth when it is, and you'll not have anythin' to worry 'bout."

Winble led the way through the streets of the large city surrounding the terminal and stopped at an impressive marble and aluminum building. Inside, they passed Marshals in both entity and corporeal forms as they moved along the corridors to the hearing chambers. Winble advised them a Chief Helper must serve as the prosecutor in any cases involving law violations pertaining to his, or her, terminal. Josh was impressed with the multi-dimensional capabilities of the Sellan people.

The Council Chambers looked nothing like a courtroom on earth. Plain marble walls sparkled in the sunlight from high windows. The mosaic floor featured intricate patterns showing scenes of what Josh guessed were mythical Giran figures. The Councilors sat behind a stainless steel table in high-backed aluminum chairs. They were all entities, but each one radiated an unmistakable aura of authority and power. Even the one female member was impressive. She looked about the same as an Earth woman in her sixties with silver hair and a wrinkled face marred by pigment spots. Hard, green eyes scanned everyone in the room; and Josh felt as if she were looking at his soul when they fell on him.

Two of the men were Girans. Josh recognized them from their long-sleeved, white robes.

Another Council member was very tall; Josh estimated over seven feet. His head was nearly bald with only a fringe of hair running from ear to ear low on the back of his head. He wore what appeared to be a military uniform with several medals dangling from his left breast pocket.

Charley pointed out that another member was a Sellan like Winble. The remaining two men were much like Earth people and wore clothes appropriate for a science fiction movie on Earth.

Winble explained the Council to Josh. "I suppose you recognize the Girans and the Sellan?"

"Yeah," Josh replied. "I know about them, but who are the others."

"The tall one is a Quazzan. They are a warrior race and quite aggressive. Their planet is constantly torn by war between various factions, but they limit the weapons available to edged types, like swords and pikes. They don't even use bows. It's quite a bloody affair, but they seem to need it to live. The woman is a Somm Truth Reader. Did you notice how uncomfortable you felt when she looked at you?"

"I sure did," Josh affirmed.

"She is the one the Council looks to for exposing frauds. You will be sworn to tell the truth, but she will advise the others when you are lying. A button she pushes with her foot sends a silent signal to the other members. No one but the other Council members know when she's doing that. The other two are from Fundor, a planet much like Earth. In fact, one of them even speaks a language similar to Earth English they call *Anglush*. He is the Grand Councilor for the rest of this year. The other is the President of the chief nation on Fundor who holds his council seat as a result of his position. Fundor is the most powerful planet in the universe because they have the ability to transmit positive matter. They've kept that technology a secret for over six hundred years in spite of many attempts to steal it."

"I'm surprised no other planet's developed the capability in that long a time," Charley mused.

"Many other scientists are actively engaged in the pursuit of that knowledge, but none have been successful, so far," Mr. Winble replied. "We believe there is something on their planet that helped them achieve this breakthrough, but they do not allow immigration; and they are very strict on exports. No one associated with the process is allowed to leave the planet, either as an entity or a corporeal. The penalty for violating any of these rules is death."

"Wow!" Josh said. "They are serious about that, aren't they?"

"With good reason, Mr. Josh. There are races in our universe which would use the knowledge for evil ends."

The sound of a chime interrupted Winble. "It is time to start," he said. "We are to sit at this table." Winble pointed out a table and three chairs in front of the bench used by the Council.

"Is there a force field in here, Mr. Winble?" Josh asked.

"Oh yes. It is a special field which allows us to handle normal objects, like any kind of exhibit coming into evidence."

They took their seats and Winble handed Josh a combination earpiece and microphone. "Here, put this on. It will translate the proceedings for you. All Council sessions are held in Giran. It is the closest thing there is to a universal language."

"It's okay, I can speak Giran," Josh assured him.

"Put it on anyway. Some of the council members have heavy accents," Winble said.

Josh put on the headset and was amused by the somewhat cryptic translation. Josh smiled broadly at Mr. Winble. "Sounds like those recordings you get on automated help systems back on Earth."

"It is a computer translation. Please excuse the awkward phrasing," Winble said.

A person Josh deduced was the equivalent of a bailiff in the television courts he was familiar with rose from a console and began to speak, "The Grand Council of Entity Affairs is now in session. Fall silent before the esteemed Councilors and learn justice." He pressed a button on a hand held unit, and four sounds like cathedral bells permeated the room. The buzz of conversation ceased immediately.

The bailiff resumed. "The Council will hear the charges of misconduct at the Earth terminal as brought by Chief Helper Winble of Gira. Is Mr. Winble present in the hall?"

"Here, Grand Councilor." Winble answered in the customary manner by addressing the head of the Council.

The bailiff went on. "Please present your case."

Winble presented a good deal of computer evidence to show the high incidence of entity anomalies on Earth, and the Council members nodded in understanding, though Josh wasn't sure he understood a bit of it.

Next he called Charley to the stand. The bailiff produced a small metal plate, and Charley placed his right hand upon it.

"Do you swear that the evidence you are about to give is the truth?" the bailiff asked.

"I do," Charley answered, and the small plate glowed a soft blue for a moment.

"What caused that?" Josh whispered to Winble as he pointed

out the glowing piece of metal.

"It is the sign the oath has been registered and that your great grandfather is sincere in his statement," Winble whispered back.

Charlie sat down in the witness chair, and Mr. Winble approached him.

"Mr. Bastin, did you make a visit to the Earth terminal on 14.2.3768.9?"

"Yes, I did."

"And, what did you find there?"

"I found a provisional terminal established in one half of the buildin', and part o' the other half bein' used for storage. On Earth they call it a warehouse."

"Was there any other facility in the warehouse?"

"Yes there was an entity fusion chamber, and machines for creatin' entity coffins."

The Council reacted in shock to Charley's statement. The Grand Councilor spoke first.

"Mr. Bastin, many terminals also serve as entity fusion facilities. Why did you find this one unusual?"

"Your Worship, the people on Earth don't know 'bout such things as that. The place is the work of some Ulans who are in cahoots with one Mr. Wycham of Earth on some sort of secret program involving entity fusion."

"Why do you say the program is secret, Mr. Bastin?" The older woman asked the question.

"My grandson took over responsibility for the Earth Cargans after I died," Charley said.

The Quazzan interrupted. "Do you mean to tell us that your corporeal body is dead, Mr. Bastin?"

"Unfortunately so, your Worship."

The Quazzan turned to the Grand Councilor. "Are we in the habit of accepting testimony from deceased persons?"

"In this particular case, I will allow Mr. Bastin's testimony. He is more familiar with Earth customs and circumstances than any of our people, having lived his entire life on the planet. Proceed Mr. Bastin," The Grand Counselor said.

"Thank you, Your Worship," Charley said. "As I was sayin', Earth don't know 'bout knowledge transfer programs. Only a small group of Earth people even got Cargans. That makes the entity fusion stuff very suspicious to my way o' thinkin', 'ticularly since it's bein' supervised by Wycham."

Winble continued. "Mr. Bastin, have you seen this type of operation before?"

"Yes, once afore, a few years back. I was part of a team that cracked an identity theft ring on Garga 4. The Ulans were also part of that operation since they got the power to manipulate entities. They provide the muscle, so to speak."

"I refer the Council to our Exhibit B, a transcription of the trial in the referenced case." The Council members consulted their computer screens. "You will note the involvement of Ulans is well documented. I have no further questions for Mr. Bastin. The Council may question him now."

Winble returned to his seat beside Josh while Charley scanned the Council members for any sign of questions. One of the Girans spoke.

"Mr. Bastin, I'm familiar with your good work as an Assistant Helper and your extensive travels around the universe, but why are you so suspicious of this man Wycham?"

"I did business with him on Earth, and I know him to be a

ruthless, power hungry man who'll stop at nothin' to get what he wants. Somehow, he managed to convince my grandson to put the Cargans in his warehouse, and that raised my suspicions in the first place. The fact that he's involved with Ulans makes me even more suspicious."

One of the Fundor members spoke next. "Your Worship, I do a lot of business on Ula, and I have been puzzled by a recent turn-around in their parliament which may have something to do with Mr. Bastin's discovery."

"Speak," the Grand Councilor said.

"For many years the Ulan parliament has been opposed to any form of mineral exploitation in one particular sector of the northern polar regions of their planet. Though they area is rich in many valuable ores, it is also sacred to the Garibbah sect, and out of respect for the Garribans, all commercial activity is banned there. That is, it has been banned until now. It seems several key members of parliament recently changed their position from opposition to support under the influence of one Manjahba who owns a good percentage of the land in question. The vote is very close now, and only a few more members would need to change sides to swing the issue in Manjahba's favor. If he were granted exclusive rights to the minerals in the area, it would make him even wealthier than he is now. I think it is no coincidence that some of those members changing their votes have also made trips to Earth in the last few weeks. Mr. Bastin's discovery of entity transfer equipment where no knowledge retention program is in place convinces me some-thing illegal involving the Earth terminal might be in process."

The Grand Councilor spoke again. "Mr. Winble, I think we have heard quite enough to order a thorough investigation of the Earth terminal, but do you have any more witnesses?"

"Only one, Your Worship," Winble said.

"Very well, present your witness," the Grand Councilor replied.

"I call Mr. Josh Smith of Earth."

Josh rose and moved to the witness chair. The bailiff placed the metal plate under Josh's hand, and he was surprised to find it was warm, almost hot.

"Do you swear that the evidence you are about to give is the truth?" the bailiff asked.

"I do," Josh answered. He noted the metal plate now glowed a light green, and wondered what was wrong. He felt a burning sensation in the back of his head and turned instinctively toward the woman Winble identified as a Truth Reader. She stared at him coldly, and he began to worry he might harm Winble's case more than aid it. The woman spoke.

"Young man, do your parents know you are here?"

"No ma'am, they don't."

"Why did you deceive them?" she asked.

"I had to. You see my Dad's not my Dad since he went to the Earth terminal. I think he's been operated on by that entity machine Great Grandpa Charley was talking about."

Several Council members suppressed laughs at the boy's naiveté, but the Grand Councilor called for order and nodded to the Truth Reader.

"What makes you think your father has been changed?" she said.

"Lots of little stuff. He likes cauliflower now, and he never liked it before."

Mr. Winble noticed the puzzled expression on the woman's

face and interrupted. "Cauliflower is a vegetable grown only on Earth, Your Worship."

"Thank you, Mr. Winble. Continue," the Grand Councilor said.

"What else, Josh?" the Truth Reader asked.

"He actually liked my loud music, and he always wanted me to keep it quiet before."

Winble broke in again. "On Earth, they have a form of music known as 'rock'. It is much like the zibble music of Phobos 3. The adult Earth people find it somewhat obnoxious while the teenaged children are enamored with it. It would be very unusual for an Earth adult to like such music."

"Thank you, again. Proceed," the Grand Councilor said.

The Truth Reader sat back in her chair and addressed the Grand Councilor. "Your Worship, the boy harbors the lie he told his parents in order to appear before this Council. I will alert the Council if I detect any falsehoods in his testimony."

"Thank you, Councilwoman Varda. You may proceed, Mr. Winble."

Before Winble could proceed, the Sellan member spoke. "Mr. Smith, did your father make any specific remarks about your music?"

"Yes, Sir. He said it 'had the harmony of the spheres'."

The Sellan smiled broadly and turned to the Grand Councilor. "Your Worship, this factor clinches Mr. Winble's case. That particular expression is only used by Ulans. No Earth person would have any knowledge of it. I think we should vote immediately."

"I agree, Councilor Pattle. Are there any objections?" The Grand Councilor looked left and right at his fellow members and noted no dissent. "Very well. All in favor of an investigation of the Earth terminal signify by the usual sign."

Seven spectral hands went into the air with one finger raised from a clenched fist. Josh found it hard to control his laughter since each member raised his or her middle finger.

"The vote is unanimous. You will be in charge of the investigation, Mr. Winble. Normal Council rules will apply, but should you deem life is in danger, you have our permission to take such action as is necessary to save lives. Otherwise, we will expect your findings in fourteen Giran days at the Council meeting to be held then. The Council is adjourned."

The bailiff pushed a button, and the cathedral chimes rang again. The courtroom stood as the Council filed out. Only Varda remained behind and glided toward Josh. She presented her cheek and Josh brushed his against it. He felt the wisdom of the ages and knew this woman was far older than her appearance would indicate.

"It is a pleasure to meet someone from Earth," she said. "I always suspected Earth people were much too devious to be trusted because of my acquaintance with your great grandfather." She shot Charley a stern glance, but he only smiled warmly at her. "But, you have shown me your people cannot hide even a justifiable lie. Your parents must be very proud of you."

"Thank you, ma'am. It's a pleasure to meet you too."

"Take good care of this boy, Charley Earth, or you'll hear from me personally," Varda said.

"Don't worry about that, Varda," Charley said as he presented his cheek to the woman.

Josh thought the two adults spent a bit longer than usual in contact, and as they walked from the room he asked, "How do you know her, Great Grandpa?"

"Varda and I are old friends. We've met on Mythos a couple of times."   Charley winked at Josh who failed to grasp the significance of the remark at first, then, he remembered the reason for Mythos' existence.

"Great grandpa! Not you and her and..." Josh stumbled on the words.

"You surprised?" Charley asked.

"Well, she is a bit old."

"Nonsense! She's a vital, active woman for 150, but she was even better at 123. Besides, it's not your body that's doin' it, it's the other creatures, and they're real go getters."   Charley laughed all the way to the terminal.

CHAPTER 38

As soon as the trio reached the Gira terminal, Winble went into action. He left Josh and Charley immediately and vanished into a section of the helper room reserved for the Chief Helper.

"Winble'll get with the Marshals and plan out the raid on the Earth terminal. There ain't much we can do now, so you might as well get back home," Charley said.

"I've only got one question, Great Grandpa. How do we get Dad back the way he was?" Josh asked.

"We'll have to get him to the Earth terminal as a entity so's we can reverse the fusion process. We can only do that when we have control over the place. I'll let you know as soon as Winble has everything set up. There's lots o' other folks that'll want to be put back in their own bodies, and we'll do every-thing we can to get them back to normal as quick as possible. The main thing is not to tip off Wycham or any o' his agents. You'll have to make sure your Dad don't get suspicious."

"That'll be pretty hard to do. Every time I look at him I see some kind of monster behind his eyes."

"Just the same, you gotta keep him in the dark about all this. If Wycham gets wind of a raid, he'll destroy or move any incriminating evidence. We're countin' on you, Josh."

"I'll do whatever it takes, Great Grandpa."

"That's my boy! Now git back home, and I'll come see you

when it's all set up."

Josh reluctantly made his way to the Hellos Cargan and soon found himself back home. He awoke to find his mother wearing her pajamas and a robe and seated in a chair commanding a good view of her son while he was attached to the Cargan.

"Hi Mom, is something wrong?" Josh asked.

"I couldn't sleep, and I came in to talk to you. I found you glued to that thing, and the room as cold as ice. What were you doing?"

"Where is Dad?" Josh asked.

"He's in bed, sound asleep. Lately, he almost goes into a coma when he finally nods off. Tell me what you were doing?"

Josh decided it was time to clue his mother in. "You gotta believe I'm telling you the truth even though it sounds crazy."

She cocked her head to one side and studied her son. She hadn't seen him this serious about anything in a long time. "Okay, go ahead."

"You also got to promise you won't tell Dad any of what I'm going to tell you."

"All right, I promise. Now, tell me."

"This sculpture is not a sculpture, it's a Cargan. You use it to travel to other planets. I just been with great grandpa Charley on Gira, and we looked in on the Earth terminal. He's been suspicious of Wycham all along, but Dad being changed after his trip to Miami convinced him something was wrong. He's going to get the Grand Council to raid the terminal so we can get Dad back."

Evelyn sat with her eyes wide and her mouth gaping open. It took her a moment to recover. "Are you on some kind of hallucinogen?"

"No, Mom, it's all real. I'll show you." Josh picked up the Mythos Cargan and handed it to her. "Grab it in the worn spots, and I'll tell you what to do."

A zombie-like Evelyn did as her son asked.

"I'll hum a note for you. It's the activation note for this Cargan. Don't forget it. It's the only way to get back home. Before I do that, you have to understand what's going to happen so you won't panic."

"Josh, you're serious about this," she said. "This is not some kind of joke is it?"

"No, Mom, this is serious stuff. Now, when you get to Mythos, you'll be a ghost with your hands inside a tree. Don't let go of what you're holding on to. You can look around, but don't leave that tree. When you're ready to come back just hum the note again. Got it?"

"I've got it. Give me the note."

Josh hummed the activation note and watched as his mother went rigid. She was only out for a few seconds before she returned to her normal self.

"Oh my God! That was surreal. Was I actually on another planet or just dreaming?"

"No dream. You were on Mythos. It's a kind of strange planet. Did you see anything going on around you?" Josh was afraid a satyr and nymph might be in action under the tree.

"No, I only saw a forest, but I did notice I was a ghost."

"You were an entity, Mom. That's how you travel using Cargans."

"What were you doing on that planet, if you truly were on another planet?"

"I only used Mythos as a way to get to Gira. That's where Great Grandpa is."

Evelyn interrupted. "Josh, your great grandfather is dead."

"I know, but his entity's alive on Gira. I went there to tell him about Dad, and we went to the Earth terminal in Miami to check it out. He said they've got an entity transfer operation going on there, and they've melded Dad with some Ulan. I had to testify about all that to the Grand Council, and they decided to raid the place. He's coming back for me when that happens so I can go along. We'll think up some way of getting Dad down there so we can make him right again, but I don't know what that will be."

Evelyn recoiled in horror. "You mean I've been sleeping with some alien?"

"It's Dad's body, but his entity's been changed."

"Well, that sure explains a lot of things. I'd begun to suspect your father was on some kind of dope, or something."

"Mom, it's important that Dad not get suspicious. If he gets wise, he could alert Wycham, and we might not be able to get Dad back. You can't let on you know about him."

"That's going to be very hard, Josh. Your father insists on having sex nearly every night, and now that I know it's not him, it'll be hard to pretend it is."

Josh thought about the situation. He had never experienced real sex, but he could appreciate the special bond between a man and a woman the activity required. He knew his mother and father were very much in love with each other, and his mother would surely feel as if she were betraying her husband by having sex with the fused entity.

"I know it's hard for you, Mom, but you have to make sure

he doesn't catch on. It's the only way we have any chance of getting Dad back."

"I understand, Josh. God! It's going to be the hardest thing I've ever done, but you're right, I have to do it. How long until this raid takes place?"

"I don't know for sure. Great grandpa seems to think it'll happen soon."

"It can't be soon enough for me. I want my real husband back. Please let me know what's going on from now on. Will you, Josh?"

"Sure, Mom. As soon as Great Grandpa tells me anything, I'll let you know."

The two parted to resume as much of a normal life as the situation would allow.

CHAPTER 39

Wycham beamed proudly as the new machine went through its paces. This device would rid them of the incriminating items left over from their entity fusion operations, the things Manjahba called "remainder entities", and destroy all indications anything was amiss at the Earth terminal. With the capability to eliminate any anomalies in entity signals caused by these remainders, they could substitute their own people for anyone unlucky enough to pass through their operation, and leave no trace of their action. Now that several of their agents were in place on critical planets, the plan could proceed more rapidly.

Manjahba even cracked a small smile as the first remainder entity vanished into the machine. The pair watched as the blinking lights on the indicator panel showed the progress of the operation, and the whir of cooling fans signaled normal operation of the vast array of electronic devices inside the large cabinet.

The Ulan at the controls was an entity, but Manjahba assured Wycham the man was capable of operating machines built on Earth. He went about his task with cold precision, adjusting levers in response to indications on the large flat-panel display. Things seemed to be going well until the Ulan turned to Manjahba and pointed to a blinking red cursor. He spoke in the Ulan language Wycham barely understood, but the old man caught enough to know there was a problem, and this was confirmed when the device suddenly shut down.

"What is it, Manjahba?" Wycham asked.

"The remainder entity was destroyed, but the clean-up operation was not complete. We will need to have your people make some adjustments before we can continue. It is not wise to leave any indication of a destroyed entity where the Marshals might be able to find it."

"Very well, I'll get my people on it in the morning. Does your man know what needs to be done?" Wycham asked.

"Yes, he will possess your technician and guide the repairs in that manner. It should only take a few hours."

"Tell him to be here at nine our time in the morning." Wycham turned to leave, but an entity appearing through the wall of the terminal caught his attention.

"Mr. Wycham, Manjahba, I have some bad news for you." It was the tall Quazzan from the Grand Council.

"What is it, Bruggar?" Manjahba asked.

"The entity called Charley Earth, and the Smith boy have discovered your operation. You have less than 24 earth hours before the Marshals will be here in full force."

"You told me Charley Earth was dead," Manjahba said as he fixed a murderous glare on Wycham.

"His corporeal body is dead, but he must have used a Cargan to escape it before he died. He complicates matters somewhat, but we can take care of him easily now that we have Smith on our side. The boy will obey his father–it's Charley Earth I'm worried about. We can't let him find any evidence of our operations when the Marshals arrive," Wycham said.

"You should have destroyed that boy while you had the

chance, Wycham." Manjahba was obviously perturbed.

"We have several hours before they get here according to Bruggar. If we hurry, they'll be too late to find anything," Wycham said. "I'll get my people in here right away to repair the entity destruction unit, and we should be rid of any remainders by morning. We can explain this machinery on the basis of our plan to create a knowledge transfer program on Earth. I'll call my people right now."

"It's the middle of your night here, Wycham. Will your people respond?" Bruggar asked.

"They will when I tell them about the large bonus they'll receive for their efforts. Never fear." Wycham left to make his calls.

CHAPTER 40

A grave-like chill enveloped Josh's body, awakening him from a sound sleep. His Great Grandfather's voice filled his head.

"Wake up, Josh! We gotta get movin'."

Josh sat up in bed and spoke a bit too loudly, "What's up, Great Grandpa?"

"Quiet, Son! Think–don't speak. We don't want ta wake up yer pa."

Josh switched to mental mode. *"Okay, what's up?"*

"The raid's comin' off in a few minutes. The Marshals'r all assembled and ready ta go with Winble leading the way."

Josh looked at his alarm clock and saw four AM. *"That was really fast work, Great Grandpa. I didn't expect you back so soon."*

Charley seemed to be very impatient. "We gotta move fast. You don't need to change clothes. Your pajamas are okay."

"I'm ready. I want to be there when you bust Wycham."

"That may not happen, but we'll sure get to the bottom of whatever's goin' on there. Let's get goin'–we gotta move fast."

"Why the big rush?"

"There was a leak. You remember Varda the Truth Reader?"

"Sure, she's the lady you take to Mythos." Josh winked at Charley.

"We don't do that no more, and that's beside th' point. Well, she happened to catch the Quazzan talking on his communicator and thought he sounded funny. She read his mind and found out he was in cahoots with Manjahba and Wycham. She called Winble right away so's he could speed up th' raid."

"*Is Dad in any danger?*"

"He could be. The first thing they'll try to do is destroy any remainder entities. We don't think they've got the capability to do that yet, but they're mighty close. You ready t' go?"

"Sure, I'm ready," Josh said.

"Then git goin'" Charley commanded as he started toward the Mythos Cargan.

"Wait!" Josh shouted at him.

"Quiet! You'll wake up yer Dad."

"How do we get Dad back to normal?" Josh whispered.

"We'll need to get him into the terminal as an entity so's we can work the process backwards, but we can take care of that later. Come on!"

"Great Grandpa, I promised my Mom I'd tell her about the raid."

Charley thought for a moment. "You can't do that without waking up your Pa, but I'll possess Evelyn and fill her in. I'll be right back. You wait here."

Charley moved through the walls to the master bedroom. Evelyn had distanced herself from the Ulan/Roger as far as the king sized bed would allow, and Charley knew this would make his job easier since the Ulan would not sense his presence so easily. He moved into Evelyn's body.

Evelyn sat up in bed and gasped at the sensation produced by Charley's entity.

"For God's sake lay down, Evelyn. It's just me," Charley transmitted his thoughts to her silently.

"Charley?" she said.

"Shhhh! Think – don't talk. Is he still asleep?"

Evelyn turned to see Roger still asleep and snoring softly.

"He's still out. Why are you here?" Evelyn thought.

"The raid's on for tonight. Josh and me are goin' to watch, but you need to keep Roger here until the terminal's secure."

"How will I know that?"

"We'll find some way of getting' him to the terminal so's we can put him back the way he was. Just go along with whatever happens like everything's normal."

"Do it quickly, Charley. I want my Roger back."

"Just don't panic and keep your cool. We should have everything back to normal by morning. I gotta go now. Talk to you later."

The cold sensation left Evelyn and she lay in bed wide awake. She knew sleep would be elusive now that the wheels were in motion. She only hoped she could keep up her act a while longer.

Charley rejoined Josh. "Now remember, leave plenty o' room fer yer pa t' grab the Cargan above yer hands. We needs t' git him ta Miami as a entity, and this is th' only Cargan we got."

"I got it. Go ahead," Josh replied.

Charlie vanished, and Josh waited a moment before grasping the Cargan as low on the grips as possible. He soon joined Charley on Gira. The terminal was a flurry of activity in every corner. Dozens of Marshal entities were assembled around Mr. Winble who was giving them instructions in a language Josh guessed was Ulan. They carried no weapons, and Josh remembered that real items could not be transported through Cargans. He wondered how they would be able to cope with the security Wycham surely had in place around the terminal on Earth, but it dawned on him that Earth weapons would be useless against entities anyway, and Wycham's goons could not transport weapons.

"We're ready, Winble," Charley shouted to the Sellan.

"Very good, Mr. Charley. We will go now. We'll see you at the terminal.

The Marshals lined up at the Earth Cargan and vanished one by one. Winble was the last one out.

"Why can't the Marshalls just grab Dad at my house, Great Grandpa?" Josh asked.

"We need him as an entity, remember. Come on, we wanna be there when the action starts. If you ain't never seen Marshals in operation, you've got a real treat commin'."

They moved to the Cargan, and when they reached the terminal the Marshals were already in action.

"Let's get over here in one corner," Charley said as he pointed the way to the only part of the terminal not involved in a strange sort of hand to hand combat between the Marshals and twenty or so Ulans. Josh needed no prodding to avoid the swirling entities. As he moved, one of the Marshals brushed against him, and he felt a sharp pain in his shoulder.

"Ouch, that hurt!" Josh blurted out as if expecting the Marshal to apologize, but the large entity was too engrossed in his battle with a shorter Ulan to notice Josh.

"You need to get out of their way, Josh. They can't take time to avoid hurting you. It looks like Wycham and Manjahba have decided to put up a fight." The two entities found a safe place and watched the battle unfold.

Josh was amazed at the sights and sounds of the scene before him. The Marshals moved like actors in a martial arts movie punching and kicking at the Ulans who defended themselves in like manner. An Ulan entity flew through the air and landed at Josh's feet. He hit the concrete floor with a thud and lay there a moment in obvious pain before one of the Marshals picked him up and threw him back across the terminal, impaling him on one of the Cargans. The Ulan screamed as if he were actually being injured and lay there for a moment before vanishing.

"Did you see that? What happened to that one, Great Grandpa?" Josh asked.

"That's the Cargan they're usin' to send these goons into custody. There's more Marshals waitin' for 'em at the other end. Winble thought we might have to put up a fight here." Charlie smiled enthusiastically as another Ulan met the same fate.

Mr. Winble interrupted their enjoyment of the spectacle. "Mr. Charley, one of the prisoners says Wycham and Manjahba are in the process of destroying remainder entities even now. Take these two Marshals and stop them."

"I got it, Winble." Charley and the two Marshals moved toward the wall separating the terminal from the deadly machinery. No one seemed to notice Josh as he tagged along behind.

On the other side of the wall, a ghoulish process unfolded. Several boxes sat in front of a machine the size of a compact car, while empty boxes of the same type stood against the far wall. An Ulan was busy manipulating the controls of a console and watching a flat-panel display. Only Wycham saw the four entities enter the room.

"Look out, Manjahba! We have company," Wycham shouted.

The large Ulan turned to face the Marshals while two more goons appeared from the warehouse portion of the building. The Marshals engaged the goons, and Josh was surprised to see his great grandfather move toward Manjahba.

"Keep going!" Manjahba called back over his shoulder as he grasped Charley by one arm and flipped the old man against the pile of empty boxes.

To Josh's surprise, the boxes clattered to the floor in disarray, but Charley shook his head free of cobwebs and charged Manjahba. They punched and kicked each other unmercifully, and Josh was enthralled by their fight until he noticed the next entity to be fed into the machine was his father. Wycham was busy moving the box into place while the Ulan at the console adjusted his dials and levers.

"Great Grandpa! They're going to do Dad next!" Josh yelled as he pointed to Wycham straining to move the metal coffin into place.

At that moment, two more Marshals appeared from the terminal and seized Manjahba. Charley looked at the box and screamed, "Nooooo!"

Josh watched in horror as Charley dove into the machine. The display in front of the Ulan operator came alive with red, flashing warnings, and the machine made grinding and shrieking sounds so loud Josh thought his eardrums were about to burst. The room fell silent as the console's indicator lights all went red and the display changed to one message Josh was surprised to see was in English. It read, "Fatal Error in Main

Processing Executable".

The Marshals were now in complete control of the terminal. The Ulan entities were being led off one by one. Even Manjahba was escorted out of the room. Wycham tried to run, but two Marshals subdued him easily, much to the old man's surprise.

Josh stood looking at the box holding his father's entity. Only the head and shoulders were inside the machine. The rest of his father lay deathly still in the coffin-like container. Josh moved to the box and placed a hand on his father's chest as if checking for a heartbeat. There was none, and the sensation was one of cold stillness. He removed his hand and began to cry.

"Oh Dad, I'm sorry we were too late." Josh knelt beside the box and cried unashamedly. He was not aware of Winble kneeling beside him.

"I'm sorry, Mr. Josh." The Sellan placed his hand on Josh's arm.

Josh felt the warm sensation and turned to see the Sellan through eyes blurred with tears. "Is he dead, Mr. Winble?" Josh asked.

"I do not know. We must obtain an expert opinion on this. Wait here while I find Doctor Bosius."

"Who's he?" Josh asked, but the Sellan was already through the wall into the terminal.

Winble returned with a distinguished looking entity following close behind. "This is Dr. Bosius, Josh. He is an expert in entity medicine."

The doctor offered his cheek to Josh who reciprocated, noticing a medicinal twinge in the process. "Help him, Dr. Bosius. He's my Dad."

"I know, Son. Give me a minute." The doctor knelt by the box and placed his hand on Roger's entity in several locations. He rose and moved to the console. After pushing several buttons, the display came to life, and the doctor fiddled with several levers and slides until the screen filled once again with various charts and graphs. Bosius smiled as he turned back to Josh and Mr. Winble.

"I think you got here just in time, but how did you stop the machine?" Bosius asked.

"I didn't. Great Grandpa did," Josh answered.

"How did he do that?" Bosius's face held a blank expression of disbelief.

"He just dove into the machine," Josh replied. "He should be around here somewhere."

Josh looked around the room and called out for his great grandfather in vain.

"Where did Great Grandpa go?" Josh asked Bosius.

Bosius looked at Winble with a puzzled expression.

"Mr. Charley is the entity of a deceased person," Mr. Winble said.

"I see," Dr. Bosius said as he tapped one of the charts on the display. "That explains the unusual readings. Charley must have known his entity would severely disrupt the machine."

"Is Great Grandpa okay?" Josh asked, fearing he had not only lost his father but also the great grandfather he had come to love in so short a time.

Winble turned to the doctor who was shaking his head sadly. "Is he gone, Dr. Bosius?" Winble asked.

"I'm afraid he is. I'm sorry, Josh, but your great grandfather must have substituted his entity to save your father's. It was his entity that was destroyed. I'm sorry."

Josh moved to the machine and placed his hands on the sides of the contraption. Once more the tears streamed down his face as he spoke to the large, white box. "Great Grandpa Charley, I'm sorry I never got to know you better while you were alive. I thought you were just a senile old man telling weird stories. I never dreamed you were one of the bravest people I've ever known. Thanks for saving my Dad. I don't know how we'll ever repay you, but Dad and I will do everything we can to make sure you're not forgotten. Goodbye, Great Grandpa."

Bosius worked frantically now. Two Marshalls moved Roger's entity to a cabinet and placed it inside.

In the rush to place Roger's entity in the cabinet, no one noticed that a very small piece of Roger's skull was missing. Evidently, the destruction machine had done some damage, but it was in a location hard to notice given the confusion and frantic activity of the moment.

Bosius turned to Josh.

"Where is your father's corporeal body now?"

"He's back home in Santa Cruz," Josh answered through his tears.

"We must get his entity, here as soon as possible, there's no time to lose. Can you convince him to come here as an entity?"

Winble broke in. "I don't think Mr. Josh would be too convincing in his current mental state, but I think I know a way to summon Mr. Smith here quickly."

Winble turned to a Marshall. "Bring in Mr. Wycham."

Two Marshalls escorted Wycham in. He protested loudly at his treatment, demanding his constitutional rights as they did.

"Be quiet, Wycham," Winble ordered. "We need you to make a phone call to summon Mr. Smith."

"Hah! Why do you think I'd help you?" Wycham laughed.

"I didn't think you would, but Marshall Mungo, here, will help persuade you."

Another Marshall moved into Wycham's body. The old man went stiff and spoke more quietly now. "What do you want him to say, Mr. Winble?"

"Make him dial the Smith's in Santa Cruz on this Earth communication device," Winble indicted the phone. "Let's see, what would bring him here?"

"My corporeal body is at the Cargan back home," Josh shouted. "Maybe if you told him I was in trouble, he'd come and bring Mom too?"

"A good idea, Mr. Josh, but with only one Cargan available at your residence, only one person may be summoned here. I think your father would respond better to another kind of message. Mungo, have Wycham call Smith and tell him there's a problem here requiring his expertise. I'm sure Wycham has some idea of what that is."

Mungo moved Wycham to the phone and forced him through the message.

"He will be here very soon, Mr. Winble," Mungo said then left Wycham.

"That's illegal, Winble. I'll complain to the Grand Council about unauthorized possession," Wycham fumed.

"I'm sure they will be very interested," Winble sneered.

In a few moments, two Marshalls appeared with Roger's entity in tow.

"Is this the man you were looking for, Mr. Winble?" one of

them asked.

"That's the guy!" Josh shouted. "How do we get him back to normal, sir?" he asked Dr. Bosius.

"It's a simple procedure, but too complicated to explain right now. We must move rapidly to save you father now that he has been exposed to the destruction machine," Bosius said. He turned and gave instructions to the Marshals in a language Josh did not understand.

The Marshals holding Roger's melded entity pulled him toward one of the large cabinets in the other end of the room. As they dragged him off, the phony Roger screamed, "No! You can't do this to me. Josh, make them stop. I'm your father. Help me!"

Winble moved to Josh's side as he noticed the tears begin to flow. "Dad?" Josh said.

"That is not your father, Josh," Winble said. "This entity faces a long prison sentence, possibly even destruction, for his crimes. He will do or say anything he thinks might save him."

"Josh!?" the entity made one last plea as the Marshals closed the cabinet door.

"Are you sure this is going to work, Dr. Bosius?" Josh asked.

"I've done this procedure dozens of times, son. It will only take a few minutes. Please wait over there." Bosius indicated an area away from the consoles and cabinets.

Mr. Winble accompanied Josh to the designated place, and the pair watched anxiously as Bosius worked the controls. The Marshals holding Wycham joined them.

"I hope the cops here throw the book at you, Mr. Wycham," Josh said.

Wycham laughed aloud. "What kind of charges would they

bring? Your father and I have a contract covering this terminal and the ultimate disposition of the Cargans. The police here in Miami will find I'm living up to the full letter of that contract. I've committed no crime here on Earth."

Winble broke in, "You have committed a host of crimes against the Grand Council, Mr. Wycham. You will probably be barred from entity travel for life."

Wycham laughed even harder. "You must stop. You're really making my sides ache from all this comedy."

"I don't think it's so funny," Josh said.

"Fools! Do you think I give a damn about the Grand Council? They have no enforcement powers here on Earth." Wycham spat the words at Winble as the Marshals holding him tightened their grip.

"Not yet, Mr. Wycham," Winble said. "But we will be taking over this terminal now, and your access to the universe will be considerably curtailed. I will also advise Mr. Smith to move the Cargans to another location as soon as possible. Take him away." The Marshals holding Wycham led him out to the terminal portion of the warehouse.

"What a jerk, great grandpa sure had him pegged right," Josh said.

"I always said Charley was a good judge of people."

Josh turned at the sound of the familiar voice and saw his father's entity standing with arms wide open.

"Dad! Is it really you now?" Josh cried as he rushed to his father's arms. In his haste he nearly passed right through him.

"Easy, easy. It really is me. Dr. Bosius says I should get back to my corporeal body as soon as possible, and I know your mother is worried sick."

The Marshalls opened the other cabinet now, and it was empty.

Josh noticed the empty box. "What happened to the other entity?"

Bosius answered him. "It's gone, Josh. Because your father's entity was exposed to the destruction machine, the Ulan entity was destroyed as a result of the residual radiation. I think your father is fine, but I'll feel better if he sees one of your physicians as soon as possible. There may be some side effects."

"I'll do that, Bosius, but we'd better get back home," Roger said. He turned to Josh. "Son, I'm proud of you."

"It's good to have you back, Dad, but did they tell you Great Grandpa's gone?"

"Yes, Dr. Bosius told me. I understand he saved my life."

"He dove right into the machine as soon as he saw you there. He was a brave guy. He even took on Manjahba, and was beating him when he saw you." Josh began to cry again in spite of his resolve to be stoic.

"I'll miss him," Roger said. "But, we need to get back so I can tell your mother the good news. Do you need us for anything more?" Roger addressed the question to Mr. Winble.

"No, Mr. Smith, we will clean up operations here and leave a small security force. I will be making my report to the Grand Council next week, and I may need you to testify then. Would you be willing to cooperate?"

"Anything you need. Just get word to me," Roger said as he offered his cheek to Mr. Winble.

Winble brushed Roger's cheek and broke into a broad smile. "I see you are really back to normal now, thanks to Dr. Bosius."

"I feel fine, but what will you do with Wycham?"

"We will take him to the Council, and I'm sure they will bar him for life. What can you do to him here on Earth?" Winble asked.

"Not much, I'm afraid. He hasn't really violated any Earth laws. I may even have to leave the Cargans in this warehouse," Roger said. "How can we prevent Wycham from starting all over again?"

"There will be a contingent of Marshals on duty here until you can move the Cargans, Mr. Smith. You need not worry about a repeat performance by Mr. Wycham," Winble said.

Roger brushed cheeks with Winble. "Thank you, Mr. Winble. We are forever in your debt."

"Not me, Mr. Smith. Charley Earth and your son are the ones deserving of your gratitude," Winble said.

Josh was next. "Thanks, Mr. Winble. I'll look you up the next time I go to Gira."

"Goodbye, Mr. Josh. I will look forward to your next visit."

Josh turned to his father. "We need to get the Gira Cargan as soon as we can. We really need two around the house now that you and Mom know about entity travel."

"Your mother knows too?"

"Yeah, I had to fill her in when she noticed you were different."

"We'll have to have a long talk about this stuff back home, but right now, the main job is to get back home. I take it you know the way."

"Sure, Dad. I'll lead the way."

Father and son made their way through the terminal, which was now swarming with entities they guessed were representatives of the press from various planets, along with some curious entity travelers.

Josh led his father back through the lengthy route to their home. Roger had to make the final transfer first as he was using the Cargan after Josh was already on it.. Evelyn was waiting in her nightgown with tears streaming down her face. She looked at Roger warily as he returned to normal.

"Is this really you, Roger?"

Roger laughed as he swept his wife into his arms. "It's me again, Darling, all me and only me. Everything's back to normal now."

Evelyn kissed him passionately, then pushed him back to arm's length to study his reaction. At that point, Josh awoke.

"It's really him, Mom. It's Dad again for sure."

Once more Evelyn kissed Roger, much to Josh's embarrassment.

"Jeez, you guys. Cut it out," Josh protested.

Evelyn looked behind Josh. "Where's Charley?"

"He's dead, Mom," Josh answered.

"I know he's dead, but where is he? He should be celebrating with us."

"I mean his entity's dead too," Josh added. "He jumped into the machine when he saw Dad was next to be destroyed. He saved Dad's life."

Evelyn stared off into space as she spoke. "Your great grandfather was a very odd man, Josh. I never thought he cared much for anybody but himself and his business, but he finally did at least one good thing in his life."

Roger turned to Josh. "Why didn't you tell me about these things?" He motioned toward the Cargan.

"At first, I was afraid to, but then Great Grandpa told me to keep it a secret as long as possible. He was afraid you'd get the government involved," Josh said.

Roger sat down and stared at the Cargan. "Do you realize what this means?" He looked to Evelyn then to Josh. Evelyn's face was blank and Josh only shrugged. "It means we're not alone in the universe. There are other people out there."

"Duh!" Josh said. "I thought we knew that all along."

"Don't be impudent, Josh," Evelyn scolded.

"I mean, it only makes sense, doesn't it Dad?"

Roger sat pensively for a moment before replying. "I guess I did always believe we'd find other people someday. I just didn't think it'd be in my lifetime. This is a momentous discovery. It makes a man on the Moon look puny."

"Are you going to get the government involved?" Josh asked.

"No, I don't think so. The shock would be too much for people to absorb. Besides, they'd take control of the Cargans, and cut off our travels. I need to give that museum another thought also. Wycham may renege on the deal anyway, now that he can't use it for his schemes. I'll have to do some entity travel myself and see what I can find out about all of the science behind these things. Maybe there's a way to ease people into the idea of entity travel?"

"Yeah, we could go together, couldn't we Dad?" Josh asked.

Roger looked at the clock, noting it was still early morning. "We can talk about all of that later. Right now, I think we all need to go to bed and get some much needed sleep, but tonight we'll go out big-time to celebrate our good fortune," Roger said.

* * * * *

That night, Evelyn completed her "just before bed" routine when she felt Roger's arms around her waist. He buried his face in her neck and whispered, "Did you know your body has the harmony of the spheres?"

CHAPTER 41

Josh punched in Mr. Karrasnik's number and waited for an answer. As he expected, the call was routed to the man's voice mail. Josh left his message and turned back to his homework. A call from Bill Thompson interrupted his studies.

"What's up, Bill?" Josh answered.

"I got that counter all fixed up. I'm ready to go."

"Good, we can talk about how we're going to make the switch at practice Tuesday. I put in a call to Karrasnik, but I just got his voice mail. I'll make sure he'll let us in early to set up by telling him we have some new sound gear and want to check the acoustics."

"The only thing that bothers me is using Julie for bait. What if he tries something?"

"I don't think he'll do anything, but I'll be watching just in case."

"Okay, but make sure he doesn't trick you like he did last time."

Josh fumed at Bill's reference to the band's deal, but held his temper. "He won't make a fool out of me again, you can bet on that."

"Okay, see you at practice."

* * * * *

Tuesday night Julie changed into the costume she planned to

wear Saturday at the performance. The top showed a lot of bosom through strategically placed slits while also exposing a good deal of cleavage, and the short shorts looked impossible for any human girl to wear. Knee-high leather boots with four-inch heels completed the outfit. She entered the practice room, and all conversation stopped immediately.

"What do you think, guys?" she asked as she modeled provocatively in front of the band.

"Holy mackerel!" was all Willie Jenkins could manage.

"If Karrasnik doesn't flip over that, he's dead," Bill Thompson said.

Rodney Barnes only stared at her with his mouth open.

"That's great, Julie, but you'd better change back to regular clothes if we're going to get any practice in," Josh said. In his mind, he secretly wished he could see her on Mythos as she really was and not as some chubby nymph.

Julie obliged and returned to find the boys huddled over a diagram of the teen club Willie Jenkins prepared for planning their "switch the counter" plot. They made a place for her next to Josh.

"God! Look at us. We're like something out of a James Bond movie," Julie said.

"My Dad always says, 'If you fail to plan, you plan to fail'," Bill Jenkins said.

"Okay, guys. Here's how we do it," Josh took over and gave each member of the team an assignment. Julie would distract Karrasnik by asking him to check out her costume to see if it was too revealing. Josh and Rodney Barnes would keep an eye on her situation in case Karrasnik got out of hand. Bill Thompson would make the switch of the counters in the club office while Will Jenkins would test out the sound gear.

"I talked to Karrasnik, and he's agreed to let us in a half hour before he opens the doors. That should give us plenty of time. Bill's got the new counter fixed so he can't reset it. That will give us a true count on the gate. Now, let's get some practice in," Josh said.

The band went through its routine for Saturday with no problems, and the boys headed for home. Julie agreed to give Josh a lift, and they walked together to her car.

"I'm glad we're over that incident on Mythos. I can't believe what a jerk I was," Josh said.

"Well, I hope you learned a lesson about the way girls feel about that kind of thing."

"I sure did, and I guarantee it won't happen again. Have you thought any more about going to Mythos?"

"Yes, and I'm still not sure I'm ready for that just yet. Be patient with me, Josh, please."

"No problem. It's easy to be patient with someone like you."

The ride home passed with small talk and gossip about school. Julie kissed Josh goodnight, but offered no more than that.

* * * * *

Saturday night Karrasnik was waiting for them.

"You guys've got a half hour to set up and test your gear. I'll be in my office if you need me," Karrasnik said and turned to leave the stage.

"Oh, Mr. Karrasnik," Julie said.

"Yeah, what is it?"

"Would you come to the dressing room to check out my

costume for tonight? I want to make sure it's not too risqué. I brought a backup in case you don't think it's appropriate."

Josh noticed the manager's agitated state. The guy was almost drooling over the prospect of seeing a lot of Julie.

"Sure, sure, I'll be glad to check it out."

"Good, I'll go change. You wait here, and I'll open the door when I'm ready, okay?"

"Yeah, I'll wait here."

The boys set up the stage and Will busied himself making sound checks. Bill Thompson slipped away in the direction of the office. Fortunately, the rest rooms were located in the general vicinity, and he could leave without arousing suspicion. Rodney and Josh helped with the sound checks but positioned themselves where they would have an unobstructed view of the dressing room door.

A few minutes later, Julie opened the door, and Karrasnik's mouth dropped open at the sight of her.

"Come in and tell me what you think," Julie said.

Karrasnik walked into the dressing room and closed the door. Josh moved to the door and checked the knob to make sure it was not locked. He leaned close to the sill to hear any sign of distress from inside.

Bill Thompson appeared a minute later holding a counter over his head triumphantly. "I made the switch, and I checked this one out. He's got it rigged to stop counting at 400. What a jerk!"

"We figured that," Rodney said.

"Let me have it," Josh said as he held out a hand toward Bill. "When he catches wise to the switch, I'll spring this one on him and let him know we're also wise to him."

Bill handed Josh the counter, and Josh stowed it in his guitar case before leaning back against the sill. The first sound he heard was a muffled, "Mr. Karrasnik!" followed by a loud slapping sound.

Josh knocked on the door. "You ready, Julie?"

The dressing room grew quiet, then a somewhat rumpled Julie opened the door.

"Give me a minute, Josh. Mr. Karrasnik was just leaving."

A sheepish Karrasnik brushed his hair back into place and rubbed a red spot on his jaw then smiled lamely as he passed Josh on the way to his office.

"I see you took care of him," Josh said to Julie.

"He tried to grope me, but I smacked him a good one, and he decided to behave after he heard you knock. I'll be ready in a minute." She closed the door, and Josh returned to the stage.

Evidently, word had spread about the band. The club filled up quickly, and Rodney returned from a trip to the restroom to say there was still a line of people outside waiting to get in.

Julie was a smash hit, and she even had the band guys sweating a bit with her outfit and her seductive moves. The crowd demanded three encores before the curtains closed and the DJ took over. Karrasnik was not waiting to pay the band off, as usual, and Josh decided he'd caught on to the counter switch. He decided to confront the manager in his office. As a precaution, he took along the rigged counter.

Karrasnik's door was closed, but Josh knocked anyway. "Come on in," Karrasnik called from behind the door.

Josh walked in to see a very disturbed Karrasnik. He closed the door and moved to the desk. "We're ready for our money now," he said.

"I suppose you are." Karrasnik picked up the new counter from his desk and hefted it in his hand. "Nice little trick, switching counters on me."

"Well, what's the count?" Josh asked.

"I don't care what this thing says, I never had more than 400 in here because that's all the fire code allows."

"I know, but you always let in more than that. Your secret's safe with us as long as you pay us for the real gate." Josh produced the old counter and laid it on the desk. "You can have this one back, but we want a fair shake or the Fire Marshal might just be tipped off to check this place out some night."

"That's blackmail!"

"No, it's doing my civic duty to report a fire code violator."

"You rat on me, and you'll never play here again."

"Judging from the crowds the last two times we've played here, I think any place in town would love to have us if you don't. By the way, we're getting popular enough we may have to join the union. Then, you'll have to pay us scale."

"Okay, you win. The count was 523 tonight." He turned to a small safe and opened it. "You got $446 coming, but I'll round it up to $450—that's an even $90 apiece." He counted out the bills and handed them to Josh. "You guys get your union cards, and I'll sign a contract with you. Call me next week."

"Thanks, Mr. Karrasnik. We'll do that."

Karrasnik stood and offered a hand to Josh. Josh took it gladly. "Nice doing business with you," Josh said.

The band was delighted with the higher take, and they agreed with the idea of becoming legitimate performers. Rodney said his father would help with the contract since he was a partner in a big law firm.

Julie helped Josh load his gear in her car, and as they settled into the seats, Josh's cell phone rang. He smiled as he finished the call. "That was my Mom. She and Dad are going to be late getting home. Want to go to Mythos?"

Julie frowned at him, but Josh could tell it was a fake frown. "Do we really have to?"

"No, it's up to you, but I was hoping we were back to normal by now."

"If it's all the same to you, I'd rather we go to my house."

Her response surprised Josh. "We can't get to Mythos from your house. The Cargan's at my house."

"We won't need the Cargan tonight, Josh. My parents won't be home until later either." She leaned across the console and kissed him with more passion than he thought possible.

"What are we waiting for?" Josh asked.

The End

- Title: The Adventures of Regen the Bremen
- Author: M. L. Hollinger
- Price: $27.99
- Publisher: TotalRecall Publications, Inc.
- Hardcover, ISBN: 978-1-59095-110-1
- Paper Back, ISBN: 978-1-59095-111-8
- eBook, ISBN: 978-1-59095-112-5
- Distribution arrangements: Baker Taylor, Ingram Book Co., American Wholesale Book Co. B&N, BAM, Hastings, Powels, Online, etc.

Regen is a Bremen. By nature he loves only his pet skeen, sensual women, money, and adventure in that order.

REGEN is an earthy, pragmatic, drug smuggler who cares little for anything but money, beautiful women, and his own highly unusual pet. The animal is a skeen, and they are usually shot on sight for the pests they are. Most people marvel that Regen managed to tame such a nasty creature. On top of everything else, he named the skeen HITLER after a 20th Century Earth dictator with a personality as evil as any skeen's. Regen is a Bremen. Bremen are known for their tough exterior, sexual prowess, and their tendency to leap before they look. I hope you enjoy following this arrogant, self-confident, egotistical and narcissistic bastard through a series of adventures in disparate sectors of the galaxy.